SWORD DANCE

A.J. DEMAS

Sword Dance

A.J. Demas

Cover art by Aud Koch
Cover design by Lennan Adams

CHAPTER 1

THE LAST LEG of the journey down to the villa would indeed have been easier on a mule. The man at the inn that morning had said so. If he hadn't followed that up with a frown and a little up-and-down flick of the eyes, and if he hadn't said, "You might find it easier, sir," with the emphasis in just the wrong place—just a little too sympathetic—Damiskos might have listened to him and left his horse behind.

Instead, as the sun began to set over the water, he was descending the steep track toward the coast on foot, limping badly, and leading Xanthe, who had refused some hours ago to proceed in any other way.

"This is embarrassing for both of us, you know," Damiskos remarked, reaching up to pat the mare's neck as they stopped for a break. "I hope you feel it as I do."

Xanthe gave a shudder which might have been agreement.

Damiskos looked down the hill toward the villa that was his destination. It perched on a heavily terraced green promontory cantilevered out into the bay below, white walls gleaming pink in the fading light. It was a smallish, old-looking place, with nothing smart or fashionable about it.

From here, you couldn't see any sign of wharfs or boats or the factory that must be somewhere nearby.

It looked like the kind of place where you might be greeted by a bearded gentleman-farmer wearing a homespun mantle with no tunic, offering you a dish of salty cheese and a cup of his own wine, and congratulating himself on not being interested in your news from the city. But, as Damiskos knew, the current owner of the villa was about as different from that type as it was possible to be.

It was full night by the time he and Xanthe reached the front gate, though with a bright moon. He had stopped to eat the last of the bread and smoked sausage he had brought with him from the inn before making the last of the descent, and when the road levelled as it ran out onto the promontory, Xanthe condescended to let him ride again, so their arrival was dignified enough.

The gate was opened promptly; they had obviously been expecting him. The slaves made no comment on his lateness or his inappropriate mount. One took Xanthe to the stables, another carried off Damiskos's saddlebags to the room where he would be staying, and a third told him that the mistress of the house and her other guests were in the summer dining-room if he wanted to join them after he had bathed.

"Thank you," he said, and winced inwardly at how grim he sounded. "I'll just wash quickly and see her directly." He should have tried to feign enthusiasm at the prospect of other guests, but the truth was, his heart had plummeted as soon as he heard them mentioned.

The slave, a lanky boy with curly hair and a crisp, white tunic, trotted ahead of him through the yard and into the house. It was a warm night, and windows and doors stood open, the moonlight supplemented sparsely with lamps burning in brackets.

How many other guests? Damiskos wondered. The villa had no near neighbours, which meant anyone at dinner would presumably be staying the night, or longer. Had Themistos sent him here in the middle of a house party?

He realized he should have been prepared for the prospect. "Think of it as a working holiday," his commanding officer had told him. "Less work and more holiday—fishing, hunting, country air, and good company—you could use it." Damiskos disliked being told things like that, but he had kept his feelings to himself.

In the atrium, the slave boy was met by a woman, big and intimidatingly beautiful, in the plain dress of a household servant. Her skin was topaz-coloured, and she wore her hair in an exuberant cloud framing her broad, strong-featured face. She gave Damiskos an unimpressed look.

"Damiskos Temnon, I think? So you've arrived after all. Thought you might. We'll put him in the yellow room, Niko," she told the boy.

The yellow room was on the ground floor, off the atrium, and Damiskos tried not to assume that this was because the intimidating woman thought he couldn't manage stairs. He shed his sword belt, changed his hobnailed boots for sandals, and unpacked a few items from his saddlebags before shoving the bags themselves to the back of the closet. Then he followed the waiting Niko to the bath. The woman—she must have been a steward or overseer—had disappeared.

The bath was an ancient, austere set of rooms to which a few modern comforts had been added. Damiskos bathed efficiently, towelled off, and emerged sooner than Niko had been expecting, to judge by the way the boy started and jumped to his feet. Damiskos gave him a smile that he meant to be reassuring. It probably just looked tired.

Niko led him out into a torchlit garden, the first sign of real luxury in the villa. Symmetrical paths were laid out between beds of flowers and herbs, black and white and rose-coloured gravel twinkling in the torchlight as though sprinkled with gold dust. In the middle of a large square pool, water trickled from a fountain beneath bronze figures of female dancers, delicate and enigmatic in the darkness. The summer dining room was set into a vine-covered arbour on the far side of the walled enclosure of the garden. Light and laughter spilled out like honey from a comb. It was full of people.

For a moment Damiskos felt a strong desire to turn around and simply leave. Mutter an excuse to the slaves, retrieve his horse and his belongings, make camp somewhere at the base of the mountain trail, and be on his way back to Pheme in the morning.

He had emergency rations and a hunting bow in his pack, and plenty of experience sleeping out of doors. He'd actually made a move to reach out to the boy on the path ahead of him, to alert him to his intention, before it struck him how insane all of this would sound if he tried to explain it to anyone. To Themistos, for instance, when he arrived back in Pheme to report on the success of his journey.

Actually, I didn't even meet with her. I arrived there all right, but she was entertaining a lot of other guests, and they were drinking and having a good time, so I turned around and came home. And what would Nione herself say if she found out he had been here and turned around without seeing her?

Instead, he let himself be led up to the glowing dining room full of people, still limping worse than usual, wishing he'd taken the time to comb his hair with something other than his fingers and to put on a better tunic.

"Damiskos Temnon of the Quartermaster's Office," the boy announced, into a lull in the talk and laughter among the couches.

"Damiskos!" said a sweetly warm voice from the far side of the dining room. "I had almost given up on you for the night."

Damiskos looked across at his host. He had not seen her in more than ten years, and she looked older, as must he too, but he would have known her anywhere. Of course, most people in Pheme might recognize her, if not from seeing her officiate at a ceremony then from her portrait in the Civil Palace. Nione Kukara, retired Maiden of the Sacred Loom: she looked the part, even three years after leaving the Maidens, in a country villa surrounded by worldly guests.

She wore her hair uncovered now, its dozens of braids swept up into a knot on top of her head. Her gown was demure and pale blue, her only jewellery a necklace of large white pearls, gleaming against her richly dark brown skin. She was tall and thin, striking without being beautiful, poised between youth and middle age. She had been not only a sacred Maiden but the chosen Speaker of the Maidens, representative of the goddess Anaxe, the only woman invited to speak before the Citizens' Assembly. She retained an air of simple holiness imparted by two decades in the most sacred temple of Pheme. In some ways her house suited her very well.

Damiskos wondered how he looked to her. Older, broken-down, with new scars and a new defeat in his eyes. And of course the lame leg.

He waited tensely for the pity to appear on her face, but she kept it well hidden. She had always been better at sparing others' feelings than guarding her own vulnerabilities. Damiskos spoke some words of apology, which were waved away with a gentle smile, and in a moment he found himself on the vacant end of a couch, a wine-cup being filled for him.

"And what brings Damiskos Temnon of the Quartermaster's Office to Laothalia?" one of the guests asked. Damiskos could not see the speaker past the woman who was serving him.

"Business," Nione answered for him. "Which of course will keep until tomorrow. And old ties of friendship.

5

Damiskos served in the Honour Guard at the Maidens' House when he was a youth."

She left it at that, not offering any further explanation or apology for a friendship that must have struck most people as unusual, even shocking. That too was how she had always been: so secure in her own honesty that she forgot to consider how things looked to suspicious people. And sometimes her conviction made itself felt. There were no obvious raised eyebrows among her guests.

Damiskos felt a sudden sense of loss for the years that had separated himself and Nione. There had been letters now and then, and he had never ceased to think of her as a friend. But the truth was that he knew as little of what her life had been during those years, and who she was now, as she did of him. He had last known her as a consecrated virgin serving the gods; she had last known him as a soldier.

"Let me introduce my other friends to you, Damiskos."

Damiskos sipped his wine and surveyed the guests on the couches as she named them for him.

"Eurydemos, on your right, you will know by reputation," she said. "He is a kinsman of mine, and I have known him since I was a child—long before he began teaching at the Marble Porches."

Damiskos looked at the man whose couch he was sharing. He had heard the name. The philosopher was a tall man with a mop of silver hair, a sparse beard, and an untidily wrapped mantle. Heavily lidded eyes swung toward Damiskos for a moment before drifting knowingly away, as if they had seen all they needed for Eurydemos to form an opinion of the man from the Quartermaster's Office.

"He has just come from founding a school in Boukos," Nione went on, "and now he is on his way home to Pheme. Helenos and Gelon here are among his current students." She indicated the young men sharing the adjacent couch, one thin and olive-skinned and handsome in a scholarly way, the other sturdier, younger, with a snub nose and freckles.

"Kleitos is a former student of Eurydemos's, and his wife Tyra a friend of mine." They were a couple of about Damiskos's age on the opposite side of the dining room. "And this is Aristokles Demotiades Phoskos, from Boukos."

For a moment, Nione's gently graceful manner faltered, as though she had to search for something to add to her presentation of Aristokles. He was a man in his mid-forties, dressed in a sumptuous dark red tunic, his thick dark hair streaked with grey, several rings on each of his large hands. He was alone on his couch, directly across the dining room from Damiskos.

Obviously unable to come up with anything else to say about Aristokles, Nione moved on to the last member of the party, the young woman who sat with her feet tucked up at the end of her own couch, whose name was Phaia. She was another of the philosopher's students, the only woman currently among them, Nione said, the admiration clear in her tone.

Phaia was remarkably lovely, dark-eyed and intense-looking, her masses of black curls pulled back haphazardly from a pale face. She looked like she could have posed for a wall-painting of a nymph—and might have done it, too, just to shock the sort of people who would have disapproved.

The introductions finished, the other guests resumed their conversation, most of them content to ignore Damiskos, who was content to be ignored.

Kleitos had been in the middle of a story, which he now resumed, about his neighbours in the city and a dispute over the upkeep of a communal garden. Somehow, by a process Damiskos wasn't paying enough attention to follow, this topic led not to a general discussion of bad neighbours but to a debate about whether or not "unmanliness" would be the death of the Republic. The philosopher and his students all seemed to agree that it would.

"You see," said Eurydemos, in a sonorous, schoolroom tone, "we may understand Order as the masculine principle, Chaos as the feminine. On the one side, the light of civilization—on the other, primordial darkness. And so the Republic cannot function, cannot order itself, if the masculine principle is not ascendant."

"How can you suggest," said Nione mildly, almost laughing, "that 'the masculine principle is not ascendant' when men everywhere control everything and always have?"

"But *are they* actually men when they allow themselves to be used like women?" This was Gelon, the younger of the two male students, speaking rather loudly.

"Practitioners of Kossian love, as they call themselves," Kleitos scoffed. "Could anything be more unmanly?"

"Our master speaks of abstractions," said Helenos, with a tolerant sidelong glance at Gelon. "Not individuals."

"Exactly," said Eurydemos, smiling at his students. "And we must understand that both the masculine and feminine forces are necessary. Just as the antithesis of the wise ruler in the masculine order is the fearsome tyrant, so the feminine principle contains both destruction and creation."

"In the Ideal Republic," said Gelon, who had possibly had too much to drink, "I maintain that unnatural half-men would be deprived of citizenship."

"Yes, yes, of course." Eurydemos sighed. "But we must distinguish between unmanly vice and pure affection."

Here he launched into a long anecdote about the heroism of the lovers Tinandros and Phoros to illustrate his point. Helenos caught Damiskos's eye and gave him a humorous look which Damiskos found somehow flattering. The whole discussion was the purest gibberish as far as he could tell. He thought Nione looked as if she had stopped listening to it.

"Well," said Phaia, rearranging herself on her host's couch

and looking at Nione, "since women are not citizens in the first place, I don't suppose any of this applies to *us*."

There was a little awkward laughter at that, and then someone else tactfully changed the subject to sea travel, and everyone began swapping stories of storms and seasickness. Damiskos waited for this to somehow turn into a political discussion too—perhaps someone would suggest that the postal ship from Boukos to the north coast of Pheme was a threat to the Republic—but mercifully it did not happen.

He sipped his wine. It was a strong, straightforward red, probably from the villa's own terraced vineyards, which he had passed on his way in. He liked it. He looked across the dining room and noticed a slave sitting on a cushion at the foot of Aristokles's couch, obviously his personal attendant, not part of Nione's staff.

The slave was a Zashian—a eunuch, to judge by his beardless face and the smooth column of his throat. He was dolled up in a way that would have made him stand out even in Zash: hands painted with henna; eyes rimmed in kohl and winged with glittering turquoise; long drops dangling from his ears. A gold stud in the shape of a flower winked in the side of his nose. Even in the warm night he wore layers of lushly decorated clothing: close-fitting trousers and silk tunic and long jacket, all patterned and embroidered. His long black hair was pulled back into half a dozen braids, threaded with beads and held together by a gold clasp on top of his head so that they fell down his back like the strands of a scourge.

Damiskos looked back up at the Boukossian aristocrat who had bought such a slave and brought him to be stared at in the home of a retired Maiden. He felt a scalding contempt for the man.

There was nothing astonishing in a Boukossian owning a Zashian slave. The trade agreement between Boukos and Zash was eight years old now. But it had not occurred to

Damiskos—just because he hadn't given it much thought—that the trade agreement might include slaves, and those slaves might include Zashian eunuchs. He wanted to ask the man on the other side of the dining room, who lay propped comfortably on his elbow, complaining about how long it took to sail from Boukos in the height of summer, what he knew about how they made eunuchs in Zash.

Had he heard how many of the boys died of infection or killed themselves afterward? Did he know that under Zashian law, eunuchs, unlike other slaves, could not earn their freedom, that they were considered neither male nor female but some other, null category, unworthy even of a name, that they were sometimes referred to in legal documents with the pronoun used for animals?

Damiskos doubted that Aristokles had travelled to Zash; the man sounded as if he could barely stand the voyage through the Tentines to the north coast of Pheme. He had probably bought the slave who sat at his feet in the market of his own city, picking him up as an expensive, exotic luxury to grace his aristocratic home, like a piece of imported carpet or a box of incense. He had outfitted the eunuch ignorantly in a half-female style, with the nose-ring and the hennaed hands that only a woman would have displayed in Zash. Though in truth the combination was not unattractive.

Damiskos reached for a dish of olives on the table in front of him. The female half of the couple on the couch beside Aristokles asked how he had found his journey around the coast from the city.

"Actually, I came overland."

"What, through the mountains?" The husband, Kleitos, looked aghast. "But why? It must take three times as long—not to mention the risk of bandits."

"I didn't encounter any trouble," said Damiskos stolidly. "There are quite good inns all along the road. It does take longer, but it was a matter of economy. My office would have had to hire a vessel and crew to transport me here by sea, but I was a cavalry officer—I already had a horse." And he strongly preferred riding to sea travel, but he did not admit that.

The guests seemed divided between approving of his frugality and thinking him mad.

"What was your legion?" asked Helenos, when everyone was finished exclaiming.

"Second Koryphos," said Damiskos, looking into his wine cup.

Murmurs of admiration and surprise circled the couches. Damiskos kept his hands in his lap, not particularly wanting anyone to notice the bracelet on his right wrist that might have told them what his rank had been. These days he often wondered why he still wore it, but somehow he had yet to take it off.

"You'll have served in Sasia, then, won't you?" said Aristokles, using the Pseuchaian name for the kingdom rather than attempting the mildly difficult consonants of "Zash." He didn't look down at his slave, whom he seemed to have all but forgotten.

"Yes," said Damiskos. "I was stationed for several years in the colonies, at Seleos."

"I *long* to see Sasia," said Aristokles. "But the journey." He shuddered. "Still, one day I will attempt it. To see the great walls of Suna, and the gardens of Rataxes!"

"I don't imagine you had much time for that kind of thing," said Helenos dryly, casting another conspiratorial look at Damiskos. "Serving in Seleos. What with the warring clans and so on."

Damiskos would have liked to agree with Helenos, but he felt the need to be honest. "We were certainly kept busy, but I was there for several years. I have been to Suna and Rataxa. They were … worth seeing."

Aristokles sighed enviously. His slave had shown no sign

of following the conversation, but sat with eyes discreetly downcast, face expressionless, apparently studying the floor.

"You can settle a dispute for us, Damiskos," said Kleitos. "We were talking of Sasia earlier, of the barbarity of their so-called 'justice.' Is it true what they say about how they punish criminals in that backward place?"

"I don't know—what do they say?"

"Oh, you know," said Kleitos, waving a hand, as if surprised to be asked to substantiate his slurs. "Horrible stuff. Cutting off hands for thieving, putting out eyes for looking at another man's wife, breaking the kneecaps of runaway slaves with—"

"Come now," Aristokles interrupted. "Not in front of ladies, if you please. Unnecessarily grisly."

"And the part about looking at other men's wives isn't true," Damiskos felt the need to add.

"But the others are?" Phaia pressed, eyes wide, casting a playful glance at Aristokles.

"Yes, the … " Damiskos gripped his wine cup. "Yes. Those are punishments that may be meted out. Amputation and the breaking of bones, as you describe. As well as various other things. But we have known equally brutal punishments in Pheme not so long ago."

"Oh, gods, let's not go into it," said Aristokles faintly, looking ill. Obviously not concerned so much about the "ladies" as about his own sensibilities.

"In the Ideal Republic," Gelon spoke up, "punishment would not exceed the bounds of reason."

"Sasia is neither a republic nor ideal," said Eurydemos dryly.

"No," Damiskos agreed, because the philosopher's remark had seemed to be addressed mostly to him. "It is a very large kingdom, very difficult to govern. Reforms have been attempted—indeed, made successfully, in certain regions—

but over such a vast territory, with so many different peoples, you cannot expect overnight change."

"But they're barbarians, though," Kleitos insisted. "Fundamentally different from us."

"Fundamentally!" Gelon echoed, raising his cup unsteadily to his lips.

"You have fought them," said Helenos, smiling enigmatically at Damiskos. "You must have a different understanding of them than those of us who have stayed at home, debating good government in the safety of our schools."

"I have no love for Zash," said Damiskos, not wanting to prolong the conversation. But that was a bare-faced lie, the bleat of a man whose mistress has left him claiming, "I never cared for her anyway."

Helenos raised his eyebrows. "Perhaps," he addressed the other guests mildly, "we should let Damiskos enjoy some refreshment after his hard journey instead of interrogating him about Sasia."

The others laughed, and Damiskos nodded gratefully to Helenos. The conversation moved off into other channels.

It was true, as Helenos had reminded them, that Damiskos had fought Zashians, but most Phemians forgot what that really meant these days. Pheme was not at war with Zash, and the job of the legions on the Deshan Coast was to defend the Phemian colonies from the local warlords, themselves rebels and enemies of the crown.

This meant that the Phemian soldiers found themselves on the same side as the Zashian king and his armies, often cooperating with the king's men to subdue troublesome warlords, camping in Zashian territory, shopping and drinking and taking their pleasures in Zashian towns. It was jarring for them to come home and hear people talk as though what they had been doing was bravely holding the Republic's last frontier against the might of Zash. Damiskos thought Helenos understood the situation better than that, and he was glad to feel he had at least one ally here.

He looked at the Zashian slave, wondering how much of their conversation he was able to understand. The eunuch was still looking at the floor, so it was impossible to tell.

CHAPTER 2

THE INTIMIDATING STEWARD, or overseer, or whatever she was, appeared at Damiskos's door the following morning while he was dressing. She was unapologetic—and apparently unembarrassed.

"The mistress would like you to join her in the garden for breakfast. I'm sure you won't want to keep her waiting."

He finished pulling his tunic over his head. "Of course not."

She gave him an approving nod and graciously waited for him to buckle his belt and fasten his sandals before marching him out into the garden to report to her mistress. He barely restrained the urge to salute when he arrived.

"Here he is," she said, presenting him as if he were a dish that the kitchen had worked hard on but that she privately thought unappetizing.

"Thank you, Aradne," said Nione, smiling at her. "Damiskos, will you join me?"

She was seated for breakfast at a table in a little secluded nook on the far side of the garden, with a beautiful view out over the bay. She was alone, and there was only one other chair pulled up to the table. Damiskos sat, a little stiffly, stretching out his right leg. His knee was sore this morning, though not as bad as it had been last night.

"Your garden is beautiful," he said.

"Thank you. It is the one part of the house I have completely redone to my satisfaction so far."

"One thing more, ma'am," said Aradne. "You asked me to tell you how Gion was doing—she's much better this morning."

"Oh, I'm so glad. Tell her to take it easy the rest of the day, and I'll visit her in her room later this morning. What about Niko? How is he coming with his lessons?"

There was a short conversation about Niko's lessons, the progress of someone else's pregnancy, and an account of how a dispute among the vineyard workers had been settled. Then the servant departed, and as she left Damiskos suddenly had a memory of a sturdy little girl with topaz-brown skin.

"There was a slave named Aradne in the Maidens' House when you were a girl."

Nione smiled. "The very same. She belonged to the House, but she purchased her freedom three years ago—at around the same time that I retired. I offered her the job as my steward. She's splendid." She passed Damiskos a dish of fruit from the table. "How long has it been since you and I met?"

"Since we first met? Fifteen … sixteen years. Immortal gods. Yes, it must be. I was sixteen when I started in the Honour Guard."

"Were you really? Only sixteen?"

He nodded. He had been young for a recruit, a rising star, beginning his glittering ascent.

"I miss the Maidens' House," Nione said.

"Yes." He should have asked about that rather than waiting for her to mention it. That was surely what a good friend would have done. "You always loved it there."

"So many of the other girls didn't. Some of them were

almost … in mourning, for the women they could have become if they lived in the world. Wives and mothers, normal things. Well, they can still have some of that, if they want—men line up to marry ex-Maidens—but I suppose it is a long time to wait for the life you want." She spoke as if making an earnest effort to understand something that made no sense to her.

"But you never wanted that life."

He had known this about her for—well, sixteen years, more or less. She had been so happy in the Maidens' House, wearing her regalia as if born to it, performing all her duties with zeal. It was why she had risen to be Speaker of the Maidens, almost inevitably. It was one of the things that had made Damiskos like her.

"I never did," she said. She glanced at him with an unreadable expression. "And so I'm doing my best to spend my retirement allowance as quickly as I can, repairing this old place and setting myself up in business."

Damiskos wasn't quite sure how that followed, but he didn't ask.

Someone had come out of the house into the colonnade at the edge of the garden. It was Aristokles's eunuch slave, already painted and decorated for the day, in spite of the early hour. His hair was in one thick braid today, and the long jacket he wore over his tunic was sleeveless, perhaps a concession to the heat, but everything else was much as the night before. He moved with a precise grace, and his figure under the close-fitting layers of his clothes was wasp-waisted and effeminate. He squinted slightly in the sunlight as he came out from under the colonnade.

"Oh, it's Aristokles's servant," Nione murmured. "He danced for us yesterday, Damiskos, before you arrived—I'm sorry you missed it. He's *very* good."

"Ah," said Damiskos, unable to think of anything else. He had seen many different kinds of dancing in Zash, but found it hard to picture any of them taking place in Nione's old-fashioned Pseuchaian villa. The idea of the Zashian being put on display like that was distasteful, but not surprising.

"Hello, my dear," said Nione as the eunuch came around the fountain to approach their bench. "Does your master need something?"

Aristokles's slave gave a slight, elegant bow and presented something in his open palms over the table. It was a small, round box, carved with stylized flowers: probably another product of the trade agreement, like its bearer. Nione's expression clouded slightly.

"Oh. How lovely. Do convey my thanks. Tell him … he needn't have, but I'm sure I will like it."

She set the box down on the table without opening it. The eunuch bowed again and retreated.

Only when he was gone into the colonnade did Nione lift the lid of the box. She looked into it for a moment, then pushed it across the table to Damiskos with a miserable expression. A pair of earrings lay jumbled inside. Zashian style, with long pendants of enamelled beads.

"A generous gift," Damiskos said neutrally. "But you look as though you're not happy with it."

Nione sighed. "No—though they're lovely." She lifted one earring out of the box, then dropped it back with distaste.

They weren't the sort of earrings that a respectable Zashian woman would have worn; the colours were flashy, and, in Zash, would have been considered masculine. Damiskos did not say that, but he thought of Aristokles's slave with his nose-ring and henna. Clearly the Boukossian knew nothing of the kingdom he professed to admire.

"I am trying not to encourage him," Nione said, "but … I don't seem to be very good at it."

"Perhaps you need to go so far as to *discourage* him."

"Well, one cannot insult a guest … "

"Of course." That was an iron law, and one a woman as sweet-natured as Nione would have a hard time even bending.

"But he isn't really in love with me. He's only been here a few days."

"You don't believe one can fall in love in the blink of an eye?" He said it with a smile, because he didn't suppose it was something she would even have formed an opinion about.

"No," she said, more seriously than he had expected, "no, I wouldn't say I don't believe it, exactly—I think sometimes one can … can develop an attachment very quickly, but only if you come to know the other person intimately in a short space of time."

"Yes," he said, feeling the need to back away from this topic now, though he wasn't exactly sure what he feared. "Yes, I expect you're right."

"And Aristokles doesn't know me at all."

"Right."

He ate a couple of spoonfuls of yogurt and said, after what he hoped was a suitable pause for a change of subject, "So your factory is down by the shore, I suppose?"

"Oh. Yes. I'll take you on a tour later."

They finished their breakfast and talked business, but Damiskos's mind kept wandering from the discussion of prices per barrel and volume discounts and fish varieties.

"Men line up to marry ex-Maidens," she had said. He could believe it. If nothing else, the retirement allowance they received could serve as a generous dowry. Damiskos would have pitied Aristokles Phoskos, pressing his embarrassing and futile suit, if he hadn't already felt such disgust with the man. And an uncomfortable thought occurred to him. What if Nione thought Damiskos was here now, on the pretext of business from the Quartermaster's Office, because he secretly harboured the same hope as Aristokles?

He had changed in the years since they had known one

another; perhaps she thought his understanding of their friendship had changed too. Perhaps she thought it might have included this all along, that he had been waiting for her to be free from the Maidens' House so that he could ask her to be his wife.

She knew he had been engaged to another woman, but she also knew he had broken it off. What if she thought that had been for her sake? What if she was planning to accept his inevitable proposal out of pity?

He was no kind of a match for an ex-Maiden, though, and she had to know that. She knew his family's fortune was gone along with their reputation, sacrificed to his parents' lavish lifestyle and bad business decisions.

Damiskos himself had risen to command of one of the most famous legions of the Republic by the time he was twenty-six, but he had only held the position for a year, and well as he liked what he did now—and he did like it, despite what everyone thought—he knew he no longer cut an impressive figure in the world.

He didn't think Nione would enjoy being married to him, either.

They had both completely finished their meal by the time Tyra and Phaia came out to the table to remind Nione that she had promised them a game of Reds and Whites that morning.

Tyra asked if Damiskos would like to join them, and he restrained himself from replying that he hadn't sunk quite that low yet. Playing a game of Reds and Whites with a trio of women, according to country villa rules and probably without betting, was no doubt exactly what Themistos had imagined Damiskos doing when he sent him on this trip. He politely declined, and the women left together.

He had not been left alone for more than a minute when the philosopher's two male students came out into the garden from the house. They had hard-boiled eggs and were peeling them and scattering shells as they walked.

"Damiskos from the Quartermaster's Office!" Gelon hailed him as they approached. "Good morning!"

Damiskos returned the greeting politely.

"We're going out to admire the view," Gelon said. "Will you join us?"

Since he had clearly not been doing anything else, Damiskos could not see an excuse to refuse. Nor did he particularly want one. Gelon seemed like a tiresome fellow, but Damiskos rather like Helenos. He followed them to a gate in the garden wall that led out onto the promontory beyond the villa.

The land here was wild, rock-strewn, and overgrown with shrubs, but there was a path leading out to the windy edge, and the students picked their way along it, eating their eggs and continuing some obscure conversation which Damiskos could not follow. They scrambled up and found seats on a large rock at the cliff's edge.

Damiskos sat lower down and looked out over the water, shading his eyes with his hand. The wide bay into which the promontory of Laothalia jutted was calm and turquoise in the sunlight, scattered with a number of tiny islets. Further out, in the open sea, he could easily make out the beginning of the island chain of the Tentines, arcing away toward Boukos.

Helenos came slithering down the rock to close the gap between himself and Damiskos. He had finished eating his egg.

"Not exactly luxurious, this place, is it?" the student said conversationally, when he had settled himself on the rock and rearranged his mantle. "A bit 'Ariatan,' as they say."

"I like it well enough," said Damiskos. "But then, I was a soldier."

Helenos smiled, and reached out to touch the wide

bronze bracelet on Damiskos's right wrist. It was an oddly intimate gesture. "You were First Spear in the Second Koryphos," he said. "You were *quite* a soldier."

To Damiskos's relief, he didn't follow that up with any expression of sympathy, just a thoughtful, sidelong look. He withdrew his hand.

"It must have been difficult for you," Helenos said, "serving in Sasia, the land of our ancient enemies, and having nothing more to do than to keep the peace between warlords."

"It was rather like bailing out a leaky boat without plugging the holes, sometimes."

Helenos laughed. "I saw you looking at the eunuch last night."

"Looking at him?" Damiskos repeated, unsure where this was going. He remembered Gelon railing against unmanly love the night before, and didn't want to get into any of that. "I—I noticed him, I suppose. It's hard not to."

Helenos nodded. "Disgusting, isn't it?"

"Yes! That's just what I was thinking."

He was relieved to find someone agreed with him about the poor fellow's situation. He had been under the impression that none of the other guests cared.

"Mm," said Helenos. "I guessed that."

"I hope it wasn't obvious."

"No—but I shouldn't worry about that if I were you. The creature might as well know what we think of him, might he not? In my view, he epitomizes the evils of his race." Helenos's tone had not changed at all; he spoke amiably, as though proposing something obvious that Damiskos would be sure to agree with.

Damiskos realized that it sounded as if he already *had* agreed with it.

"That's—not what I meant by disgusting," he said stiffly.

"Oh?"

"I find the practice of making eunuchs repellant, and I cannot approve of a Pseuchaian owning one, but … "

But what? A moment ago he had felt sure Helenos meant something specific by "epitomizes the evils of his race," something that Damiskos didn't agree with at all, but now he wasn't so sure. It would be rude to jump to conclusions.

"Well, it's not his fault," he finished lamely. "The slave's, I mean."

Helenos smiled. "The sentiment does you credit, First Spear."

"I don't hold that rank any more," said Damiskos. "You should not call me that."

"Ah. No such thing as a First Spear in the Quartermaster's Office, is that it?"

"That's it."

"Our hostess said you were here on business. Is that true?"

"She owns a factory that makes fish sauce. I've come to see whether she may be able to supply the legions."

"You're joking," said Gelon from above them.

"Not at all. The legions go through a great deal of fish sauce, and our current suppliers are not adequate to our needs."

"You must admit it is a little bizarre," said Helenos equably.

"I suppose so," said Damiskos, though he didn't see it.

"A *little* bizarre?" Gelon protested. "A retired Maiden of the Loom runs a fish-sauce factory, and a retired First Spear of the Second Koryphos is her customer! It's like something out of one of those modern novels that everyone wants to ban for corrupting the youth."

"I wouldn't know anything about that," said Damiskos stiffly.

Helenos laughed warmly. "Indeed not. Shame on you, Gelon."

"What? You know what I'm talking about. Petris Akrotis and that. There was one where the hero's patron had made his fortune buying houses that were on fire, or about to catch fire, or something. Absurd."

Damiskos gave him an unfriendly look, and Helenos said, "Just leave it, Gelon," as the younger man opened his mouth again.

In the afternoon, most of the male guests trooped down to the fishing pier with rods and nets. Damiskos excused himself, pleading sleepiness. The truth was that he didn't fancy the walk. The fishing pier sounded as if it was a good distance away, and in some fit of vanity he hadn't brought his cane.

He had seen the villa's library: an airy and well-lit room on the ground floor near his bedroom. He was looking forward to it as a place of solitude as much as anything. He returned to the house and found of course that the library wasn't empty.

"I don't know how you could ask it, after the way I suffered on the voyage over," Aristokles was saying when Damiskos entered the anteroom.

When he stepped through the inner door, he saw that the other person in the room was Aristokles's eunuch. He looked as though he had been about to say something before he saw Damiskos, and he dropped his gaze instantly to the floor. The snatch of conversation which Damiskos had overheard struck him as odd for a master talking to his slave.

Aristokles made a huffing noise. "I am going to take a nap," he announced, and brushed past Damiskos on his way to the door.

Damiskos looked at the eunuch, surprised that he wasn't

following his master. It was the first time Damiskos had looked closely at him in daylight.

He was very striking, something between pretty and handsome, the intermediateness of it entrancing as a complex melody. He had very white skin and very dark eyes above high, sculpted cheekbones and delicately shaped lips, and—well, he was attractive, in a way that Damiskos found rather interesting, that was all.

He was looking at Damiskos now with a flicker of curiosity, and Damiskos realized to his embarrassment that he must have been obviously staring.

"I—er—I hear that you dance," he said. At least that was what he hoped he said; on some impulse of the moment he tried saying it in Zashian, which he had barely spoken in years. "What kind of dance … uh … do you do?"

The eunuch's eyebrows went up, but the rest of his face remained neutral, and Damiskos thought at first he was just surprised to hear a Phemian speaking his language. But the pause before he replied was long enough to suggest that actually he was trying to decipher what Damiskos had said. Or at least that he wanted Damiskos to think that he was.

"Vishmi kokoro," he said finally, a dialect term which was unintelligible to Damiskos. He had a cultured, courtier's accent, and his voice had a timbre that Damiskos associated with sophisticated older women. He reverted to Pseuchaian: "Sword dance. You know it?"

"Ah," said Damiskos. "No."

"Well," he said after a moment, his expression still neutral, "it's a dance with swords."

His Zashian accent was strong, but he seemed to have a surprisingly good grasp of idiomatic Pseuchaian.

"Hm," said Damiskos.

There was a moment's awkward pause. Damiskos couldn't think of anything polite to say about dancing with swords. That was not what swords were for.

The eunuch tucked a strand of hair behind his ear with a hennaed fingertip and gave a little nod before turning to depart the same way as his master. Left alone in the library at last, Damiskos wandered to one of the book-cupboards and stood staring aimlessly at the scrolls for a minute before he could collect himself enough to pick one.

He had looked on the Zashian strictly as an object of pity before, but now he felt the stirring of a personal dislike. He'd been trying to be friendly, and the eunuch had just been very demurely rude to him. Which was fine. You could pity a fellow perfectly adequately without liking him.

CHAPTER 3

CONVERSATION AT DINNER that night was much the same as the night before. Gelon ranted about effeminates destroying the republic, and Aristokles and Kleitos spouted their different flavours of ignorant nonsense about Zash.

Eurydemos read aloud a poem of his own composition about a man in love with a beautiful tree without fruit. That struck Damiskos as an obvious non-starter. Nione might not have children, but it was because she had spent most of her life serving in the Maidens' House, and anyway she was only in her thirties; if she *had* wanted children, the option was surely still open to her.

After that, the philosopher and his students became very animated on the subject of something they called "Phemian purity." Damiskos honestly could not work out what it was supposed to mean. Pheme was a huge, cosmopolitan city, the biggest in the world. It was the centre of a web of conquest and influence and trade that had long ago filled its streets with almost every race and language and religion. All of that wasn't some kind of accretion; it *was* Pheme. What did "purity" have to do with any of that?

He didn't speak up; he knew better than to get involved

in a conversation where they were quoting philosophers he had never heard of and talking about the Ideal Republic as if they had spent their summers there growing up.

He left them still debating and went in to bed early, fidgeted about for a while, rearranging his portable shrine and oiling his sword belt, then lay staring at the moonlit ceiling and listening to the subdued night sounds of the villa around him.

He heard voices in the atrium outside his room, a man's and a woman's.

"It's a disgrace, isn't it?" said the woman's voice. "The way the master drools over him."

"It's a disgrace, and it's a godsdamned fucking nuisance," the man replied angrily. "Where did this fucking Sasian-lover come from, anyway, and why have we got to contend with him now of all times?"

Damiskos fell asleep eventually, though he didn't feel as if he'd been asleep long when something woke him. The house was very quiet now, but there must have been some noise. He heard it again: low voices from the atrium, these too quiet for him to make out the words, and then the slight creak and thump of a heavy door opening and shutting.

Probably Nione's household slaves, working late and headed back to their quarters. Damiskos turned over in bed and tried to go back to sleep.

Once more, he couldn't settle. Very soon he found himself sitting up, swinging his legs over the edge of the bed, and searching in the shadows for his sandals. He would get up and take a walk, and hopefully that would help him fall back to sleep. He left his room, crossed the moonlit atrium, and went down the short passage toward the garden.

From the colonnade, he saw that there was someone already there, sitting by the fountain. The moon was almost full, and he could identify Eurydemos by his mane of grey hair. Damiskos had no desire to be drawn into a philosophical discussion or listen to soggy poetry in the middle of the night. He headed back through the house toward the front door.

The yard in front of the house was a wide, gravelled space, with the slave's quarters along one side, the kitchens and other domestic workshops along the other. Between the kitchen range and the paved path leading to the gate stood a well with a waist-high stone coping and a pulley. As soon as Damiskos stepped through the front door, he saw the two figures on the other side of the well.

He saw the glint of moonlight on a knife-blade, and he was running—or doing the closest thing he could to running these days, ungainly and not very fast—across the gravel and around the well. He collided with the Zashian eunuch, pinioned his arms from behind, and caught hold of his right wrist. The knife dropped to the gravel. Gelon, backed up against the coping of the well, gave a startled grunt.

Sword-dancing probably demanded some strength as well as grace. The body Damiskos had hold of was more wiry than he had expected, and twisted in a very determined effort to escape. This took up enough of Damiskos's attention that he almost didn't notice Gelon stepping forward and snatching up the fallen knife until it was too late, and the young man was lunging forward with it.

Damiskos swung his captive out of the path of the knife and felt the blade catch in the sleeve of his own tunic and graze his upper arm. He let go of the Zashian to push Gelon back, catching him across the throat with his forearm and slamming him into the coping, unbalancing him enough to threaten him with a fall into the well. He wrenched the knife out of Gelon's hand and stepped back defensively.

"What's going on?" Damiskos demanded, glancing between the two of them. The eunuch was leaning with his hands on his knees, catching his breath.

Gelon coughed and pushed himself off the well.

"He knows what he was trying to do with his unnatural Sasian ways!" the student rasped. "I wasn't going to *kill* him —I was only going to frighten him, the chicken-hearted dog that he is."

Having delivered this speech, Gelon fled, thudding away over the gravel toward the house. Damiskos let him go, mostly because he couldn't have hoped to catch up to him.

He flipped the knife around, point down, and looked back at the eunuch. His eyes looked black in his bone-white face, and the hand that he lifted to push back his hair was shaking badly. His hair was loose, dark strands sticking to his face and throat, the eye-makeup washed off for the night, his only remaining ornament the little flower-shaped stud in his nose.

"I take it this knife was his?" said Damiskos.

The Zashian nodded.

"Are you all right? He didn't hurt you?"

"I'm fine."

"I'm extremely sorry. If I hadn't interfered … You had the situation under control."

He gave a shaky laugh. "I'm not sure that I did." He fumbled in the folds of his broad sash. "You're bleeding," he said, holding out a patterned handkerchief.

"Oh." Damiskos took it and hitched up the sleeve of his tunic to press it to the shallow cut which was dripping blood down his arm. "Thank you."

Damiskos looked him over assessingly. The elaborate Zashian clothes were disordered but not actually torn or pulled off, which could mean that Gelon hadn't attacked with rape in mind, or only that he hadn't got very far with his attempt.

In the pale moonlight, with his hair down and his face unpainted, Aristokles's slave was lovely in a way that seemed somehow basic and elemental, as if he were really neither male nor female, but a being of his own unique nature with a beauty that had no relation to either.

Which was of course nonsense. He was a young man who had been deliberately mutilated as a child, who had survived, and was obviously tougher than he looked.

"Pharastes?" said a querulous voice from behind Damiskos. "What's going on?"

Damiskos turned to see Aristokles standing in the kitchen doorway, absurdly frozen with a raisin cake in each hand, one with a bite taken out of it.

"It was one of the students," the eunuch said quickly. He pushed both slender hands into his hair, in what Damiskos suspected was an attempt to stop them shaking. It didn't quite work. "He had a knife, which First Spear Damiskos took away from him. He has gone back into the house."

Damiskos opened his mouth to say something, but realized he didn't know what. He wanted to protest that he had not been nearly as helpful as this explanation made it sound, but that seemed slightly churlish when the slave had gone out of his way to present him to his master in the role of a saviour.

"He attacked you?" said Aristokles stupidly. "With a knife?"

"He was not able to do any serious damage," said Damiskos, feeling he ought to say something. "Fortunately."

Though who was he to say, really? There were ways to damage a man that didn't involve blood or bruises.

Aristokles ignored him and did not wait for his slave to reply. "Are they going to come after me next?" he quavered, looking around him.

"I shouldn't think so, sir," said the eunuch. Damiskos had to give him credit for not laughing. He himself barely managed to avoid it.

"I don't know," his master muttered fretfully. "I don't know. Are we really safe here? Milos didn't tell me that—"

"Sir," his servant cut him off with a surprising briskness. "We should return inside. And we should let First Spear Damiskos return to his bed also."

"Oh," said Aristokles. "Yes." He shook himself slightly, and only then seemed to remember the raisin cakes he was holding. He took another large bite out of the one in his right hand, and advanced out of the doorway, holding out the other. "I got you one, too. They're very good."

"I'm not hungry," the eunuch muttered, but he took the offered cake.

Aristokles looked at Damiskos and gave a little gasp. "You were injured in the affray!" He pointed to the handkerchief which Damiskos was still holding to his arm, not so much because he was still bleeding as because he had been rooted to the spot with puzzlement at the strange scene playing out between master and slave.

"Oh. Not really. Slightly grazed." He unclamped the handkerchief and then didn't know what to do with it. He realized he was also still holding Gelon's knife.

Aristokles shuddered. "Ghastly business. I tell you, Pharastes, if I'd had any idea … "

"Yes, sir." The Zashian put a hand on his master's elbow and steered him toward the house door. Aristokles took another bite of his raisin cake and moved as directed.

Damiskos followed them at a polite distance. That their relationship was something more than master and slave was obvious, but it only partly explained the strangeness of what Damiskos had just witnessed. Why had Aristokles not asked what made Gelon attack the eunuch? If he had made the obvious inference—that it was a rape attempt—why leap immediately to the conclusion that he might be in danger himself? And what had any of them been doing in the yard in the first place?

Ahead of him, Aristokles was talking earnestly and not

very quietly. "It's shocking, Pharastes, absolutely shocking. If you really were my slave—"

The eunuch drew in a sharp breath, but Aristokles had already stopped, seeing Damiskos behind him. Damiskos stopped too, looking at Aristokles with raised eyebrows.

"I ... that is ... " Aristokles floundered.

"You will be surprised, First Spear," his servant said smoothly, turning back to Damiskos. "On account of your familiarity with Zashian customs. In Zash, of course, a eunuch cannot be freed. But in Boukos it is not so. I was once Aristokles's slave, but I am so no longer."

"Ah," said Damiskos. "I see. My congratulations."

Aristokles gave an awkward laugh. "Yes, yes. You see, people often don't understand, which is why we, er ... "

The eunuch laid his hand on Aristokles's arm again, a gently shushing gesture.

Damiskos said no more, but he wasn't at all convinced he had heard the whole story. Their explanation wasn't unbelievable, but it was a little thin, and it didn't account for how alarmed Aristokles had looked when he realized he'd let this bit of information slip.

They reached the front door, and the Zashian, to Damiskos's surprise, did not follow his patron inside to his room, but saw him through the door and then turned back.

He must have seen Damiskos's puzzled look in the moonlight, because he gestured toward a building on the other side of the yard, and said, "I'm headed back to my own room," rather dryly.

"Oh," said Damiskos. He hoped it wasn't obvious that he had assumed the eunuch shared Aristokles's bed. But if he didn't, then Damiskos was at a loss all over again. He realized the building on the other side of the yard was the slave quarters. "Why did you let them put you out there?"

The Zashian sighed in a way that seemed somehow very

33

genuine. He looked at the ground for a moment, and then he shrugged, looking up. "It is what I'm used to."

"I see." That was rather sad, but it made sense. "Let me see you safely there?"

"That's ... unnecessary, but thank you." He made a gracious, automatic gesture, something between a nod and a bow, which Damiskos had seen often among Zashian courtiers.

Pharastes, his master had called him. It was the Pseuchaian rendering of an old and dignified Zashian name that meant "warrior."

"Your name is Varazda, isn't it?" Damiskos ventured.

"Varazda son of Nahaz son of Aroz of the clan Kamun." He made a more studied version of the same courtly gesture. "In Boukos I generally go by Pharastes."

Son of Nahaz son of Aroz. He had been an aristocrat. He was probably from one of the warring clans in the southeast, whose territory and conflicts Damiskos knew well. Many of their women and children ended up as slaves when their men were massacred in raids. Damiskos's throat felt suddenly painfully constricted. Whatever he had meant to ask after that—and he wasn't at all sure what it was—went unsaid, and they crossed the yard to the slaves' quarters in awkward silence.

At the bottom of the exterior stairs that led up to the second-storey rooms, Varazda turned and bowed once more.

"I—am very grateful, truly," he said in a subdued voice. "For your intervention. I cannot thank you enough."

Damiskos shook his head. "I am sorry I couldn't have done it in a more ... couldn't have intervened without causing you more distress. I'm sorry I misinterpreted what I saw."

It must have been awful, especially for a civilian, to think you'd got the better of your attacker only to find yourself seized from behind by someone who might easily have been

34

his accomplice. Worse still if you had ever spent time in slavery.

Varazda looked slightly surprised. "You sorted it out," he said. "That's the main thing." He looked down rather ruefully at the raisin cake Aristokles had given him, then held it out on one decorated palm. "By any chance were you going to the kitchen for a snack yourself? Because I don't think I'm going to eat this."

CHAPTER 4

WHEN DAMISKOS WOKE the following morning, the first thing he saw was Varazda's floral-patterned handkerchief on the table by the head of the bed. He propped himself on one hand and lay looking at it and recalling the events of the previous night. Gelon's knife was on the table too. Damiskos had eaten the raisin cake.

He wondered what he should do about last night's incident. His instinct, born of a career in the army, was to report it to someone. But who? If Aristokles hadn't been there at the time, it would have been appropriate to report it to him, as involving his slave—or his freedman, or whatever Varazda was. But Aristokles had been there, and frankly his response had been one of the more peculiar parts of the incident.

He should tell Nione—though Aristokles would no doubt do so himself, perhaps already had. Aristokles might also complain to Eurydemos about the behaviour of his student. That would be very appropriate.

Damiskos got out of bed and went to the portable shrine to Terza that he had set up in a suitable corner of his room the previous morning. It was a day for burning incense, but he had used up all his small supply on the journey over the mountains. The rubrics specified only a sweet smell, so it was possible to use something other than incense. His eyes fell again on the handkerchief by the bed.

On impulse, he picked it up and brought it to his nose. It smelled of perfume. He had rinsed out the traces of blood the night before, and it was still slightly damp. He shook it out and draped it over the incense burner in his shrine and made his customary brisk and unemotional morning prayer.

He heard voices from the winter dining room on the other side of the atrium as soon as he emerged from his room.

"Gelon says your slave attacked him last night—and I say you should have him beaten for it!"

"I suppose it's my business what I choose to do with my own slave, sir."

"Not when he begins attacking free Phemians, *sir*! Then it's everyone's business to see he's punished."

"Some of us"—here Damiskos thought he recognized the voice of Helenos, calm and reasonable as ever—"wonder that you would see fit to bring such a slave into a Phemian household."

Damiskos stepped through the dining-room door. The men inside looked up at his arrival.

Along with Aristokles and Helenos, Gelon was there, looking distinctly shifty and rather sick, his white face decorated with a livid bruise under one eye. Kleitos was there too; he was the one who had been remonstrating with Aristokles. Varazda was not present, and Damiskos did not know whether to think this a mercy or not.

"First Spear," said Helenos smoothly. "Ah, my apologies —Damiskos, I mean. You and I were speaking yesterday of the matter."

Damiskos frowned at him.

"You agreed with me," Helenos continued undaunted,

"that no Pseuchaian should own a creature so contrary to nature. I believe the word you used was 'repellant.'"

Damiskos carefully said nothing. Behind Helenos, Gelon was looking as if he wished he was dead. Aristokles was looking rather queasy too, come to that.

"Repellant!" Kleitos exclaimed. "That's a *polite* word, especially coming from a soldier." He laughed heartily and looked as if he would have slapped Damiskos on the shoulder if he had been standing nearer.

"What exactly are you speaking of?" Damiskos asked severely. It would be bad form—and giving up a tactical advantage—to admit he had overheard any of their conversation.

"Ah." Kleitos took over eagerly. "Gelon here appeared this morning with a bruised face, as you can see, and when I asked him about it, he said the Boukossian's eunuch lay in wait for him last night and launched a cowardly attack. I naturally sought out the slave's master and laid the matter before him, but he refuses to take action—perhaps because he doesn't believe Gelon's word, or perhaps—"

"He shouldn't believe it," Damiskos interrupted, "because Gelon is lying."

Kleitos gaped, but Damiskos thought it clear he was enjoying himself. He was obviously a busybody.

Damiskos had been told that he had no flair for the dramatic. He went on stolidly: "It may have been Aristokles's servant who gave Gelon that bruise, but I think it more likely I did it myself. I came upon the two of them fighting last night, and it was very clear to me that Gelon was the aggressor. He ran when I took away his knife."

Kleitos turned on Gelon. "Is this true?"

"No! I mean, I did have a knife, and I was—but I didn't start it. He attacked me—or, anyway, I thought he was going to. I was defending myself."

"You interrupted the eunuch in some suspicious activity, didn't you?" Helenos prompted.

"Well, I—that is, I—we're not going to talk about that?" It was an appeal to the older student, as if Gelon feared they were veering off some script agreed beforehand. That was interesting.

"I'm sure we can all imagine the sort of thing," said Helenos delicately.

Kleitos shuddered. "Well, however it got started, it ended with a Sasian eunuch laying hands on a Phemian citizen, and I remain firm in my opinion that he should be whipped."

"I feel bound to say," said Damiskos, "that I saw nothing to support that judgement. If we were in the city and the matter were taken to law, I would testify to it." He would also mention the fact that Varazda was apparently free, which changed the legal character of the matter considerably.

"Thank you," said Aristokles with a pathetic dignity. "I shall consider what you have said and decide what to do with my own slave, as is my right."

After a little more muttering and blustering, the two students and Kleitos left the dining room. Aristokles lingered as if anxious to let them get well ahead of him. He glanced back at Damiskos with a wan smile.

"Much obliged, I'm sure."

"What are you doing pretending that Va—Pharastes—is your slave if you've freed him?"

"What am I ... oh, well, it's just easier. Everyone assumes, you know."

Damiskos frowned. That didn't make much sense. "Still, you were there last night. And surely Pharastes told you what happened. I am surprised you did not defend him more strenuously."

"Surprised" was maybe not the right word. "Disgusted" might have been a better one.

"I—I don't know what happened," Aristokles protested—nervously, Damiskos thought. "I mean, Gelon's a monomaniac, isn't he? Perhaps he saw Pharastes outside that philosopher's door and thought he was sneaking in for an assignation!"

This was such a strange answer that it took Damiskos a moment to absorb it.

"Was Pharastes outside Eurydemos's door?" he said finally.

"Well, I don't know! He might have been."

"He's your servant. Shouldn't you know where he is?"

"Not all the time! I can't keep track of him all the time!"

"I see." Then Damiskos remembered something. "He can't have been having an assignation with Eurydemos last night—at least not in Eurydemos's room—because Eurydemos wasn't in his room. I saw him in the garden, and then I met him coming in from the garden on my way back to bed."

"I *know* he wasn't having an assignation with—with … But the point is, Gelon doesn't know that, does he?"

And anyway, Damiskos was about to add, *Eurydemos is in love with Nione.* Then he remembered that he had assumed Eurydemos was in love with Nione on the strength of that poem about a fruitless tree … which possibly meant something else entirely.

Had Eurydemos been waiting in the garden for Varazda, who hadn't arrived because he had retreated to his own bed after the scene with Gelon? Somehow that didn't quite fit. What had Aristokles been doing, if that were the case?

"Well," said Damiskos, "as you say, he is a monomaniac. I hope he will not cause you or your servant any more trouble."

Aristokles shuddered.

"Have you told our host?" Damiskos asked.

"What? Told her what?"

"Told her," said Damiskos patiently, "what happened last night. That one of her other guests attacked Pharastes."

"No, no." Aristokles waved a hand. "Nothing to do with her."

"I beg to differ. If it had happened under your own roof, to one of your own guests, I'm sure you would want to know."

"Yes, yes, of course, and I will tell her at the—at the appropriate juncture." Aristokles had been looking away impatiently toward the door, but now he glanced back sharply at Damiskos. "I beg you would not say anything yourself."

That sounded quite sincere, and Damiskos found it somewhat alarming.

"I don't know what you're up to, Aristokles," he said, "but I don't like it. Refusing to take action when one of the other guests attempts to rape your freedman—"

"Attempts to—? No, no—you've got it quite wrong. That wasn't what he was doing at all." The Boukossian seemed surprised by the suggestion.

"How do you know?" Damiskos countered. "Did you ask your servant what happened?"

"Of course I did," Aristokles snapped. "Look, you simple little soldier, you have *no idea* what is going on here. There are things in motion—affairs of the highest—you have no idea."

"Really."

"Really. Now leave me and Pharastes alone."

Damiskos narrowed his eyes at the Boukossian. "I will … if you'll leave Nione Kukara alone."

"Oh, yes, yes, yes," Aristokles crowed. "I knew this was about jealousy at heart. I could tell you—the things I could tell you. You've no idea."

"So you keep saying."

Damiskos could tell that Aristokles was making a colossal

effort not to tell him absolutely all about it, and he had a feeling that if he just waited long enough, and looked unimpressed enough, the Boukossian would lose the struggle. Unfortunately, they were interrupted by a slave with a broom peeping through the dining-room doors to see whether she could come in to sweep, and this gave Aristokles all the distraction he needed to think better of whatever he had been about to say. He pulled himself together, sleeking back his hair with one hand, and cast Damiskos a dark look as he stalked out of the room.

Still turning the conversation over in his mind, Damiskos went out to the garden, where he was met by an entirely normal scene of Nione breakfasting at her private table with Phaia. She beckoned him over to join them.

"Shall we take a walk down the shore to look over the factory this morning?" Nione suggested when he had taken a seat.

"Yes. Excellent."

He was startled to catch an obviously hostile look from Phaia. It was gone in an instant, and he thought perhaps it hadn't had anything to do with him. Sometimes he himself was accused of frowning forbiddingly at people when he thought he was simply giving them a neutral look.

"May I come too?" Phaia asked, turning to their host. "I haven't seen the factory."

"Of course, if you like." After a moment, almost shyly, she added, "I should love to show it off to you."

Damiskos ate in silence while the two women talked. He wasn't inclined to honour Aristokles's request that he say nothing to Nione of what had happened last night. But he wasn't inclined to talk about it in front of Phaia either, so for the moment he had little choice but to keep quiet.

After breakfast, the three of them walked down from the villa to the complex of buildings by the shoreline that housed the fish-sauce operation. The path descended the cliffside with the aid of several steep flights of stairs. Damiskos was embarrassed by how slowly the two women were forced to go for his sake.

"Will you be staying long?" Phaia asked him coolly.

"At least a fortnight, I hope," said Nione before he could answer.

"Really?" said Phaia. "That seems a long time to spend buying fish sauce."

Nione laughed.

"My commanding officer thought I needed a holiday," said Damiskos, "after … There was a lot of trouble with the grain shortages in the winter. I hope I hadn't complained, but I suppose I must have been looking tired."

Once he'd been able to lead troops into battle after days of hard riding through the hostile coastlands of Zash, but these days apparently a few late nights in an office were enough to make him look like he needed a holiday.

"I see," said Phaia. "Well, for my part, I'm sure I shall never want to leave." She smiled, intimately and dazzlingly, up at Nione.

"Oh, come," said Nione, but she looked as if she was suppressing a smile of her own.

Damiskos wondered if that was what it looked like—women had different ways of behaving with one another, so it didn't do to make assumptions—and whether Phaia *had* been glaring at him after all because she thought he was trying to flirt with Nione too.

He also thought that he was going to need another holiday after this one.

The fish-sauce factory was set on a white sweep of shoreline below the promontory that held the villa. The buildings, of whitewashed stone, stood near the waterline, and a pair of neat fishing boats were moored at the end of a stone jetty. Workers were busy processing the morning's catch at a long table on the shore.

The smell hit them almost as soon as they arrived on the beach: a wave of fishiness, with undercurrents of decay and fermentation and salt. It got stronger as they approached. Damiskos tried to think what to say about it, but couldn't come up with anything polite.

"Occasionally, when there's a stiff wind, you get a whiff of that in the garden," said Nione. "But only occasionally."

"I suppose you wouldn't be out in the garden much in a stiff wind," said Damiskos.

"No," said Nione, "that's true."

Phaia looked nauseous.

Inside, the factory was a model of efficiency, everything well-appointed and clean. There were outdoor tanks, a fermenting house, a smaller building where the finished sauce was bottled, and a warehouse which contained jars of sauce ready to ship, along with some wine and olives and other products of the estate.

Nione introduced her foreman, who proudly pointed out the improvements they had made, all the new work that had been done to the buildings since Nione bought the operation. The work of the factory was done by a small staff, six slaves under the oversight of the foreman, while the crews of the two fishing boats that supplied them were free contractors who leased their vessels from Nione and also sold fresh fish up and down the coast.

"The factory didn't belong to my family," Nione explained, as they came back out of the bottling house onto the sunlit shore. "It just happened to be for sale at the same time that I moved back to the neighbourhood. We haven't changed the recipe or the method of production at all. My focus has been on improving distribution."

"Very sensible," said Damiskos.

He was envious, actually. She seemed to have found a new passion after leaving the Maidens. He wished he had something similar. He would have loved to run a business, to renovate an old house, to live quietly in the country—though to tell the truth he liked the city just as well. But his father had sold the family home years ago, and his parents lived in rented rooms. Damiskos had forfeited his pension by going back to work, and there had been no dowry for him when he left the Second Koryphos.

The foreman reappeared, followed by a boy carrying a tray with several small cups. Damiskos hoped fleetingly that this wasn't what it looked like.

"I thought you would like to sample our product," said the foreman.

"Of course," said Damiskos neutrally.

The factory made three different grades of fish sauce, and the foreman had brought samples of each. Damiskos dutifully sipped them all. Phaia declined, not very politely.

Damiskos wasn't picky about food; he didn't mind a dish strongly flavoured with fish sauce, but he wasn't one of those people who liked to slop it on everything. He certainly had never felt inclined to drink it straight, and the experience didn't change his mind.

"Let's walk a little further down the beach," Nione suggested, after her foreman had departed.

"Yes, let's," said Phaia.

She tucked her hand through Nione's arm, murmuring something about how hard it was to walk on the soft sand. She wore stout sandals, and Damiskos doubted that she was really having difficulty. They made a striking pair, Phaia wispy and delicate and pale, Nione tall and lean, with her braids and her dark brown skin.

He tried to fall behind discreetly, but they were walking slowly enough even for him. He was steeling himself to admit that his knee hurt—it did, but that wasn't the main reason he wanted to go back to the house. He felt very much in the way, and was more and more convinced that Phaia resented his presence. He couldn't even really blame her.

They rounded a spur of rock that jutted onto the beach, and a small, exquisite cove opened up before them. A pair of tiny, whitewashed, slate-roofed stone huts nestled at the top of the wide, white beach. They were sheltered from the smell of the factory here, and it was very quiet.

"Those were ancient houses," Nione said, pointing to the little buildings. "The walls have been here as long as anyone can remember. I had roofs put on and turned them into beach huts."

"How perfect," Phaia breathed. "The whole setting. It will make an ideal exercise ground for our school, Nione. Running along the beach at sunrise—ah! So invigorating. Of course I can't exercise with the men, but you'd keep me company, wouldn't you?"

"Running?" Nione laughed. "Blessed Orante, I don't think so. Not unless something were chasing me."

"Just watching would be perfect."

Nione turned to Damiskos, who was just opening his mouth to say that it was time he headed back to the house. "Did I tell you, Damiskos? Phaia is trying to convince me to let her fellow students take up residence at Laothalia."

"Oh. Really. I see."

"Yes, you see, Eurydemos is my first cousin, and he was robbed of his inheritance by our grandfather—it's a long, sad story. But I do feel myself obligated to make things right, as best I can. I don't mean to suggest that he views himself as having a right to my property … "

"Of course not!" Phaia chimed in. "He would never say such a thing—even though it is true. He is happy just to be invited to stay here. But no one suggests—no one would dream of suggesting—you ought to give up the villa to him. We simply think it would be a lovely gesture if you made room here for his school. Besides, Laothalia would suit us so well."

"It is so far from the city, though," said Nione doubtfully.

Damiskos thought he knew what Phaia would say to that.

"Oh, but that is an advantage! To be able to escape the clamour of the city would be bliss. To leave behind the cries of the marketplace and the wrangling of politicians … "

Yes, that was about what he had expected.

So the philosopher was leeching off Nione on the strength of some injury two generations back, and his students were badgering her to give over part of her home for them to discuss their claptrap and go running on the beach. In Nione's place he would have shut the whole thing down when it was first proposed.

Or maybe he wouldn't. She missed the communal life of the Maidens' House, just as he missed the camaraderie of the army. Maybe she would enjoy living among the students.

Finally he found an opportunity to announce his intention to return to the villa, but to Phaia's obvious annoyance, Nione agreed that it was time for them all to go back.

"What about Aristokles Phoskos?" Phaia asked on the way back, in the midst of a conversation that Damiskos had been trying not to listen to. "Is he here to buy fish sauce too?"

"No! He's here to meet Eurydemos—well, mainly. He's a kinsman of a friend, who asked me to invite him as a favour because he was dying to meet your master."

"Really? But he's hardly spoken to our master. At least I haven't seen them speak."

"No? Oh, well. Perhaps he's just shy."

"That's odd, though," Phaia persisted. "Don't you suspect something?"

"Suspect something?"

"Yes, that he's up to something—you know."

47

"I—I don't, really. What do you mean? He's … he's trying to court me, if that's what you mean. But that's not suspicious, just … well."

"Unwelcome?" Phaia suggested archly.

"Oh, very much so, I'm afraid."

Phaia glanced over her shoulder at Damiskos, eyes narrowed. He looked back at her blankly.

As they climbed the steep track toward the villa, he considered the question of what Aristokles was doing there. It was, as Phaia pointed out, odd. He had clearly come under some form of false pretences and was lying about more than one thing. To learn that Nione didn't really know him at all but had invited him at the request of a friend—that was unsettling.

Had he really come expressly to court Nione, ready with imported Zashian jewellery to offer her? It was certainly possible. But it didn't explain his bluster that morning about "things in motion."

Damiskos could think of one way he might find out more.

He spent the rest of the day in a less sociable—and less enjoyable—version of the sort of thing Themistos had recommended to him when sending him to Laothalia. He worked up the courage to ask the steward if she could arrange a packed lunch for him, and she did, without comment, and he took Xanthe out for a ride in the country-side around the villa. The cleared land of the estate was surrounded by thick scrubland, with a fringe of taller trees planted around the villa proper. There were not many places to ride, and he was preoccupied and out of sorts anyway. The lunch, which was excellent, was the only high point.

In the evening they dined outdoors again. Gelon was not

there, but Varazda stood against a column behind Aristokles's couch. His hair was done up like a scourge again today, and he wore a sleeveless coat of bright blue silk embroidered with poppies over a shirt of paler blue. His trousers matched the colour of the embroidered poppies. Damiskos thought that he looked tired.

Several times in the course of the meal, Damiskos found himself looking at Varazda and realizing that Varazda had noticed him doing it. Finally, towards the end of the meal, Damiskos looked across the couches and saw Varazda's eyes on him. The eunuch tipped his head discreetly toward the twilit garden beyond the summer dining room. Damiskos tried to convey that he had got the message without being too obvious about it. He didn't dare look at his fellow diners to see if he had succeeded. He waited, wine cup frozen in his hand, to see what Varazda would do.

Varazda was leaning down to speak to Aristokles, and Aristokles was nodding and reaching up to pat his attendant on the arm, gently dismissing him. Varazda moved around behind the couches and slipped out into the garden. Damiskos finished his wine.

"I think I had better ... had better head to my room," he said, reaching for his sandals.

"Of course," said Nione, just as Eurydemos said, "So soon?" and Kleitos said, "What, already?"

Damiskos mustered a yawn. "I'm ... rather tired."

"Not to worry," said Nione. "You are supposed to be on holiday, after all. Take the opportunity to rest."

Helenos was yawning too, and murmured something about following his example. Damiskos got his sandals on and made his escape back toward the house.

Varazda materialized from the shadows at the head of the passage that led into the atrium. Exactly like a court eunuch in a Zashian romance, Damiskos thought. Varazda disappeared down the passage, and Damiskos followed.

A lamp was burning halfway down the short corridor. Varazda stopped before reaching its pool of warm light, still in the shadows. He turned to Damiskos.

"So. What do you want?" He spoke Zashian, with his courtier's accent.

"Want?" Damiskos repeated.

"You've been looking at me all evening."

"Divine Terza," Damiskos swore. "It was so obvious?"

"Maybe only to me." He managed to make that sound patronizing.

"I—just—I wished to talk to you." Damiskos's Zashian was stilted and rusty, but he did his best.

"Yes," said Varazda, with an air of great patience. "So I gathered. We are talking now."

"Yes."

This was a different person than the one who had thanked him the night before, who had looked surprised when Damiskos apologized. This was the same lacquered rudeness that had made Damiskos dislike Varazda initially. Only now Damiskos knew there was more to him than this.

"And?" Varazda prompted. "Perhaps you wish to remind me that you saved me from a flogging—or worse—this morning?"

"I told the truth about what I had seen—but you couldn't have been flogged, you know. You're no longer enslaved."

"True."

"I was in the army for a long time," Damiskos offered. "Sometimes I forget that I can't be reported for dereliction of duty anymore."

Varazda leaned one shoulder against the wall. It was a relaxed pose, but he didn't look relaxed. Damiskos found himself wishing that he could see him better, without the concealing shadows.

"Well?" Varazda prompted again. "What ... do ... you ... want?"

"I don't—Well. There is one thing. Something I wanted to ask you."

There was a pause. Damiskos could not read Varazda's expression in the dark, but he didn't need to see him to feel the tension coming off him. Obviously Damiskos had said something wrong, but he couldn't work out what.

He wanted to offer some kind of help, but didn't know how to do it in a way that wouldn't seem both condescending and overbearing. Besides, he had so little idea of what was going on here. He wasn't sure whether to say, "I've got my eye on you two," or "Call on me if you need anything."

"Yes?" said Varazda finally.

A female slave emerged from the dark atrium and slipped past them. Damiskos waited for her to exit to the garden.

"We shouldn't talk here. It's hardly private."

"Hardly."

There was another pause. Varazda seemed to be waiting for something. Then abruptly he pushed himself away from the wall, hennaed fingers flicking back a stray braid.

"Lead the way," he said. He had switched to Pseuchaian too; it didn't put him at a disadvantage.

Damiskos took the lamp from its bracket and went down the hall and around the corner to the library anteroom, where he opened the door. Varazda stopped, a faint look of surprise on his face. He had obviously expected them to go somewhere else.

"Oh," said Damiskos. "I forgot, I still have your handkerchief. Come, I'll give it back to you."

He led the way to his own door and held it open, noticing as Varazda walked through it that his posture and movements were much more masculine than they had seemed earlier, almost stiffly so.

"It's right here," Damiskos said, closing the door and gesturing toward the shrine in the corner.

Varazda frowned. "You appear to have dedicated it to your deity. I would not dream of taking it." He walked closer and leaned in to inspect the figure in the shrine.

Damiskos plucked the handkerchief off the unlit incense burner and held it out. "I didn't dedicate your handkerchief. Just the scent on it."

He gritted his teeth in anticipation of whatever delicately snide comment was coming. Zashians loved to make jokes about the number and behaviour of Pseuchaian gods and the rituals with which they were worshipped.

"Oh." Varazda took the handkerchief. "I'm sure Terza will have appreciated it. It's very expensive." He tucked the colourful cloth back into his sash. "And … your question?"

"I know it's none of my affair, but … last night, Gelon tried to force himself on you, didn't he?" He didn't believe Aristokles's assertion to the contrary, any more than he had believed Gelon's weird, weak story about what had happened.

Varazda's eyebrows went up. He had elegant, effeminate eyebrows, well matched to his painted eyes. "He didn't, no. What gave you that idea?"

Now Damiskos was completely at a loss—and more than a little embarrassed. What *had* given him the idea?

"I—I don't know, I just … "

In fact, he remembered very clearly. He had looked at Varazda in the dark and been struck by how beautiful he was. Somehow this had suggested what Gelon's motivation must have been. He could see now that this didn't really make sense.

"Because he was carrying on about Kossian lovers at dinner?" Varazda suggested. "Did that seem a little pointed? Well, it doesn't matter. That wasn't what happened."

"That's—that's good. I wouldn't have said anything, only I thought … you hadn't told your master—former master, and that you ought to, because ... But if that wasn't what happened, then ... That's good."

"Is it?" Varazda's tone was very dry.

"Yes, but—what did happen?"

"What did happen ... " Varazda considered him thoughtfully for a moment, clearly deciding what to tell him —clearly not caring that it was obvious this was what he was doing. "Aristokles wanted to visit the kitchen for a snack. I was waiting for him in the yard, alone, and Gelon snuck up on me and threatened me with a knife. We fought briefly— he found me more of an opponent than he had expected— and then you arrived, and you know the rest."

"He ambushed you? But—immortal gods—why? Do you have any idea?"

"Mm. I have some idea."

Damiskos looked at him expectantly. "And?"

"I appreciate that you're trying to make this your business, First Spear. I'm grateful for your intervention last night, and for your defence today. But it isn't, really. Your business."

"Ah," said Damiskos, chastened and—once again— embarrassed. Also annoyed, but he thought Varazda was being deliberately annoying, and he wished he knew why. "Well. You can't say fairer than that, I guess."

Varazda made his courtly little gesture.

"Having said that ... " Damiskos began.

"Yes?"

"Having said that, your patron is obviously up to something under my friend's roof. You've more or less admitted as much, though it was already clear enough before you did. I don't want harm to come to Nione, but I also wouldn't wish to see you hurt—and you've obviously already been put in danger. I don't think Aristokles is doing much to look out for you. I want you to know that if you need help, you can count on me.

"Also, if you're up to something even slightly shady in my

friend's house, be assured that I will stand in your way."

Varazda had been looking more and more surprised throughout Damiskos's speech, and at the end he actually smiled, a broad, genuine, captivating smile.

"What was the phrase you just used? 'You can't say fairer than that'?"

Varazda moved toward the door, and Damiskos followed. He didn't want to leave it like this. He sought for something more to say, something that might help to get them on the same side.

"If you're showing loyalty to Aristokles because … "

Varazda's hand was on the door handle. He looked back, his expression guarded again. "Because … "

"Because you're lovers. I mean, I assume you are, and … "

"Holy God." Varazda dropped back into Zashian for the oath, and his accent was briefly provincial, no longer the polished syllables of the court. "You never stop. That is *irrelevant* to you, First Spear. That is the very definition of none of your business. Go back to negotiating about your rotting fish guts, or whatever it is, and forget about me and Aristokles."

He pulled open the door, and would have slipped out and closed it behind him in one motion if Damiskos hadn't caught it. Instead the two of them were framed there in the lamplight from the room, in full view of Helenos, who was crossing the atrium, headed for the stairs.

"Goodness," said Helenos mildly, stopping to give them a humorous look. "I'm sure this can't be what it looks like."

"Certainly not, we were—"

"Don't be silly," said Varazda, in a girlish tone and thick Zashian accent that Damiskos had not heard before. "Of course it is just what it looks like."

And he turned in the doorway and lightly, precisely kissed Damiskos on the lips.

"Good night, First Spear."

CHAPTER 5

SOMEHOW DAMISKOS MANAGED to get the door shut without looking at Helenos. What his own face might have betrayed he had no idea, but he had to hope that between the lamplight behind him and the shadows in the atrium, it had not been much. At least he could be reasonably sure that it hadn't been dismay or disgust.

The kiss lingered on his senses like a vanished phrase of music, tantalizing and irrecoverable. The cool softness of Varazda's lips; the tiny, fleeting brush of his fingertips along Damiskos's jaw; the scent that he wore, citrus and something spicy, neither masculine nor feminine. Damiskos felt a warmth sinking into the core of his being, as if that strange moment echoed in some hollow place inside him.

It had been a long time since anyone kissed him. Years. Not since Shahaz, he thought. Was that true?

Not that Shahaz had ever kissed him—that would have been very bold—but he had kissed her, and it amounted to the same thing. And since then … there had been encounters here and there, but kissing hadn't been involved. It was an odd thought.

He sat down heavily on the bed. His own reaction to the

kiss was the least important thing here. He tried to sort out the things that had just become clear to him.

Helenos had seen Varazda slipping out of Damiskos's room, and—perhaps because he still thought of Damiskos as a kindred spirit, perhaps because he was so attached to his own prejudices that he didn't see Varazda as attractive—he hadn't wanted to believe he had witnessed the end of a tryst. But Varazda had been at pains to prove that he *had*.

Why? Well, possibly just to be a bastard. But more likely because there was some other interpretation that he didn't want Helenos to put on the scene.

He didn't want Helenos to think that he and Damiskos had just been talking.

Of course he wouldn't have kissed Damiskos otherwise. From the beginning of their exchange in the passage, he'd been afraid Damiskos had been coming onto him, and he hadn't welcomed it. In fact—*Terza's balls*—he'd thought Damiskos was trying to blackmail him into his bed.

Staring at him all through dinner, following him out into the hall, wanting to talk to him alone after intervening to defend him from guests who wanted him whipped. That was what "What do you want?" had meant. Then Damiskos had capped it all by asking whether Varazda was sleeping with his former master. Immortal gods. "It's irrelevant to you," Varazda had said—meaning, *Even if I'm not, that doesn't mean I want to sleep with you*. And then he'd felt compelled to kiss Damiskos in front of Helenos. He must have had a very good reason.

Of course Damiskos wanted to know what that reason was, but it was quite true that this was all very much none of his business. Still, it would be only decent of him to let Varazda know he hadn't misinterpreted the kiss. "I realize you didn't do that because you wanted to, and don't worry, *I* didn't want you to either—there's no question of my being attracted to you, that was all just a misunderstanding, and I spoke in your defence because it was the right thing to do."

That was true, wasn't it?

Shahaz was in his mind again—naturally enough, since he had just been thinking of her. He found himself comparing his memory of her to Varazda, which was perhaps less natural. They were really nothing alike. Shahaz's hair was lighter, a warm brown, her skin honey-hued, her cheeks soft, dimpling when she smiled. She had plump hands and wore subdued colours, as befit a modest girl of her class. Or she had, six years ago. She was probably—certainly—a married woman by now.

Perhaps her accent and Varazda's were similar; it had been a long time, and he didn't remember Shahaz's accent clearly, though he did remember her singing voice. He wondered whether Varazda sang. Some eunuchs were trained to it—but of course Varazda was a dancer.

After that, it was perhaps not surprising that he had another bad night's sleep. Voices from the atrium woke him some time before dawn. They sounded agitated, but he couldn't identify the speakers. A man and a woman, he thought. Or at any rate a man and someone with a higher voice. A third voice growled something about "calming down" and "dealing with it." Damiskos heard brisk footsteps receding toward the back of the house, and then silence.

Damiskos woke the following morning wondering how soon he could decently leave Laothalia. He had only been here two days, but his business with Nione was virtually complete. He had satisfied himself that Nione's factory would make a good supplier for the legions, and they had negotiated the details of the contract. He needed only to make payment for the first shipment of sauce and settle on a date for its delivery.

He should probably stay out the week; it would be insulting to Nione not to do so. He could manage five more days, and then he would make his excuses and apologies and go home.

He would tell Nione about Gelon attacking Varazda, and what Aristokles and Varazda had said to him about it afterwards—he'd do that as soon as possible. If she wanted him to stay longer to help her deal with them, well, of course he would. But he doubted she really needed his help. She had a whole villa full of staff, including her formidable steward, who could help her evict Aristokles if it turned out he was here to rob or defraud her or otherwise cause trouble. It wasn't, as Damiskos had been repeatedly reminded, any of his business.

Having made this decision, he felt a weight lifted from his spirit, and paradoxically found himself determined to enjoy what was left of his stay at the villa.

Nione was not in the garden, and her servants thought she was not up yet, so he went down to the fishing pier. He found Kleitos already there, with a line in the water, wrapped in a mantle and looking like he hadn't slept. Helenos arrived while Damiskos was baiting his own hook.

"Good morning," said Damiskos.

Helenos looked at him assessingly for a moment, then sat on the pier beside him. "What's going on, Damiskos from the Quartermaster's Office? What was the Sasian eunuch really doing in your room last night?"

He seemed genuinely to expect an answer to that, not just to be teasing. It left Damiskos at a loss.

"I'm not going to give you a detailed account," Damiskos said, feeling that this struck the right note while being literally true.

Helenos looked at him for a moment with plain confusion. "Oh," he said finally. "Well, I suppose you must take your pleasure where you like. Far be it from me to dictate the terms of your private life."

"Not at all," said Damiskos equably. Aside from those remarks about Sasians the other day, the fellow had been quite friendly.

"I seem to have been mistaken about you," Helenos remarked. "I see that now."

"Do you." That wasn't so friendly.

"Yes, I had imagined you were an ally to our cause. Given your military record. I thought you saw the importance of preserving Phemian purity and felt a distaste for the Sasian slave."

They sat in uncomfortable silence for a few minutes. Damiskos was becoming more and more annoyed. What possible business was it of Helenos's whether he and Varazda were sleeping together?

Maybe it had to do with their rubbish about masculine and feminine principles. Damiskos had no bent for philosophy, and had always thought the ascetic strictures of the Marble Porches—what he knew of them—incompatible with a soldier's life.

They would say it was natural for men to desire women, but if you spent too much of your time with women, or took them too seriously, it made you unmanly. Men ought to reserve their purest affections for other men, they said. But they meant something quite specific by that. They liked to trot out examples of legendary heroes dying in each other's arms, and primly remind you that the poets said nothing about them doing anything else in each other's arms beforehand—as if that proved anything, except about the philosophers' own preoccupations. Their idea of the virtuous man was someone who didn't love anyone, male or female, really heartily. He wouldn't have any use for a person so ambiguous as Varazda, except as an object-lesson on the unnaturalness of barbaric Sasians.

Of course, Damiskos had no use for him either. Obviously.

It wasn't a matter of "use." Anyway, it was irrelevant.

"What does it really mean, 'Phemian purity'?" Damiskos asked suddenly.

"It means purging the Republic of the poison—"

"Not the metaphors. What does it actually mean?"

Helenos looked at him. "It means our ancestors were great men, and we are pitiful by comparison. It means banishing the foreigners from our streets and from our shores. It means putting pressure on Boukos to do the same. It means—as I'm sure you realize—war with Zash. The Republic was forged in the fires of war and has never been stronger than when it has stood against Zash. That is what I mean when I say 'Phemian purity.' And how are we to achieve that, you ask? Wait and see, my friend. Wait and see."

That was deeply unsettling, and Damiskos did not immediately know what to say to it. Helenos did not look as though he expected an answer. In fact, he looked rather like someone who had picked up an edged weapon in the middle of a training bout and felt pleased with the result.

Damiskos knew how to turn away a sharp sword with a wooden one, but he didn't really know what to do here.

"I cannot agree," he said stiffly at last. "I cannot approve of any of that."

"Mm," said Helenos. "As I said, I was mistaken about you. Still, respect is due to the service you gave the Republic."

At that moment Damiskos's line jerked in the water, and he was occupied with landing a large bonito, so it was Helenos who had the satisfaction of getting up and walking off without another word.

By the time Damiskos's fish was safely in a basket on the pier, Phaia had come down to speak to Helenos. She looked worse than Kleitos, her eyes dark-ringed and her hair wilder

60

than usual, though it suited her in a way. Helenos drew her away to talk privately.

Eurydemos arrived, with his mantle over his head, and sat down on the pier beside Damiskos.

"So how was he?"

Damiskos looked up. "Excuse me?"

"Aristokles's exquisite Sasian. I hear you've beaten me to the finish line there."

The words were archly coarse, but his tone was wistful.

"I didn't—don't know what you're talking about," Damiskos managed stiffly.

Of course that wasn't true. He remembered that poem about the unfruitful tree. But Eurydemos smiled and let the subject drop.

Terza's head, what a lot of ghastly people Nione seemed to have gathered around herself. Did he really have to stay out the week?

Damiskos took his fish and went back up to the house. He asked for the mistress, anxious to have that conversation that would determine how much longer he need stay in this wretched place. He was told she was out in the vineyard.

He took the fish to the kitchen himself—the slave offered to do it, but he said there was no need—and from there went across the yard to check on Xanthe. He spent some time chatting with the stable hand about the merits of different feed and grooming techniques. He felt as if there was something else he needed to be doing, but he reminded himself that he was on holiday; he was supposed to be enjoying himself. He enjoyed talking to people about horses.

He left the stable feeling somewhat more sanguine about the world again.

The villa's stables lay next to the slave quarters, and there was a small, sunlit yard between the two. As Damiskos emerged into this space, a trio of domestic slaves—two young women and an elderly one—sat working in the yard and watching an impromptu performance. Varazda was practicing, dancing without music in a flat, sandy area between the stairs and the wall.

He was barefoot, his hair loose down his back. He wore a plain dark coat that swung around him, the fabric as much a part of the dance as the two swords that flashed in his hands. They were long, Zashian-style, singled-edged swords, and he handled them effortlessly, twirling them in elaborate arcs and slices as he moved. It was delicate and martial at the same time, a far more impressive and dignified use of the weapons than Damiskos had imagined. He stood with his hand on the stable door, watching, transfixed.

Varazda flipped the two swords to hold the hilts together, the blades pointing in opposite directions, and spun them as if they were one fearsome, twin-bladed weapon. He leaned gracefully back, long hair swinging free, as he flipped them up above his head. Then he separated them and swept them out to the sides as he dropped to one knee, the skirt of his coat settling around him. His audience—the ones he was aware of—applauded.

He got to his feet, smiling a kind of modest, genuine smile that Damiskos had not seen on his face before. Neither he nor the women had noticed Damiskos.

"Finished already?" said the older women, obviously disappointed, as Varazda picked up his swords and tucked them under one arm.

"It is getting late—I must go dress and attend my master."

The women made regretful noises.

"If you want help with your hair or your makeup," said one of the younger women, "let me know."

The others laughed. It was at that moment that Varazda

looked across the yard and saw Damiskos. His smile faded slightly.

"Thank you," he said, replying to the women. "I think I'll be all right."

He turned and disappeared into the space under the stairs along the front of the slave quarters.

"Good morning, sir," said the older woman, noticing Damiskos at last and scrambling to her feet. "Can we help you? Are you looking for someone?"

"No, no, thank you. Don't mind me."

The slaves went back to their work. Damiskos crossed the yard to the shadowed space under the stairs. He would compliment Varazda on his dancing and then bring up the subject of last night, he decided, after having established a more friendly mood.

Varazda was stripping off his coat in front of the fountain set into the wall of the slave quarters. He wore dark trousers under it and no shirt. It was a little surprising, Damiskos thought, that he would strip down more or less in public. Zashians were peculiarly reluctant about displaying skin; it was one way they held themselves distinct from the barbaric westerners. And after all, most of the kingdom was cold for large parts of the year, so they could afford their taboos.

Varazda scooped up water from the fountain, splashed his face, and ran his wet hands over his throat and underneath the heavy fall of his hair. He looked up and saw Damiskos. He snatched up his coat exactly like a nymph caught bathing by a satyr.

Damiskos started and gabbled out an apology. Gods. He'd *just* been thinking that Zashians had different customs; he should have had the decency not to sneak up on Varazda when he was half naked. Not that he'd intended to sneak up, of course, but that must have been what it looked like.

Varazda had tossed down his coat and was simply glaring at Damiskos now, and Damiskos wondered if he should back away, or if he had already been standing there for too long to do that, or what in the world he should do.

Somehow it didn't help that Varazda stripped to the waist was absolutely a sight that would have been worth sneaking up to see. He was thin but very fit, the muscles of his arms and torso crisply defined under his pale skin. It was not surprising, of course, after seeing him dance, but it was a beautiful contrast with the flowing grace that he presented when fully clothed.

"I'm sorry," Damiskos repeated leadenly. He realized Varazda was probably less embarrassed to have been caught without his shirt than annoyed at having been startled into acting as if he was embarrassed.

Varazda narrowed his eyes at him. "For what?"

Really, the fellow was impossible. "For—for—I don't know." He gestured unhelpfully. "You seem offended by something, and I'm sorry for it. I saw you dancing just now. It was very impressive." He sought for something more specific to say. "The swords that you use, are they weighted like real swords, or … "

The swords were lying across the corner of the fountain. Varazda reached back and picked one up and tossed it to Damiskos. He caught it awkwardly.

"Ah," he said, weighing it in his hand. "They *are* real swords. I see."

"They're not very sharp," Varazda admitted.

Damiskos turned the blade to catch the light from the yard. It was beautifully crafted, made of bronze, and looked as if it might be quite old. "Not completely dull, either."

He lifted the sword in his right hand, put his left on his hip, angling his body and the point of the blade in the best approximation of shu, the "ready" stance, that he could remember.

"It's been a few years," he said ruefully.

Varazda picked up the other sword. His stance was

elegant and precise—and he held it for only a moment before his sword flashed out and rang against Damiskos's. Blade skittered against blade, and the tip of Varazda's sword caught in the tracery of Damiskos's hilt, gave a sharp twist, and sent the sword spinning out of his hand to clatter on the stones of the yard.

"Nicely done," said Damiskos. He limped out into the yard to retrieve the sword.

Varazda dropped his sword's point. "Mm. It's a trick, and you were ready for it—you let go just as I caught the hilt."

Damiskos shrugged. "Makes the sword fly further—and prevents me getting a sprained wrist."

"I wasn't trying to give you a sprained wrist. I'm aware I'm no match for you. I don't really know how to fight—just tricks like that."

Damiskos handed him back his sword, and Varazda laid both weapons on the edge of the fountain again.

"I used to be pretty good with a Zashian blade," Damiskos said, "but it was only what you might call a hobby —professionally, of course, I used a Pseuchaian short sword." He still wore one, much of the time, but only as a mark of status, a familiar weight at his side. "And of course, on horse-back a spear and shield. The sword being only for close combat … "

He realized he was on the verge of becoming boring—if not well past it. He cleared his throat. "I haven't had much call to draw any kind of blade in the last five years." And he wasn't much use with one now either, with one knee unable to bend even halfway.

They stood a moment longer, regarding one another. The moment was different, somehow. Not less tense than their previous encounters, perhaps, but tense in a different way.

Damiskos remembered he had wanted to assure Varazda that he hadn't put the wrong interpretation on that kiss in the doorway. He quickly decided this was not the right time for that.

It was Varazda who broke the silence—which, after all, had not gone on very long. "I have work to do. Was there something you wanted?"

"Yes. I mean no—I just happened by, and—yes, I'll leave you to it. I really did enjoy the dance."

"Thank you," said Varazda in Zashian. "You are very kind."

He went back into the house and asked the young slave at the door, Niko, whether the mistress was back yet. Niko didn't know.

A female slave was coming down the stairs with a tray.

"Niko," she called from halfway down, "you told me Aristokles was still in bed, but—oh, I'm sorry, sir," she caught herself when she came down far enough to see Damiskos.

"Not at all. Is Aristokles up early this morning?" He put the question casually, but an instinct for trouble tugged at him.

"How can he not be in bed?" Niko demanded. "He hasn't come down, I know that."

"He's not in his room," the woman insisted. "I've just come from there." She held up the breakfast tray with its untouched bowls of food.

Niko looked at Damiskos as if for backup.

"Had his bed been slept in?" Damiskos asked. It seemed the next obvious question.

The woman considered. "No, sir. Now that you mention it. I don't believe it had. That's odd, isn't it, sir?"

"It would seem so," said Damiskos.

"All the other guests are up, and the mistress, so … you know … I'm not sure where he can have got to."

"He was still in the dining room when I left last night," Damiskos said. He remembered the voices he had heard in the early hours. "Does either of you know when he retired?"

He realized his attempt at sounding casual had rather broken down, but he couldn't think of any way to pursue the inquiry without sounding worried. And he was worried.

"Around midnight," said Niko. "By then it was just him and our mistress and that woman with the big eyes."

"Phaia," the female slave supplied.

"Yes, her. They all went in at the same time, but Aristokles has Pharastes to attend him, so none of us would have seen where he went."

A useful cover for skulking about the villa undetected, Damiskos thought.

"You should probably tell your mistress one of her guests is missing."

Niko looked sceptical. "Missing, sir?"

"Well, I mean. If he doesn't turn up."

"Of course, sir."

"Here, you take this," said the woman, pushing the untouched breakfast tray into the boy's hands. To Damiskos she said eagerly, "I'll run up again and see if his things are still in his room!"

She took off up the stairs, and Niko gave Damiskos the closest thing to a withering look that a respectful slave could allow himself. Damiskos smiled wryly back.

They were both still standing there when the woman came running back down and reported breathlessly, "They *aren't*! All his clothes and his trunk are gone! He left in the night!"

"Well, so, he left in the night," said Niko, striving to remain blasé. "People do sometimes."

"Around here? Where there are no neighbours? And there was no ship this morning. It's *odd*, Niko. Isn't it, sir?"

"It is rather odd," said Damiskos. "Might he have moved to another room?"

The slaves considered this.

"Maybe," said Niko. "But not without one of us knowing about it. Rhea and I are the ones who would have been called if a guest wanted to change rooms. I do luggage, and she does beds and breakfasts. Aradne would have told us if someone was being moved."

"Yes," said Rhea, "and anyway, all the rooms that are fit to be slept in right now are occupied. The others have got no beds, or leaks in the roof, or the floors are being retiled."

"I see," said Damiskos. "Well, there must be some other explanation."

"We had better tell the mistress, though," said Rhea.

Niko looked doubtful. "Don't you think she, uh, probably already knows?"

"What do you mean?" Rhea asked innocently.

"Well … " Niko glanced hopefully at Damiskos. "You know what I mean, sir, don't you?"

He guessed the boy was suggesting that Aristokles and Nione had arranged some kind of tryst. That seemed completely implausible. If they were together, Nione was not there willingly. But she had been seen going out to the vineyard earlier, so kidnapping didn't seem likely either. And neither possibility explained why Varazda was still here.

Varazda had said, "I must go dress and attend my master." He didn't know—or was pretending not to know—that Aristokles was gone.

"I think," Damiskos said slowly, "that you should go and speak to your mistress—or I suppose it would be more proper for you to report it to the steward. It may be that she knows all about it, but even if she does, I think she cannot fault you for noticing and being concerned. And if she does *not* know, well—obviously she will be grateful to you for telling her."

"You go tell Aradne," said the boy to Rhea. "She likes you better than me."

"That's not true, Niko!"

"You know it is. She's got an anti-whatyoucall, antithesis to men."

Rhea snorted. "Oh, and you qualify, do you? Fine, I will go tell her. You take that breakfast tray back to the kitchen."

Damiskos had noticed that Nione's household was composed mostly of women. He wondered if Aradne had been in charge of choosing the slaves.

CHAPTER 6

THERE WAS no one in the courtyard of the slave quarters when Damiskos entered for the second time that morning. He had gathered from the way Varazda spoke last night that he wasn't lodged in a dormitory but had his own room, or at least a shared room, which probably meant he was in one of the chambers on the upper level of the slave quarters, their doors opening onto a gallery along the front of the building.

Damiskos laboured up the wooden stairs at the end of the gallery, grateful there was no one in the yard to see how much effort it cost him. He was almost at the top when he glanced up at a noise to see a door halfway along the gallery open and Varazda emerge, in green silk patterned with white roses, with a comb in his hand, his hair still unbraided.

Varazda stood still, watching Damiskos finish climbing the stairs, a dubious expression on his face.

"Aristokles left in the night," said Damiskos quickly, in Zashian, once he had reached the gallery. "Did you know about it?"

He'd intended to spring this on Varazda to catch him off guard, if possible. He also wanted to speak first to shut down whatever dry remark Varazda had been planning to make.

"You want something, First Spear? Again? You must want it pretty badly, too, to brave those stairs."

It worked on both counts. There was, for a moment, a look of complete shock on Varazda's face. It melted away to be replaced by his usual haughty composure, and there was a tense pause.

"Who told you that?" Varazda asked finally.

"Some of the household slaves—Niko and Rhea. His bed had not been slept in, and his belongings are gone."

"Couldn't he have moved to a different room?"

"Apparently not without their knowing about it."

"I see."

"Did you attend him last night when he went to bed?"

Varazda looked for a moment as if he was going to remind Damiskos again that this was none of his business. Instead he said, with an air of being very forbearing, "No. My excuse for leaving the dining room to talk to you was that I wanted to go to my own bed. And after our conversation, I did."

Damiskos considered that and decided that he believed it.

"But the household slaves thought you would be attending Aristokles, so they left him alone. So actually, nobody knows where he went when he left the dining room."

He almost added, "And it's too late for you to pretend you do know." He knew Varazda was thinking it.

Varazda pulled his hair forward over his shoulder and twisted it around his hand to lift it off his neck, as if he was too warm. "First Spear ... " He sighed. In Zashian, he said, "Who do you work for?"

Damiskos blinked. What did that have to do with anything? "The office in charge of provisioning the Phemian army. In Pseuchaian my commanding officer is called the 'Quartermaster'—I don't know the Zashian word."

"No, no." Varazda waved his free hand irritably. "Really. Who do you *really* work for."

"I don't ... I don't think I understand. Do you think I am lying to you?"

Varazda's dark eyes were inscrutable. "No. I see. You are actually here on behalf of the Master Provisioner of the Phemian legions to buy fish sauce."

"Is there something about that that's hard to believe? Eurydemos's students seemed to think it was funny—like something out of a modern novel, they said."

Varazda's shapely eyebrows went up. "The comedy of the absurd? They have a point. That's not what I was getting at, though. I'm trying to account for your interest in Aristokles and me."

"I'm not *interested* in Aristokles. Nor—nor in you." That didn't come out sounding nearly as convincing as he wanted, or as polite. "I mean ... "

Varazda sighed. "I, ah ... Aristokles is here on behalf of the Boukossian government."

Damiskos blinked at him for a moment. "He what? Doing what? Courting Nione?"

"No," said Varazda dryly. "That part is what you might call extra-curricular."

"Oh. So he's—he's what? A spy?"

"Something like that." He seemed to be thinking for a moment, then he nodded decisively. "Look, I'll tell you the whole story, if you want. I probably owe you an explanation after that ... after last night." He looked through the open door into his room for a moment. "You'd better come in."

The room beyond the door was small and very full of Varazda's belongings. There were two beds, but only one had a mattress; evidently Varazda had the room to himself.

For someone who had, presumably, been a domestic slave, he was surprisingly untidy. There was a trunk against the opposite wall, its lid open, clothes flopping out of it.

More clothes were draped over the disused bed, along with a box containing a jumble of jewelry and a makeup kit: little brushes, vials, and pots of colour. There was a faint scent of incense in the air.

Varazda tossed the coverlet halfheartedly over his own bed and pushed aside some of the clothes on the other bed to make room for Damiskos to sit. Damiskos sat.

"If Aristokles didn't actually come here to court Nione—those earrings he gave her, were they … "

Varazda made a face. He sat cross-legged on the end of his own bed. "They were mine. My favourite pair. I made him promise to get me a replacement when we're back in Boukos."

"Ah." *Made* him promise? *None of your business, First Spear*, Damiskos reminded himself.

"So," said Varazda, "I said I'd tell you the whole story. I hope it goes without saying that this is in utter, *utter* confidence?"

"Of course."

"Good. You know Eurydemos opened a school in Boukos about a year ago?"

"I think someone mentioned that."

"It's very popular—he was flooded with students as soon as he opened. As far as anyone knew, what they were teaching there was nothing out of the ordinary. Whatever it is they normally teach in these places." He waved a hand airily. "Don't ask me—I'm a dancer, not a philosopher. Anyway, a week ago there was a riot."

"A riot? In Boukos?" He hadn't known such things happened there.

"Well, probably not something you'd consider a riot in Pheme. A disturbance. Nobody was trampled to death in the streets. It started in the Vintners' District, near Eurydemos's school, and we think—the captain of the public watch thinks—some of Eurydemos's students started it. At the very least, they were heavily involved. They broke into the home of a Zashian merchant, looted a couple of shops that stock Zashian goods, and finally marched across town and tried to set fire to our embassy."

"No! But that's appalling!" Damiskos was shocked. "An anti-Zashian riot? But I thought the trade agreement had been well received."

"It has been. This seemed to come out of nowhere, which makes the authorities think the anti-Zashian sentiment was being stirred up deliberately in the school. Anyway … the fire at the embassy was quickly put out. Officially, there were no fatalities."

"Officially."

Varazda nodded grimly. "In fact, there were three men murdered that night on the grounds of the embassy. The fire may have been arranged to cover up the evidence, although it didn't work. All the victims were connected to the embassy. An aide to the ambassador, a Boukossian liaison, and a visiting court official from Suna."

"Daughters of Night," Damiskos swore. "Is the motive known? Was it simply spite against Zash, or … "

"Spite, certainly—or something worse than spite—but there were also documents stolen from the court official. His secretary was able to confirm that he'd had them with him, and they were gone. The other two men seem to have been killed because they were with him. It was a ruthless crime, but not a particularly expert one."

"And the students are suspected."

"They are. The public watch was able to find a witness who saw several armed men leaving the embassy and got a clear look at one. Her description didn't match any of the students currently at Eurydemos's school, but there were a lot of men from his old school in Pheme visiting that week, and they'd left by the time the investigation got underway."

"So Aristokles is here to investigate Eurydemos and his

students. Who may well be murderers." It was a lot to take in. Aristokles didn't seem like Damiskos's idea of a secret agent. But then, presumably that was the point. "I thought he was up to something, but I'd never have guessed it was anything like that. Do they know who—I mean—presumably the philosophers are working for someone?"

They had to be; it was hard enough to imagine them doing more than sitting around talking about the theoretical desirability of assassinating someone in their tedious Ideal Republic. Someone else must have done the practical planning.

"They may be," said Varazda. "We're not sure."

"And what they stole, the documents—obviously I don't expect you to tell me what they were, but I assume they were sensitive?"

"Very."

"And the embassy needs them back?"

"Urgently."

"Terza's head. I know what they're doing. They want war with Zash."

He told Varazda about his conversation with Helenos on the fishing pier and Helenos's explanation of "Phemian purity."

"They think war is good for the Republic," Damiskos said, "and I think they may have a plan to bring it about."

"You don't agree?"

"About war? What, just because I happen to be good at it? No. Does a physician wish for a plague so he can exercise his skill?"

Varazda looked momentarily taken aback. "I'm sorry. You're quite right."

"Never mind. The point is that Helenos seems to believe this, and I suppose his fellow students may too."

"They may. Eurydemos himself seems to be rather more

pro-Zashian than anything. He certainly … ” Varazda winced. “He certainly fancies me.”

“Ah. Yes. But Gelon attacked you.”

“Yes. That was related. He saw me … lurking, I suppose … outside Eurydemos's room, and he followed me out to the yard, thinking he was defending his master from my unnatural Sasian what-have-you.”

“Right.” And why had Varazda been outside Eurydemos's room? *None of your business, First Spear.* “Aristokles said something like that, actually, when I asked him about it.”

“Did he.” Varazda looked tired.

“They didn't exactly send their best, did they? The Boukossian government.”

Varazda gave him a sour look for a moment, and Damiskos wished he hadn't said that. It wasn't fair to ask a freedman to speak ill of his old master, whatever else they might be to one another.

“You may be right,” was all Varazda said.

“So I suppose … Do you think Aristokles has gone now to make his report to someone, or meet some contact, or … ” He knew very little about the practical workings of espionage.

“I don't know where he's gone,” Varazda admitted, “or why, or when—whether—he'll be back. I don't know why he left me behind.”

Damiskos was startled by his candour, although he had spoken calmly enough. “You think something sinister has happened to him.”

“I do. We are potentially dealing with dangerous fanatics. If they happened to learn what he was here for … ”

“Right.” And that wasn't the least likely thing in the world. Aristokles had come perilously close to telling Damiskos himself.

“In any case,” said Varazda, “I'm going to have to lie and say I do know where Aristokles has gone. That's why I thought I had better come clean to you now. Since you would of course know that I was lying." He looked up at Damiskos through his lashes.

"I thought perhaps you wanted my help," said Damiskos frankly.

Varazda's brows rose archly.

"You're in a vulnerable position," Damiskos persisted, then hoped that didn't sound bullying.

"It's kind of you to be concerned, First Spear. I'll be fine."

"I know you can handle yourself. I just … With your patron away … And as you said, these men may be dangerous. If there's anything I can do … "

"Thank you. I will keep it in mind."

"Good. Well, I won't keep you any longer. I do … I am … Thank you for taking me into your confidence. If there's anything I can do." He'd already said that. Idiot.

Varazda uncrossed his legs and stood, the movement liquidly graceful.

"One thing more," he said as he reached for the door handle. "About last night."

Damiskos got awkwardly to his feet. "Oh, you mean the, um … No, no explanation necessary. I quite understand. You and Aristokles being here on confidential business, obviously you don't want Eurydemos or his students to think you're up to anything underhanded, conspiring with any of the other guests or whatnot. No, I—I understood that."

"Yes. But what I was going to say was: We needn't keep up the pretence."

"Oh. No, I didn't think … I mean, if you're sure."

Varazda reverted to his mannered court Zashian: "I mean the pretence of a continued liaison between ourselves. It will do to let it be thought that I am simply promiscuous." After a moment he added, very precisely, "That is also a pretence."

"Yes," said Damiskos, and couldn't suppress a smile. "I'd figured that."

He was surprised to see Varazda's cheeks colour slightly. He realized how his remark might be taken.

"I didn't mean just because of the, um … " He made an unfortunate gesture.

"Out," said Varazda, holding open the door.

The more Damiskos thought about what he had just learned, the more disgusted he was with Aristokles. Maybe the man knew what he was doing with his mission—appearances to the contrary—but why had he thought it necessary to bring his very Zashian freedman into a nest of suspected Zashian-haters? Aristokles and Varazda obviously had a close and friendly relationship, even if they weren't lovers. Look at all the details Varazda knew about his patron's mission; it was obvious they talked almost as equals and that Aristokles had few secrets from Varazda. All the more reason to take better care of him, Damiskos thought. Advise him to tone down the jewellery and the makeup, at least—those were bound to attract the anger of the philosopher's students with their mania for manliness.

Though it would have been a shame. All that finery did suit him.

When Damiskos came into the house, Niko hurried up to tell him that the mistress was back and discussing with Aradne at that very moment the question of what had happened to Aristokles Phoskos.

It came as rather a strange shock to recall that when he had last been looking for Nione it was with the intention of telling her a vague story about Aristokles acting suspiciously and Gelon menacing Varazda for unknown reasons. He knew so much more about it now, and he couldn't talk to her because he was committed to keeping Varazda's secret, and he didn't yet know what story Varazda was going to give to account for Aristokles's disappearance.

If it was true that Eurydemos's students had murdered men in Boukos and stolen valuable documents, did Nione know about it? Damiskos did not want to believe that possible. But she had invited these people into her house, was apparently seriously considering letting them move into her house permanently. Did she had any idea what they were really up to?

No. No, surely not. She was tolerant to a fault, but she must draw the line somewhere, and Damiskos felt sure she would not be embracing the students if she knew them to be criminals and fanatics.

Someone had proposed a game of Reds and Whites for that afternoon, and everyone else seemed enthusiastic. Damiskos thought joining the game would be the best way of keeping an eye on the other guests.

It was deathly dull. No one was much of a player except Kleitos, who had won a cup in the Pan-Pseuchaian games as a boy and took every opportunity to mention it. He and his wife obviously played together at home, and she would have been quite good too if she hadn't been so busy trying to make sure to let him win.

Nione seemed distracted and not herself. Damiskos might have been imagining it, but he thought he could see evidence that she had been crying. Several times in the course of the set she was called away by members of her staff and returned looking even more harried and unhappy.

Helenos was exactly the sort of Reds and Whites player that Damiskos would have expected him to be: carelessly unskilled but not bothered by it, just a little aloof from the whole thing. Eurydemos was the same, only he also seemed to feel it was beneath him to remember the rules, and kept having to pause to hitch up his mantle.

Gelon was missing from the party, the only one absent besides Aristokles.

The Reds and Whites court was squeezed in between the summer dining room and the cliff's edge, with a strip of scrubland preventing the balls from rolling off and landing on the beach below. In the final game of the set, Phaia, who was a bad player but seemed to take the game very seriously, sent her red ball flying into the undergrowth. Damiskos, who was standing nearest—and had almost been hit by the ball—volunteered to wade in after it. He was the only person present not wearing a gown or a long mantle, so no one objected.

He battled through the bushes, wondering whether he could feign some sort of shrub-related injury that would allow him to retreat to the house and escape the rest of the boring game, when something out in the bay caught his eye. It was a small ship, arriving from the city of Pheme, to judge by the direction it was pointed. The sailors had just dropped anchor and were lowering a boat.

He found the ball, nestled right on the edge of the bluff, and as he was manoeuvring awkwardly to retrieve it without losing an eye to one of the bushes, he noticed something else below. Someone was crawling about in the tall grass and shrubs below the cliff, dragging something.

Damiskos straightened up and nudged Phaia's ball with the toe of his boot. It tipped over the edge and bounced and rolled down to plop into the undergrowth below. The crawling person started, turned around, and looked up, and Damiskos recognized Gelon.

"I'm afraid the red's gone out of play," he reported when he had made his way back to the court. "Over the cliff edge."

"Automatic forfeit!" Kleitos cried, as Damiskos had known he would.

"Why don't we call it a match, in that case?" said Damiskos, who had been winning the set. "There's a ship coming in—maybe we should go down to meet it."

"Oh, that will be our fellow students from Pheme," said Phaia. "Come, Nione—let us go welcome them."

She held out a hand, smiling, head tilted winsomely to one side. Nione gave her a look that Damiskos had seen on the faces of men on the battlefield who had received their mortal wound. There was an awkward pause before Phaia dropped her hand and laughed carelessly. Everyone seemed to have noticed; no one said anything.

"I must go speak to Aradne about accommodating our extra guests," said Nione finally. "I was not expecting them so soon. You will excuse me."

She left, and after a moment Tyra followed her back toward the house. The others headed for the stairs down to the beach. Damiskos kept up as best he could.

Helenos and Phaia were walking ahead, deep in conversation. Helenos was obviously annoyed; Phaia seemed to be trying to justify herself.

By the time they reached the beach, the boat was almost ashore, its passengers waving and hailing the approaching party. Damiskos let the others get ahead of him here, and turned back to scan the fringe of grass and shrubs for Gelon.

He spotted him, crouching among the bushes with leaves in his hair. When Gelon realized he'd been seen, he crawled out and got to his feet, attempting a casual air.

"Damiskos from the Quartermaster's Office!"

"What are you doing out here?" He looked past Gelon at the bushes. There was certainly something else in there—a dark, inert object—but he could tell nothing more about it from here. "Not looking for another opportunity to ambush Aristokles's slave, I hope."

He wondered if Gelon, who had brought a knife with him to a house party and been willing to use it, had been one of the assassins in Boukos. He hadn't been very skilled with the knife, so perhaps not.

"Don't be silly," said Gelon cheerfully. "Helenos is very disappointed in you, Damiskos."

Damiskos glanced over his shoulder at the group by the shore. They were paying no attention to him and Gelon.

"Why should I care what Helenos thinks?"

"Why should you care?" Gelon looked genuinely surprised. "Because he's the rising star. He's the one everyone is going to be listening to at the Marble Porches in a few years—maybe less. Eurydemos is past it. That's a fact. He's been seduced by the gods-cursed Sasians, that's what it is. Mentally seduced, I mean, though who knows about the other—anything's possible. He is a soft half-man. Maybe he's let some trousered dog bend him over." Gelon shuddered. "It all goes together, that's what Helenos says: degeneracy of the mind and body. Barbarian ideas infect like a disease, infect the individual, infect the state."

Damiskos laughed harshly. "Helenos doesn't know what he's talking about. He's never been to Zash, has he? Those people are so hemmed in by taboos and euphemisms and elaborate clothes—it's a wonder anyone in the kingdom ever has sex at all."

Gelon was shaking his head. "Helenos has seen the Sasian plague infect Boukos and Master Eurydemos. He says we have to take strong measures to prevent the same thing happening in Pheme. And he saw you last night with the Sasian gelding—he saw the two of you coming out of your room. We thought you agreed with us that a barbarian dog has no business in a Maiden's house. How did he get at you? You're not a degenerate yourself—First Spear of the Second Koryphos, I wouldn't dare suggest it!"

"And *you've* obviously never been in the army. Soldiers on campaign sleep with whomever they like, and don't go about calling each other degenerates—nobody's got time for that kind of thing when you're facing death on the battlefield. What are you doing down here?"

Gelon adopted a prim expression. "I probably shouldn't tell you. I don't know if we can trust you."

"If it involves knifing innocent civilians in the night, you can trust me to stop you."

Gelon gave him a sharp look, as if Damiskos had said something unexpected.

"Well, you should stay away from the Sasian, is all I'm saying. Don't listen to his lies."

"I have no idea what you are talking about," Damiskos said sternly.

The new arrivals from the ship were ashore now, and the whole party was headed their way.

"Hestos! Phaidon!" Gelon called, waving. "Giontes? Good to see you!"

Damiskos hoped briefly that Gelon would take off across the beach to greet them, but he had enough sense to stand his ground and wait for them to come to collect him and Damiskos.

"So this is to be our new home, is it?" one of the students was saying to Eurydemos. "It's all settled?"

"It will be soon," Helenos interposed smoothly.

Gelon introduced Damiskos to the newcomers as a war hero, and they were all exaggeratedly deferential.

"First Spear of the Second Koryphos," Gelon reported.

"We're honoured!"

"Served in Sasia," Gelon added.

"Like your cousin, Helenos."

"Like my cousin. Only Damiskos came home alive."

"Injured on the battlefield, though," said one of the other students in a sententious tone, "in defence of the Republic. I hope they give you a generous pension for that."

"I wasn't," said Damiskos. "Injured in battle."

They didn't know what to make of this, and so pretended he hadn't said it.

There were five of them, all about Gelon's age, all with the same prototypical Phemian looks as Damiskos himself—dark hair, olive skin—as if they had walked off of a painted cup. There was a fat one, a tall one, two utterly generic ones, and a shaven-headed one with a badly-healed broken nose. Gelon mentioned their names, but they did not stick in Damiskos's mind.

Of course they wouldn't leave him alone to poke around in the underbrush, but wanted to hear details of his war record and make pronouncements about the glory of Pheme. In this way Damiskos found himself herded back up the stairs to the garden in the midst of the party. Gelon followed, looking pleased with himself. He'd shown more cunning than Damiskos had given him credit for.

So Helenos was the one to watch. Damiskos could see it now that there were more students present: the way Eurydemos, their supposed master, faded into the background, not exactly ignored but subtly condescended to, while Helenos cooly dominated the conversation.

Was Eurydemos uninvolved in the events in Boukos? That fit with what Varazda had already ascertained about his sympathies. Perhaps Helenos and his cronies had masterminded the riot and the theft from the embassy without their master's consent. But what, exactly, were they planning now?

There were no Zashian shops or embassies here for them to loot. There was just Varazda, abandoned by his patron. A completely innocent bystander, who had already been attacked once.

Varazda was in the garden when they arrived at the top of the stairs. He was sitting on a bench by the fountain with his feet tucked up, looking decorative and very, very Zashian. His hair was in two braids, looped up on either side and pinned behind his ears, framing the long pendants of his earrings. His eyes were dramatically painted.

"You there, slave!" one of the students called out. "Fetch us some wine."

"Why is he still here?" Gelon asked loudly as Varazda swished away. "Didn't I hear his master had been urgently summoned back to Boukos?"

There was a little pause.

"Did you?" said Helenos blandly.

"Uh," said Gelon. "Oh."

"The Sasian does not belong to the mistress of the house," Helenos explained to the newcomers, subtly redirecting the conversation. "Her staff is more conventional, in keeping with the style of her house. It is a fine, old-fashioned place, don't you think?"

Damiskos looked around, anxious to get back to the beach and investigate the place where Gelon had been hiding in the bushes. But Gelon was staying put, glancing in Damiskos's direction every so often. There was no chance to sneak off without him seeing, and no opportunity to follow him surreptitiously down to the beach either. Damiskos ground his teeth as the students launched into a debate about virtue like caricatures of themselves.

Varazda returned with wine, followed by a female slave with cups. When they had finished serving everyone, the woman departed, and Varazda remained. He came over to the bench where Damiskos was sitting, and elegantly but rather fussily arranged himself on the ground, with his legs tucked to one side, at Damiskos's feet.

"If you could try not to act surprised … " he murmured in Zashian.

"Of course," Damiskos replied automatically.

He took a swallow of wine, trying to think what a man

who wasn't surprised to have Varazda sit down at his feet would do. He had no idea.

They were seated at a slight remove from the rest of the party, and one or two of the students had cast them curious looks, but no one said anything to Damiskos. Varazda folded his hands in his lap and looked at the ground.

Nione arrived and was listlessly polite to the newcomers. She gave Damiskos a strange look and did not speak to him.

"When you offered to help," said Varazda in a low voice, still speaking Zashian.

"Yes. Anything. What can I do?"

"You can corroborate the story I've recently told our host."

"Yes, of course. What have you told her?"

"I have told her that before Aristokles left, he sold me to you."

That landed on Damiskos like a rockslide, though he realized he should have guessed it as soon as Varazda sat at his feet.

"You've … uh. Yes, I see how that will help. I suppose I should have thought of it myself."

"I am very glad you didn't. I would have refused any such proposal coming from you."

"Oh. Yes. I quite see that. Rightly so. Why did I, er, buy you, do you think?"

"Well," said Varazda dryly, "it could be that you are buying up slaves to work your olive farm. But I think it might go over a little better if we say you appealed to Aristokles's sentimental side to let you have me at a price you could afford because you've developed a fondness for me."

"Don't be so hard on yourself," Damiskos managed. "I'm sure you could do a fine job of picking olives."

Varazda looked as if he was struggling, very prettily, to suppress a smile.

"First Spear, I do appreciate that this puts you in an

awkward position, and I wish I could have thought of a better story to account for my presence. If it is any comfort, you should know that I would not have told this particular lie if I had thought you would take advantage of it."

"Yes, I see. Thank you. I won't."

"I know," said Varazda patiently.

Aradne had come out, followed by the cringing Niko, to glare at the new guests and take a headcount.

"Tell the kitchen five more for dinner, Niko. I'm off to find something for them to sleep on." Her tone suggested whatever she found would not be very comfortable. "Can I put some of them in Aristokles's room?" she asked Nione.

"Yes, for now. His, um—Pharastes—told me this morning that he took the coast road to Laokia on an errand he wished to keep secret. I'm not sure when he will be back."

Damiskos looked down at Varazda, wondering what gesture he could make to signal to the students that Varazda was now his property. He could touch him casually. That would be the sort of thing a master might do to a slave, especially one to whom he was supposedly attracted. He could reach out a hand and brush his fingers around the outside of one looped-up braid, flick a dangling earring in passing, perhaps graze the pale shell of Varazda's ear with his fingertips.

He sat picturing the exact route his hand would travel, the movements his muscles would make. He couldn't bring himself to make them.

It was repellant. It would make him no better than the sort of man he had imagined Aristokles to be.

What would Nione think of him?

Well, whatever it was, she probably already thought it, and he wasn't helping Varazda by sitting here looking awkward.

"May I touch you?" he asked in Zashian.

Varazda glanced up, surprise flickering in his eyes for a moment.

"Yes," he said stiffly. "I think you had better."

Damiskos put out his hand and laid it on Varazda's shoulder. It wasn't the right kind of gesture at all. It looked like something you might do to comfort a grieving friend. Probably he had a frown on his face to match.

Varazda's shoulder tensed, then relaxed minutely as he looked down at Damiskos's fingers. He lifted his own hand to Damiskos's, interlacing their fingers, turning the gesture into something else, something intimate and emotion-laden. It told a completely different story than the proprietary brush of the hand that Damiskos had contemplated and baulked at. It suggested Varazda might be glad to have been bought by Damiskos. Maybe they had talked about it beforehand; maybe Damiskos had promised to treat Varazda better than Aristokles Phoskos. It was perfectly judged.

Varazda looked up at Damiskos through his lashes, and Damiskos thought he was awfully good at this. Much better than Aristokles had been.

"You're the Boukossian agent," Damiskos said, as it flashed into his mind. "Not Aristokles."

Varazda looked shyly down at the ground. "Mm. Perhaps we could talk about that later."

Damiskos looked up and realized they were the centre of attention. Most of the students were looking disgusted. Helenos was frowning deeply. Eurydemos looked ready to compose another poem.

Nione was the only one who was smiling, but she also looked ready to burst into tears.

Looking flustered and embarrassed was probably the best thing Damiskos could have done, and if so, he played his part admirably.

Nione stood up abruptly. "Damiskos! I meant to ask you if your—if Pharastes—could dance for us tonight? We're having a bonfire on the beach. The men who run my factory follow Opos, and it's Hapikon Eve tonight. I like to hold some celebration for them. You are all welcome to join us."

Damiskos looked down at Varazda for guidance. He was smiling and looking shy again, so Damiskos said, "It is up to him. I've no objection."

Varazda gave Nione his gracious agreement, and she beamed at him and Damiskos. After a strained silence, it was Kleitos who spoke.

"Why did you ask *his* permission? I thought the Sasian belonged to Aristokles?"

"Well, they, they came to an agreement." Nione had sat back down again, but fidgeted as though she wanted to get up and leave.

"I bought him," said Damiskos bluntly. He wanted to get this over with. "Yesterday afternoon."

"Really?" Kleitos looked surprised. "Yesterday afternoon? Huh." He glanced around at Helenos, who showed no reaction.

"What for?" one of the new students asked, with a rather unpleasant, half-lidded smile.

Damiskos raised his eyebrows. "I need workers for my olive farm."

CHAPTER 7

It was late afternoon by the time Damiskos was able to get down to the shore again. The students had quickly recovered from their shock at learning that he had bought Varazda. Gelon and Phaia still looked slightly disgusted, and Helenos was inscrutable, but the others seemed to have decided that if Damiskos, who was obviously very manly, had done this, then it must in some way be a very manly thing. They had discussed the question at length.

By this time, Damiskos was reasonably sure that Gelon had already been down to the shore—he had lost track of him at some point in the afternoon, to his annoyance—and whatever had been hidden in the undergrowth would be gone. But he had told Varazda, when they had managed to snatch a moment alone together, that he would go down and look, so he did. Varazda had gone back to the slave quarters, ostensibly to practice for that night's performance.

Damiskos made his way back down to the beach and began methodically searching the bushes where Gelon had been hiding earlier.

At first he thought he wouldn't find anything. He made it all the way down the stretch of brush where he remembered seeing Gelon—he was reasonably certain of the general area—and there was nothing hidden in among the bushes.

Then he retraced his steps, looking for something that wasn't there, and he found it: an area of broken branches and disturbed leaves, and a sharp-cornered depression in the sand where something heavy had rested. Something square or rectangular, a couple of feet in length. About the size of a sea chest.

He could see a faint trail of disturbed undergrowth leading away from the spot, showing where Gelon had crawled down with the object, and when Damiskos had struggled to follow it for a few paces, he was rewarded with a glint of metal in the sand. He bent and dug out a leather belt with a round gold buckle, chased in a typical Zashian style.

He wrapped the belt around the buckle and hid it in the fold of his tunic for safekeeping, then he made his way back to the beach and up the stairs to the villa. He seemed to spend all his time here trudging up and down these gods-cursed stairs.

He made a token search around the house for Varazda, without result. He didn't like to go to the slave quarters, as that didn't seem like something Varazda's master would do, or to send for him, as that very much did. What an absolutely ridiculous situation this was.

Like many Phemians, Damiskos had never personally owned a slave. There had been slaves in his parents' house when he was a boy, so he had grown up taking the concept for granted, and there had been slaves attached to the Second Koryphos to whom he had given orders, but he had never owned another person, certainly never purchased one. The pretence made him surprisingly uncomfortable.

By this time, his knee was throbbing fiercely, and when he sank onto a bench in the garden, he could not move from it for some time.

As the sun was setting, the guests trooped down together to the beach, where the factory workers and many of Nione's slaves were already assembled and preparing the bonfire. They were on the sheltered stretch of beach that Nione had shown Damiskos and Phaia the day before, happily out of range of the smell of the factory. Some of Nione's women were putting down blankets and cushions, and the guests settled themselves comfortably.

Cups were passed around and filled, though most the students had been drinking steadily all afternoon. Only Helenos seemed quite sober.

Nione sat with Tyra and got up frequently to play host to the larger gathering. All the women and the few men from Nione's household were there, along with the factory slaves and people from the nearby villages.

Varazda appeared from somewhere, wearing a long, thickly embroidered black coat over his green silk from the morning. He served Damiskos his wine and then went to talk to the musicians.

Since they were there to witness a ritual in honour of Opos, the students took up the subject of foreign cults in Pheme. Of course they were opposed to them. They wouldn't go so far as to criticize their host, whom they held in the same sort of overdone reverence as Damiskos because she was a retired Maiden. But they clearly thought she shouldn't be encouraging her slaves in their worship.

Damiskos, himself a follower of the "foreign cult" of Terza, like most cavalry men, kept quiet. He watched Varazda standing on the other side of the unlit fire, taking down his hair while he chatted easily with the musicians, smiling and laughing. How did he *do* it? He wasn't unconcerned or careless of the danger of his position at the villa; when he'd spoken to Damiskos in the garden, it had been clear that he took the situation very seriously. Damiskos had even thought he sounded a little afraid. But he was able to carry on playing his role as naturally as if he weren't in a house full of fanatics who had murdered his countrymen and in all probability his … whatever Aristokles had been. His colleague?

The conversation had moved on from foreigners to women. One of the students, Phaidon, began to expound an unpopular opinion. The others shouted him down with appeals to reason and virtue.

"No, no, no!" Gelon cried. "In the Ideal Republic, since all cosmetics would be forbidden, women would lose their power to deceive men, and so what you say is absurd! Don't you agree, Phaia?"

"What? Oh, yes, quite absurd. In the Ideal Republic."

"Fuck the Ideal Republic," Eurydemos growled, flinging himself to his feet. He strode off into the crowd of revellers.

There was a shocked hush among the students, as if someone had just cursed a departed kinsman.

"What did he mean by that?" one of the newcomers asked finally.

"Perhaps, in a sense, our master is still wise," said Helenos. He had everyone's attention. "The Ideal Republic is a fairytale for children. This is the real world, and in the real world Pheme is beset on all sides by barbarians, degenerates, half-men—there is too much at stake for us to indulge in idle talk. We must become men of action and do things we have never thought possible. 'Fuck the Ideal Republic' indeed. It will become our new watchword."

This was met with the kind of approving laughter that acknowledges that what was said was only partly a joke. Helenos looked directly at Damiskos for a moment and raised his eyebrows slightly. Damiskos looked stonily back at him.

The bonfire was lit as the light died from the sky. Grilled

fish and fruit and spicy-sweet Hapikon cakes were passed around, along with more excellent wine. There was music: several musicians, some from Nione's household and some hired from the villages, alternated reels and popular songs for the crowd to join in with accomplished solos and ensemble pieces. Nione's steward sang, in a big, rich voice of amazing range and sensitivity, a song from a popular new tragedy. It should all have been quite enjoyable; in other company, it would have been.

Some of the students were mixing with the villagers now, and one had brought back some of the free fishermen to join their party. The fishermen did not themselves worship Opos, and were complaining that they were expected to take on extra work for the next week while the Oposite slaves and their foreman went to a shrine in the Tentines. The students sympathized as heartily as if any of them had ever done a day's labour. Surely, Damiskos thought, these men couldn't be dangerous. They were too ridiculous.

Since people seemed to be moving about now, Damiskos got up and left the blankets where the villa's guests were reclining to go sit closer to the fire and watch the entertainment. That was just before Varazda got up to dance.

It was fully dark by this time, but the beach was warmly lit by the bonfire. A space had been cleared in the sand for dancing, and the amateurs retired from it to sit around the edges in expectation. Damiskos had a good view.

There were no Zashian musicians, but there was a Gylphian drummer with a big, hide-covered drum, and she now took up a slow, familiar beat. The sound seemed to catch and twist at something in Damiskos's gut. He had never seen Varazda's style of dancing in Zash, but he knew its rhythm well.

Varazda stepped out of his shoes at the edge of the cleared area and walked out barefoot into the centre of it, his long coat swinging around his ankles. He had unpinned his hair and wore it loose as he had that morning.

He laid one sword down in the sand and began dancing slowly, almost lazily with the other, spinning it lightly as if exploring its properties, like a graceful visitor from another world who had encountered a sword for the first time. Then the drummer sped up, varying the rhythm in a way that stabbed Damiskos through again with familiarity, and the dance quickened, Varazda's bare feet flying over the sand as he twirled and swung the sword.

He was a constellation of beautiful details in the firelight: bronze and henna and embroidery and long hair flying. He slowed his steps just a fraction, swooped down with his free hand, and added the second sword to the dance. His audience erupted in an awed cheer.

He ended with the showpiece that Damiskos had seen in the yard, spinning the two swords as one, then dropping to his knees, his coat fanned out like a peacock's tail, while the onlookers shouted and clapped.

"That was marvellous, Pharastes!" Nione cried, emerging from the fire-lit circle of watchers with hands clasped raptly. "Oh, will you dance another for us?"

Varazda had stripped off his coat already and twisted his hair around his hand. The night air was cool on the beach, but dancing in the bonfire's warmth in all those clothes must have been sweaty work.

He bowed assent. Nione looked delighted, and there were murmurs of approval from the audience. Whatever the philosopher's students thought of it, the workers and the slaves were enjoying it.

"What a shame we don't have more music for you," Nione said. She appealed to the crowd of factory-workers. "I don't suppose anyone knows any Sasian dance tunes?"

Damiskos cleared his throat. "I do."

Heads turned in his direction as he got awkwardly to his

feet in the sand. He had noticed that the Gylphian musician had a stringed instrument that was more or less the same as the Zashian long-necked lute; he didn't remember what they called it in Gylphos. He approached and asked the musician's permission, and the woman handed her instrument over.

"Do you mind if I retune it to the Zashian mode?"

"Please."

It was a light, well-made instrument, more like the one Shahaz had played than those that the men had brought out around the watch-fires on campaign. It was easily retuned to the scale of the Zashian lute. Finding a comfortable position in which to sit to play took longer. Sitting cross-legged in the approved style was no longer feasible, so at home when he played he generally sat on a stool. He arranged himself as best he could in the sand, with the instrument cradled in his lap.

Now that he had committed himself to this, he had a moment's panic when he couldn't think what to play. He strummed a few experimental chords and then began the first thing that came to mind, hardly even knowing what it was. He looked at the drummer, who nodded and picked up the beat readily. The tune was a lively, cheerful one, one of Damiskos's favourites, and now he remembered what it was and wished he had picked something else.

He looked up at Varazda, half-expecting to see him glaring. The tune was a wedding-dance from the Zashian coast, danced at the marriage banquet by the young women of the village.

Varazda was giving him a quizzical look, but it was not exactly a glare. He had already laid aside the swords and the embroidered coat. After a moment he raised his hands above his head, palms out, long fingers poised, the gesture flawlessly feminine. He swayed his hips, and someone in the crowd whistled.

It wasn't the way the village girls danced; it was more like the dance of a Suna courtesan, although by Pseuchaian standards it was very demure. It would have been a fine show even if he had actually been a woman, but in the sword dance he had moved like a man, and now it was hard to believe that the delicate hand gestures and swaying hips belonged to the same person. The audience ate it up, and Damiskos could have sworn that Varazda was enjoying himself. What a mass of contradictions the fellow was. Who would have imagined he would voluntarily dance like this in front of an audience of labourers? He could have done a different dance; no one but Damiskos would have noticed.

Damiskos wrapped up the wedding dance and segued into another tune with a slower, more delicate rhythm, to let Varazda wind down his performance, which he did amid wild applause. Nione got up to entreat Damiskos to play some more for them while Varazda retreated from the fire-lit stage. He obliged her with a couple of tunes he had learned in Suna. They were well received, though nothing like so popular as Varazda's dancing.

He considered singing, but didn't quite feel up to it. Besides, Varazda had disappeared into the shadows, and Damiskos was anxious to keep him in sight.

Fortunately, by this point it was nearly midnight and time for some ritual related to Hapikon, from which Damiskos excused himself. Many of the other non-worshipers did the same, drawing back from the fire a little while the followers of Opos joined in a hymn and threw incense-laden logs onto the flames to produce clouds of fragrant smoke that billowed up into the dark sky.

Damiskos looked around for Varazda, whom he would have expected to join him by this time, and spotted his shoes and swords and folded coat abandoned on the edge of the firelight. He gathered them up and went looking for their owner.

He found Varazda, at length, at the back of the crowd,

looking like he was trying to think of a polite excuse to get away from Eurydemos, who was just taking a seat beside him in the sand.

Varazda had taken off his shirt and sat with it bunched up in his lap, his hair pulled forward over one shoulder. As Damiskos approached, the philosopher offered Varazda his wine cup. Varazda waved it away delicately. He looked up and saw Damiskos as Eurydemos leaned in close to say something to him, and, for reasons which escaped Damiskos, he glared.

It was a pointed glare, as if he was trying to tell Damiskos something. Damiskos stopped, looked round, and saw the students approaching.

Whether their intention was to mock their master or to rescue him from the clutches of his new favourite, Damiskos didn't care to find out. They looked drunk enough—still with the sinister exception of Helenos—that it would probably amount to much the same thing either way. They came up behind Damiskos and circled the pair on the ground, looming over them, threateningly close. Eurydemos looked up, frowning, and Damiskos thought he could see the question forming behind his eyes: was he still in control of these young people at all? Damiskos felt sorry for him, but didn't feel that the philosopher's problems were his responsibility.

"Do you usually fetch and carry for your slaves?" said someone at Damiskos's shoulder.

He looked down at the bundle of Varazda's belongings he was holding. Of course. That was what Varazda had been glaring about. Damiskos managed a laugh.

"No, but I never owned a slave before."

"Really?" said Helenos. "And yet you could afford to purchase such an exotic specimen."

"Perhaps he saved up," Phaia suggested with a snicker.

"I beg your pardon," said Eurydemos belatedly to Damiskos.

The philosopher hauled himself to his feet, spilling wine from his cup onto the sand. He offered a hand to Varazda, who accepted it lightly and uncoiled himself from his seat in the sand. Eurydemos presented him with the air of a father handing over his youngest daughter to her groom on their wedding day. Damiskos tried not to grimace too obviously.

"When did you say you bought him?" Helenos inquired silkily.

"What business is it of yours? Yesterday afternoon, as it happens." That was what he'd said before, and it seemed best to stick to his story until someone provided proof that he was lying.

He was sure that was what was about to happen, but Helenos merely said, "Hm," and then Gelon, drunkenly earnest, pushed aside a couple of his companions to come face-to-face with Eurydemos.

"Master! Settle a dispute for us. Do you not agree that the Sasian capon is an abomination against nature, and do you not think that Furs Smear—Surst Fear—him—is a disgrace to the legions if he—"

"That's enough!" Eurydemos's voice cut across Gelon's with the ease of one long practiced in public speaking. "If this is what you've taken from my teaching, Gelon, my boy, I have failed you."

"Don't you call me your boy," Gelon breathed. "I'm not your boy."

Damiskos took Varazda's arm. "Let's—"

"I have never taught," Eurydemos drowned him out, obviously rather drunk himself, "that the citizens of the Ideal Republic would live like—like—would deprive themselves of the fruits of love. I have never taught that!"

Damiskos stood still, waiting for a better moment to shoulder his way out of the knot of students. He tried to take his cue from Varazda, who was looking blank and demure.

Phaia spoke up again. "The 'fruits of love,' Master? I don't think Damiskos has such a thing in mind. Do you?" She looked at Damiskos, a slight smile on her lips. "I thought your interests lay elsewhere."

"I have many interests," said Damiskos woodenly.

Some of the other students hooted appreciatively. "Many interests! Do you hear that, Phaia?"

"Why don't you loan the Sasian to Master Eurydemos for the night?" someone suggested.

Someone else chimed in, hilariously: "We could conduct them to the marriage bed and sing the wedding hymn for them!"

"*O blessed night, eya, eya,*" someone began to sing tunelessly. "*O gather round, ye gods …* "

"How dare you?" Eurydemos was protesting weakly. "This vicious mockery—"

"Perhaps you would rather we sang the hymn for you, First Spear," Helenos suggested.

"Excellent idea!" someone cheered. "I wouldn't mind seeing a Sasian subdued by the pride of the Phemian army— if you take my meaning."

"*O blessed night, ai-ai-ai-ai …* "

"Or perhaps," Helenos continued, as if none of the mayhem around them were going on, "you wouldn't. I was surprised to see the Sasian kiss you last night. But then, I rather think you were surprised yourself."

Divine Terza, he had really made a dog's breakfast of this. He didn't know exactly what Helenos suspected, but if Damiskos wasn't selling the story that he'd bought Varazda because he was in love with him—if there was a chance the students knew he hadn't bought Varazda at all because they knew where Aristokles had been yesterday afternoon—it wouldn't be hard to guess that what Damiskos was really doing was trying to protect Varazda.

"*O BLESS-ED NIIIIIIGHT!*"

"Sure," said Damiskos, looking Helenos in the eye. "Maybe a bit."

"Because you're not the master's rival in love at all, are you?" Helenos continued. "I think your interest in the Sasian is something quite different. Pity, for instance."

That just made Damiskos mad. Terza's head. If he were Eurydemos's rival, he wouldn't be ashamed to admit it. Varazda was stunningly good-looking, and he'd just kept the whole crowd on the beach enraptured with his dancing; it would be a shock if Eurydemos were the only man there who wanted to sleep with him.

"Oh, well, there you're wrong," Damiskos spat back. "It's true all I got last night was a kiss, and I wasn't even expecting that—but tonight I'm counting on a bit more." He slung his arm around Varazda. "Come on, we're done here." He pushed past the students still singing their off-key hymn, and tossed back over his shoulder, "So long as you make the wedding offering, I don't care what you do. Takes more than that to put me off my stride."

CHAPTER 8

Damiskos had set off more or less at random, anger stiffening his gait and lending him a burst of speed. They were headed in the direction of the ruined huts that Nione had shown him the previous day.

Behind them, the students were marshalling in an impromptu procession.

"Torches!" someone cried. "Torches for the wedding party!"

"*Eya! Eya!*"

"That," said Damiskos, "uh, didn't go entirely as planned."

"I daresay it didn't." Varazda's voice was toneless.

Damiskos withdrew his arm to unsling Varazda's coat from his shoulder and offer it. Varazda took it and draped it around his bare shoulders.

"It's just that I was annoyed," Damiskos tried to explain. "They keep assuming I share their wretched preoccupation with 'Phemian purity,' which is a load of balls, and I'm sick of it. But please don't think—I didn't mean it. I wouldn't—won't—take advantage of you."

Varazda gave him a sour look and glanced back at the

students, who were laughing and gathering up sticks to wave in lieu of torches. He turned to walk on, reaching out to take Damiskos's hand. "You're going to have to, now."

"I—uh—oh?"

"They are clearly prepared to follow us, and they're going to watch—as you invited them to."

"I didn't—I—that wasn't—I was just being rude. Are you sure—"

"For God's sake, don't let go of my hand." He was walking close to Damiskos, nestled against his side. His grip was hard and unfriendly, but it probably looked good from a distance. "We're going to have to put on a show for them. We can't afford not to. I told you we had a description of the one of the assassins? 'A young man with a shaved head and a broken nose.' Sound familiar?"

"Shit. It *was* them."

"It seems that it was."

"You might have told me sooner."

"In Zashian, in front of all of them? Yes, I can see that working beautifully. You would have remained completely stone-faced, I'm sure."

That stung. "Look, I'm doing my best."

Varazda made no reply. The students had organized their procession and begun singing in ragged unison. People from the bonfire were looking over curiously. Eurydemos was waving his wine-cup and ranting about pure affection. You could feel the violence simmering under the surface of the scene—the crude violence of the mob, but also, perhaps, the cold violence of the fanatic.

"Most of them are just drunk," said Damiskos. "But Helenos isn't, and he thinks I was bluffing."

"Well, you were."

"Yes! I mean, of course. I mean—as it happens—I prefer women."

"You'll just have to pretend I am one. It is dark—that should help."

"I'm not going to—"

"Stop saying you're not going to take advantage of me. If you don't want to compromise me further, you'll have to lie down with me. If Helenos is trying to prove you haven't really bought me, he'll egg them on to watch, and if they don't see what they want—"

"This'll turn ugly," Damiskos finished for him. "What should we do?"

"We can go in one of those little tumbled-down houses up ahead—they don't look like they'd offer the slightest privacy. And since I suppose 'You won't put me off my stride' was the biggest bluff of the lot, we'd better attempt something that doesn't require you to do too much acting. Leaves of the Lily, maybe—although that won't look all that spectacular for our audience. I'm not very good at Stalk of the Lily, but I suppose it doesn't matter—you can at least pretend to enjoy it. You wouldn't like Heart of the Pomegranate, and Planting the Rose is out of the question."

"What are you *talking* about?" Damiskos was torn between laughter—of the strictly hysterical sort—and plain horror. "I—I mean, I don't know what any of those things are, and—"

"And I don't know any other names for them. I've never had to discuss any of this in Pseuchaian, because I've never had to *do* any of it in Pseuchaia—"

"And we're not going to do any of it now, if it means anything like what I think."

Damiskos drew a deep breath. He had fucked up at every turn, rousing Helenos's suspicion and bringing this whole situation down on Varazda's head. He owed it to Varazda to do what he could to fix it.

They had reached the nearer of the two beach huts, and Damiskos turned Varazda toward him, lifting their joined hands into a clasp between them. Varazda stepped in, very close, every muscle rigid with tension, plainly about ready to throw up with some combination of anger and fear and disgust.

"Here's what we're going to do," said Damiskos quickly, to forestall any further suggestions about flowers or fruit. "We're going to lie down together in there and talk, and—I don't know—maybe pretend to kiss and cuddle a bit. It's going to be very boring to watch, and they'll go back to the bonfire before long. But it should be convincing. It's what I would really do, if this weren't all a setup."

It took Varazda a moment to unclench his jaw sufficiently to reply. "Don't be ridiculous. You, a soldier? No one would believe that."

Damiskos sighed. "It's not what I'd do with a camp follower, or a fellow soldier, but it *is* what I'd do with someone like you. Not that I—"

"Yes, I heard you the first time. You prefer women."

"So—is it all right?"

The students were getting close, chanting snatches of obscene poetry in the style of wedding blessings and holding their sticks aloft. Eurydemos had dropped behind, but Helenos was there with the main group, arm draped around Phaia's shoulders. If they persisted in their parody of a marriage procession, they would end up surrounding the beach house for the singing of the consummation hymn.

Varazda moved back toward the open front wall of the hut, pulling Damiskos with him in what he managed to make a graceful, shyly flirtatious gesture. Considering how strung up he actually was, Damiskos thought that was impressive.

The interior of the hut contained a pair of masonry couches, padded with rush mats, positioned on opposite sides of the small space. Varazda led Damiskos around to the couch on the left, where he sat, and Damiskos deposited the shoes and swords he had been carrying on the floor. Varazda swung his feet up onto the couch. Damiskos remained standing. He could hear the students outside laughing and talking. It was dark in here, but not dark enough; as Varazda had predicted, there was nothing private about it.

"When you say 'someone like you,'" said Varazda, "you mean a boy, don't you?"

They were both still speaking in undertones. "I don't court boys—I know Zashians think all Pseuchaians chase boys, but there are plenty of us—"

"*I heard you the first time.* And I'm not a boy. I'm thirty."

Damiskos stared. "Thirty?"

"Thirty. Just turned."

"Well." Damiskos sat on the edge of the couch. "We're almost of an age. I'm thirty-two. I knew you weren't a boy, but still—you don't look thirty."

"Thanks." He looked, for just a moment, just a little pleased. "Look, First Spear, I realize this situation is my fault."

"What? No, it isn't."

"If I hadn't surprised you by kissing you in the passage in front of Helenos—"

"You didn't have any choice. You had to deflect suspicion."

"I could have done it some other way. And I could have come up with some other explanation for why Aristokles left me behind, rather than forcing you to pretend to be my master."

"I'm really not sure what else you could have done. The problem was just that I haven't played along very well."

"What's going on in there?" one of the students called from the beach outside.

"*Eya, eya for the ploughing of the fertile field—*"

"Fertile! Hah!" Loud guffaws.

Varazda draped a wrist over Damiskos's shoulder. "This

isn't going to allay their suspicions, First Spear," he murmured. "You literally said you were expecting more than a kiss. We'd better do something out of the Garden of Jasmine, at least."

"The garden of what? Why can't you say 'fuck' like a normal person?"

"Oh, I can *say* it, but I'm not going to let you *do* it—and much as I'd love to do it to you, it's not really in my repertoire." He must have been able to see Damiskos's eyebrows rise, because he cringed. "Oh, God, it was meant to be an insult, that's all—because you're supposed to find it humiliating, you all think that sort of thing is humiliating, don't you? I didn't mean that I literally want to … ugh, you don't actually like it? What happened to preferring women?"

"I like a lot of things," said Damiskos repressively, annoyed that his expression had betrayed anything. "But listen. If I was really courting … someone like you … here's how I think it would go."

He slid his hands behind Varazda's shoulders and eased him down onto his back on the couch. He turned to kneel over Varazda, carefully moving his stiff leg. Varazda's long, wavy hair was pooled on the cushion beneath him, and his coat had slipped off one shoulder, baring his white chest. Damiskos was acutely aware of how unequal the situation was for the two of them. There was nothing unpleasant about having Varazda under him, his skin blue-white in the moonlight, his eyes wide and dark. The memory of his dancing, fierce and elegant and alluring, was fresh in Damiskos's mind. He could easily have enjoyed this, but the same was obviously not true for Varazda.

It had been very gracious of Varazda to apologize, but Damiskos was still convinced this situation was mostly his own fault. Even if it wasn't, trying to handle it sensitively was the least he could do.

Some of the students had brought real torches now, and

the shadows of their swaying forms danced over the interior of the beach house as they chanted vulgar nonsense and laughed at their own wit.

"At this point—" Damiskos paused to clear his throat, finding his voice betrayingly husky. "At this point, assume I'm still expecting more than a kiss. So I'm forging ahead … " He ran a hand sketchily over Varazda's hair, not really touching him, and down past the edge of the open coat. From a distance, he hoped, it would look like a long, slow caress, down to the waistband of Varazda's trousers. It took a definite effort to keep from thinking about what it would feel like to really do what he was feigning. "But you don't like where you think this is going."

"Right." Varazda mimed a very convincing reluctance, flinching and twisting away from Damiskos's hand. Damiskos leaned down and kissed into the soft nest of his hair, then drew back.

"And then I say something like, 'Don't worry, there's no rush'—because there isn't, honestly, when we've got an audience. I don't see how anyone could find that suspicious. Move over a bit?"

Varazda shifted over on the couch to give Damiskos room to stretch out beside him. Damiskos lay on his side, propped on one elbow, effectively blocking the view for the watchers from the beach. They seemed to be tiring of their chanting. Varazda tugged his hair out from under him to make himself more comfortable, and looked up at Damiskos.

They lay very close on the couch. Varazda smelled good, his citrusy perfume mingled with sweat and smoke from the bonfire. He had gathered his coat around him again. Damiskos reached across and fingered one of the smooth bone buttons on the opposite side, to make it look like he was doing something.

"So, First Spear—all those years in the colonies, what

were you doing that you don't know what the Garden of Jasmine is?"

"Who was I doing, I think you mean. The wrong people, obviously."

Varazda gave a little splutter of laughter. "It's a book. *The Three Gardens*."

"Oh, I've heard of that. But not read it."

"It's mostly pictures."

Damiskos considered that for a moment. He tried to remember the times he had heard people mention *The Three Gardens*, wondering how many conversations would have taken on a different cast altogether if he had known they were talking about a book of sex pictures.

"Well, that's … interesting. I don't think I ever slept with anyone in Zash who, uh, owned a lot of books."

"Right."

From outside the beach hut came sounds of grunting and scrabbling. Someone climbing up onto the roof. Others laughed and called up encouragement.

"I'm going to look through the smoke hole," the one on the roof called down. "There's nothing going on in there. I think they're *both* eunuchs."

Damiskos looked down at Varazda, and Varazda rolled his eyes expressively. Damiskos bit his lip to hold back laughter, and after a moment saw that Varazda was doing the same. From the roof came the sounds of one of the students crawling across the tiles. Damiskos braced his hand on the far side of the couch and leaned over Varazda.

"Is he looking in?" Damiskos whispered.

Varazda glanced up. "Yes."

"Ah."

"You know, at this point, it might be simpler if we just kissed."

"Yes."

Damiskos leaned over a little further, and Varazda pushed

109

himself up on the couch, and their lips met. It was certainly simpler than pretending to kiss. It was very simple, in fact. For a time, there was nothing but the act of kissing, the feeling of Varazda's lips, his slender hand on the back of Damiskos's neck, the warmth of their bodies barely touching.

They drew apart just the width of a breath, and Damiskos was aware of other things: soft notes of music and laughter borne on the breeze from the bonfire, the tang of incense-scented smoke, the cool of the night air. Then they were kissing again, still exquisitely light, and this time he let his fingers trail gingerly through Varazda's hair, trying hard not to sink down into the kiss and enjoy it too much.

More grunting and scrabbling came from the roof, then a sound of sliding, a yell, a thump, and a groan from the side of the hut. Damiskos and Varazda, parted again, looked at one another and shook with silent laughter.

The chanting had stopped, the torchlight moved off. The group of watchers was breaking up and losing interest. Damiskos could hear them collecting the fellow who had fallen off the roof and heading back to the bonfire to refill their wine cups and argue some more about virtue. He propped himself on his elbow again, looking down at Varazda.

"Before you ask," said Varazda, "no, 'that wasn't so bad.'"

Damiskos chuckled. "I *was* going to ask."

"I knew you were."

"I suppose we ought to wait a while before going back."

"Mm. Yes."

He didn't want to look round to make sure they were really alone, so he still spoke quietly in Zashian. "Do you think it … worked?"

Varazda glanced past Damiskos's shoulder toward the front of the hut. "They're gone. I don't know if Helenos will be entirely convinced, but I think he operates mostly by manipulating his underlings, and he'll have a harder time now convincing them that you're up to anything more complicated than romancing your new slave. Thank you for suggesting ... " He gave an elegant little gesture.

"You're quite welcome. It was ... really the only option. I'm not sure what kind of demigods you've been acquainted with, but, er, there's no way I could have performed under those circumstances."

"Oh." Varazda looked deeply embarrassed. "I do apologize. But—I am sure you could have."

"Now, look! I'm not confessing to impotence. *Nobody* could get it up with an audience like that, jeering and looking down the smoke hole and making rude jokes."

"Is that ... not what they do at Phemian weddings, then?"

"You're joking, right? No, it's not what they do at weddings. They sing a *decent* version of one of those hymns, they process to the couple's house, they sing another one while the bride and groom go inside, and then they leave. They don't *watch*."

"Oh. Oh, I see." He sounded entirely sincere.

"You really didn't know that."

"Well, it's not what they do at weddings in Boukos, I knew that. I'd just—honestly—never known an intact man admit there were times he couldn't get ... you know, ready to perform ... unless it were his partner's fault."

"That's a Zashian thing—I remember that. You say, 'Sorry, my dear, I'm a bit tired,' and she bursts into tears because she thinks it's something she did."

"Ah. I thought it was ... I didn't know it was a Zashian thing."

The voices of the students had long since receded into the distance. Of course now that they had started talking about it, Damiskos found that he was aroused after all, with a fierce and urgent warmth. It warred with the instinct of protectiveness he had been feeling for Varazda all evening, but it fired it up, too, because now he felt he needed to protect Varazda from him.

He turned carefully to lie on his back, propping his good leg up, knee bent, so that the skirt of his tunic draped discreetly. He tucked a hand behind his head.

"When I was serving at Seleos, I got engaged to a girl from Suna."

Varazda gave him a curious look. "Did you?"

"It was an entirely respectable thing. Her father hosted a dinner for the officers of my legion, and I met her when he invited her to play the lute at the party. I asked the family's permission to call on her again, we met a number of times with a chaperone, and eventually I asked if she wanted to marry me and negotiated a bride price. Then I found out how her father made his living."

"Oh yes?"

"Well, he was a merchant, I had known that. I thought he dealt in Parkan rugs, but it turned out that was only a part of his business. His main trade was in boys. Eunuchs. I found that out when he explained the business to me. Because I was set to join the family, you see."

"But then you didn't."

"No. The whole thing horrified me. I wanted no part of it. I considered asking Shahaz, my fiancée, to run away with me, but that wouldn't really have made either of us happy—she wanted a respectable marriage, and I wanted … well, I wouldn't have wanted to disgrace her. So I broke it off."

"I see." Varazda's voice had become remote. "I wonder what lesson about you it is that I'm meant to learn from that."

That was an annoying way of putting it, but as an insight it wasn't too far off. "I wanted to settle in Zash. Shahaz is a beautiful and talented woman, and would have made an excellent wife—is, I'm sure, an excellent wife now, to someone else—but it was the city of Suna that I was really in love with."

"And then we spoiled it for you with our barbarian ways. I see."

"No, you don't! I was trying to … oh, forget it."

Trying to express sympathy, he'd been about to say. Trying to show that he understood, better than the average Pseuchaian, that he'd even been willing to make some personal sacrifice on account of that understanding.

They lay for a little while in silence, Damiskos feeling irritable and slightly nauseous with cooling lust. Sounds from the bonfire were fading as revelry gave way to quiet conversation. The oldest and youngest of the merrymakers were probably heading home to bed.

"Will you be safe when we go back up to the house?" Damiskos asked finally.

"Probably." Varazda sounded irritable too. "Who knows. They'll expect me to be in your room, and I don't think they want to deal with you right now. If they're still suspicious of me, they'll wait until they can get me alone."

"Had you better be in my room, then?"

"I'm sure that would be delightful, but I don't believe it's necessary."

"Look." Damiskos pushed himself up on his elbow again, looking down at Varazda. "I'm not going to press the point. I know you know what you're doing. But if I haven't already made it quite clear that I would not take advantage of you, in any way—I wish you'd tell me why."

Varazda looked up at him for a long moment. The air between them felt heavy as a thunderstorm, but what it was charged with, Damiskos could not have said.

"No, First Spear, I know that," Varazda said finally, reverting to his old, acerbic tone. He moved away from Damiskos a little to sit up. "I think we have drawn this out long enough."

"Absolutely."

They both moved at the same time, Varazda pushing himself up and swinging a leg over Damiskos to get off the couch, Damiskos turning on his side to manoeuvre his stiff knee, and there was a very slight collision. Very slight but very telling.

Varazda had slithered off the couch in an instant and was grabbing up his shoes and his crumpled shirt and pretending it hadn't happened. Damiskos wasn't entirely sure it had.

"Was that … Are you … uh … turned on?" That changed things considerably.

Varazda's dark eyes flashed up at him, furious.

"Holy God. You just can't leave anything unsaid, can you? It does work, yes, after a fashion. And I don't—as it happens—prefer women."

"Oh," said Damiskos, at a loss. "I see."

CHAPTER 9

A LETTER from Aristokles arrived the following morning. Damiskos was at breakfast with Nione and Tyra when the young slave Niko brought it in. The students, mercifully, were too hungover to be present, and their master had not come down either.

Damiskos and Tyra waited politely while their host opened the tablet and read its contents. Nione set it on the table by the basket of bread, frowning. She shook out her skirt as if to rise, then subsided into her chair and looked at Damiskos.

"I don't want to embarrass you, Damiskos," she said, clearly embarrassed herself, "only I wondered if you might have some idea why Pharastes lied to me about his master's—his former master's—whereabouts?"

Damiskos desperately wanted to unfold the full story to her on the spot, but he couldn't do it in front of Tyra—couldn't do it at all, in fact, without betraying Varazda's trust.

"I ... I can only think that Aristokles must have instructed him to do so."

"Yes, I suppose that may be."

"Would you like me to speak to him for you?"

"Perhaps we could send for him now."

Well, it had been worth a try.

She sent Niko to fetch Varazda. Damiskos half expected the boy to come back alone to report that Varazda had vanished now too, but he didn't. He came back followed by Varazda, who looked to Damiskos's eyes as though he had neither slept much nor had any breakfast. His hair was pulled back in a simple twist, and he had no earrings in or kohl around his eyes. He was wearing the trousers he had worn yesterday, with a plain white shirt.

"May I speak to him?" Nione asked, before Varazda had arrived at their table.

"What? Oh, yes, of course."

"Pharastes, I hope you can clear up a misunderstanding for me," Nione said. "I received a letter from your previous master this morning. He says he was called away by a family crisis—he had a message from home yesterday and left on the same ship that brought the letter. I do not know what ship that was, or where it docked—it cannot have been the ship from Pheme that we saw yesterday afternoon. And all this is quite different from the account of his departure that you gave me."

Varazda let a moment pass in uncomfortable silence, an expression of shocked distress on his face.

"Indeed, my lady," he said finally. "I knew nothing of this. He told me that he was travelling to the village—I can only think that his plans must have changed suddenly. But by the time of his departure, of course, I was no longer his slave. I suppose he does not mention me in his letter?"

Damiskos saw an opportunity and leaned forward to pick up the letter before Nione could do so. He flipped it open, turned it around, and held it out toward Varazda.

"You can see for yourself that he doesn't," he said.

Nione took the letter back from Damiskos, giving him a

rather annoyed look. "He did not," she told Varazda gently, assuming that of course he could not read.

Damiskos didn't know that he could, but he was hoping that he might at least recognize Aristokles's writing. If it was Aristokles's writing.

"I suppose what you say must be true," said Nione. "I can think of no other explanation. But it is strange that he should have packed all his belongings for a journey down to Laokia, and strange that he should not have told anyone when he decided to take ship suddenly instead. After all, he had time to write this message for me and leave it with one of the fishermen."

"It is very strange, my lady."

"He's a bit of a strange man," Tyra put in. "I had a really peculiar conversation with him. He kept talking about being afraid of something."

"Perhaps, Damiskos," said Nione, "you might inquire in the stables for me—did Aristokles take a horse when he left, and do they know where he intended to go?"

"Of course."

"I'm sure it will all prove to be some kind of misunderstanding."

"I expect so," said Damiskos. He pushed back his chair. "I'll go right now, if you don't mind."

He and Varazda left together.

"Do I find he took a horse, or no?" Damiskos asked when they were in the hallway leading into the house.

Varazda ground the heels of his hands into his eyes for a moment, an uncharacteristically inelegant gesture. "Yes. I think we want my story to hold up while theirs doesn't. Or— I don't know. This is rather a mess."

"It is that."

"Anyway, you can ask in the stables—I already paid the grooms to say Aristokles took a horse and someone from the village brought it back. And no, Aristokles didn't write that letter."

"I was going to ask. You're sure?"

"Quite sure. It was nothing like his writing, wasn't sealed with his ring—nothing about it looked right."

"Divine Terza."

"I am going to spend the morning on a tour of the villa, looking for places where one could hide a body."

Damiskos digested that for a moment. "If that's what you're doing," he said firmly, "I'm coming with you."

"No, you're not."

"I *am*. I'm besottedly in love with you, remember? No one will think it odd if we're inseparable all day. And no one will have the opportunity to murder you, either."

Varazda gave him a look that could only be described as a silent snarl.

Damiskos did not exactly follow Varazda around all day, but only because it didn't take all day to search the villa. He accompanied Varazda to the wine cellars, where he browsed among the bottles while Varazda looked in corners and behind barrels. When one of the household slaves came down to fetch some wine, Damiskos engaged him in conversation so that he would not notice Varazda, and accompanied him upstairs and then loitered around the cellar door, pretending to admire some mosaics, until Varazda returned.

"Oh, good," said Varazda sarcastically. "You're still here."

"You didn't find anything."

"Of course not."

In the stables, much the same process was repeated, with Damiskos chatting with the grooms while Varazda sneaked about. This time it was Varazda who was waiting outside the stable-yard gate, leaning against the wall and looking elaborately bored, when Damiskos finished admiring the horses and finally emerged.

"Sorry about that. Got caught up."

"Mm. Fun for you."

Damiskos sighed.

In the kitchen wing, Damiskos pretended to want a snack while Varazda pretended to be looking in the store-rooms for the ingredients to make a special Zashian dish.

"I wouldn't have thought he knew how to boil water," the head cook remarked, looking after Varazda. "Begging your pardon, sir."

Damiskos shrugged and laughed.

He probably didn't. He came back empty-handed, claiming that they didn't have whatever it was he needed; he also claimed, wisely, not to know what it was called in Pseuchaian.

"Still nothing?" said Damiskos when they had left the kitchen.

"Still nothing."

"Well, I suppose in this context, 'nothing' is good."

Varazda shook his head. "I don't know. I'm going down to the fish-sauce factory to look around there, and then I'm going to walk to that village that I pretended Aristokles went to. Please don't come with me, First Spear. I will be fine, and I think … I'm sorry, but I think you have already walked enough today."

That caught Damiskos by surprise, not only the words but the tone in which they were said. Clearly Varazda realized he wouldn't like to hear that—even seemed to understand, or at least to care.

"I—" Instinctively he wanted to say he was fine, but he wasn't. His knee had been hurting all morning after walking so much yesterday without his cane, and the prospect of sitting down and resting it for a few hours was pitifully appealing.

"Wait for me in the garden or the library," Varazda suggested, "and I'll come find you when I've done. If I'm not back by sunset, you have my leave to raise the alarm."

"I don't like it, Varazda."

"Neither do I, First Spear. I don't like anything about it. I will see you soon."

It was still well before dinner, and the sun was still high in the sky. Damiskos had been reading in the library—well, sitting in the library with a book open in his lap—for an hour when Helenos, Gelon, and Phaia came in.

"Oh look," said Gelon, "it's Damiskos."

"First Spoon of the Quartermaster's Office," Phaia supplied.

Gelon giggled. "Oh, that's rather good!"

"Stop it, you two," said Helenos mildly. "It is not a laughing matter."

"I thought it was sort of funny," said Damiskos equably.

"You took a wrong turn, Damiskos Temnon," said Helenos, "but you could have the respect of the whole Republic again, if you tried. I don't believe you are really so far gone."

In a moment he was going to say something that would really hurt. Something about Damiskos searching for meaning, not being the man he used to be—Helenos's solution would be that Damiskos should join with him in fomenting war with Zash so that he could restore his lost honour, and Damiskos didn't think he would find that tempting, but he really had no desire to find out for sure.

While he was searching for something to say to shut Helenos up, he looked past the students and saw Varazda arrive in the doorway.

Varazda had been out walking, and it had put some

colour in his cheeks. His hair was a little tugged-about by the wind, a few strands escaping the neat knot from the morning. His sleeves were rolled up to his elbows, his shirt unfastened at the throat.

Damiskos swung his legs down from the footstool and stood, dropping his scroll, which unrolled across the floor. He heard a scornful laugh from the students. He honestly didn't care.

"Darling," said Varazda. He said it in Zashian, but the way he said it, one didn't need to speak the language to know what kind of term it was.

Damiskos remembered kissing him the night before, the scent of his perfume, the softness of his lips.

"Uh. You're back."

Varazda came across the room to pick up the dropped scroll, roll it back up, and hand it to Damiskos.

"Let's go," said Damiskos.

"*The Painted Urn*?" Varazda said as the door closed behind them.

"What?"

"*The Painted Urn*. What you were reading. An interesting choice. Not Tyreus's most popular play, but a good one, I've heard."

Damiskos looked at him. "You don't need to prove to me that you can read."

Varazda said nothing, and Damiskos thought he might have scored a rather roundabout point there. He wondered why he felt the need to think of it that way.

"So did you find anything?"

Varazda gave a one-shouldered shrug. "No one saw Aristokles in the village or down at the factory—though there's no one there but the fishermen now. The man who received the note to give to Nione said he got it this morning from one of the students, but he couldn't remember which one.

"Oh, and a rowboat went missing last night and reappeared on the beach this morning, and the factory workers think someone broke into one of their outbuildings and moved things around without taking anything."

"I see." Damiskos didn't like to spell out what that might mean in connection with Aristokles's disappearance.

Apparently neither did Varazda. "It's not much and may not be related, but it is what I've been able to come up with."

"You've been very thorough," said Damiskos, because it was the truth. "I think you have done all you can for today."

"Mm. You may be right."

"I'm going to ask Niko about getting a mattress for that extra bed in your room," Damiskos said. It would look odd to the other slaves, but no one would protest; he was a free man and entitled to his eccentricities.

Varazda groaned. "Oh, First Spear."

"You call me that to annoy me, don't you?"

"If it's not working, I'll stop."

Damiskos snorted. "Is there a lock on your door?"

"No, of course not."

"Well, then. I'm sleeping on that other bed. I'll sleep there without a mattress if I have to."

"No, no, I will personally find a mattress for you. I wouldn't want you to enjoy yourself *too* much."

"Good. So that's settled."

They stood for a moment in the yard. Varazda's expression lost its mocking cast and became thoughtful.

"You haven't told Nione the truth yet, have you?"

"No, of course not," said Damiskos.

"It's just that she said you are her friend." Varazda shrugged. "And she was very understanding about … well, my alleged situation. When I went to tell her that Aristokles had left and sold me to you, she congratulated me on having a good master now. She seemed to think you would free me directly."

"She's probably wondering why I haven't."

"I defer to you, as you know her better, but *I* think we could trust her with at least some of this. And as it is all happening in her house, her assistance could be very beneficial."

It struck Damiskos that what Varazda was really doing here was trusting *him*, and he was rather moved by it.

"I think you're right," he said after a moment. "But let me take some time to consider how best to talk to her."

"Of course. On an unrelated note, how's your leg?"

"Much better, thanks."

"Do you fancy sparring a little?"

"Do I what?"

"Fancy sparring. With me. I expect you could teach me a few things."

"I expect I could."

He smiled, surprised. It had been a friendly overture, unmistakably. Even if his leg hadn't been better—and it really was—he would have wanted to say yes.

"And they might come in useful."

"What?"

"The things you might teach me. Or at least—it might be useful for you to be seen teaching me."

"Ah. Yes. Can't hurt to let it get around that you know how to do more with a sword than dance."

"Exactly."

Varazda fetched his swords, and they squared off in the slaves' courtyard. They began with some easy exercises to warm up. Varazda already knew some of these, and the ones he did not know he picked up quickly. By the time they began fencing in earnest, they had an audience, loitering under the stairs and leaning over the railing above.

The two blades met, ringing with an unexpectedly pure note, like a bell. Varazda was caught off-guard by it; Damiskos was too, but he recovered more quickly. He slipped his sword free and brought it down on Varazda's arm, in what would have been a devastating slash if the swords had been sharp and Damiskos had put power behind it. Varazda jumped back, startled, and laughed.

Then he recovered, meeting Damiskos's next attack with a stylish little flourish and a precision that Damiskos had not expected. They fenced a few more passes, Varazda clearly giving it everything he had, Damiskos not remotely so—just observing, learning his opponent's limits.

If his life had followed its first trajectory and he had grown up as the son of a noble Zashian household, Varazda would have made an excellent swordsman. But he had not, and the skills he had cultivated were not all ones that mattered in an actual fight. His instinct was to sacrifice speed and force for style, and he was used to thinking only about his own movement, not predicting the attacks of an opponent. He was beautiful to watch, but he was no match for Damiskos. When Damiskos began to really press him, he gave ground quickly.

He was very fair-minded, though—or perhaps 'considerate' was a better word for it. His biggest advantage against Damiskos was that he was much faster on his feet, but he refused to use it. He would dodge Damiskos's attacks, but without moving more than a few steps, effectively neutralizing Damiskos's weakness.

Damiskos had sparred with other men, in the years since his injury, who had done the same, but none that he could remember who had done it so gracefully—without saying anything about it, without seeming to have to work at it. If he hadn't been having so much fun, it might have brought tears to his eyes.

He swung in earnest, hitting Varazda's blade with his full strength, once, twice, three times, driving him back. Varazda actually shrieked.

It was put on—he obviously wasn't really scared—but it was very funny, and Damiskos lost all form and composure and burst out laughing. Varazda seized his moment and swatted him on the flank with the flat of his blade, not hard enough to hurt. The watchers hissed and hooted.

Varazda had not been joking when he had suggested he could learn something, and after this he insisted that Damiskos teach him a couple of attacks, and put serious attention into learning them. Damiskos suggested techniques that would take advantage of Varazda's strengths: his height, his speed, his dancer's ease of movement.

This part was less entertaining to watch, and their audience gradually melted away so that by the time they were both tired and the light was fading, they were alone in the courtyard.

"Thank you," Varazda said, taking back Damiskos's sword and making a crisper, more military version of his usual courtly bow.

"My pleasure," said Damiskos sincerely.

They stood there for a moment, and it struck Damiskos suddenly that if they had still had an audience he would have had an excuse to lean in and give Varazda a kiss. But they didn't.

It was time for Damiskos to be going in for a bath before dinner, time for Varazda to rejoin the slaves as they prepared for the evening. Neither of them moved from where they stood.

Varazda said, "It has been five years since you left your command, I think you said?"

"Five years in the autumn."

"You must have been superb."

Damiskos shrugged and looked at the ground in the middle distance. "I was good."

"You're very good now, even with a foreign blade."

"Well, it's a style of fighting I've always liked. And I liked to challenge myself."

"I'm sorry they took that from you."

Damiskos looked up, surprised. "What do you mean, 'they'?"

Varazda's eyebrows went up a fraction. "I don't know. I must have misspoken."

But Damiskos was pretty sure he hadn't.

"Well," said Varazda after another moment, "I must let you go in. I don't think you want to join me in the slave baths—they're one of the unimproved parts of the house. Rather ghastly."

Damiskos chuckled, as he was obviously meant to do. "I am glad to be spared that."

"I'll see you later, then," said Varazda.

Damiskos watched him walk away toward the door into the slave quarters. He felt a pull, somewhere in his soul, strong as a river running downhill, an urge to follow Varazda. He didn't care how ghastly the slave bath was, what the slaves were having for dinner, or when they got to eat (he was used to a soldier's life, after all). He just wanted to be near Varazda.

He hadn't felt that pull, that helpless yearning, in years. But he *had* felt it before, often enough, when he was younger, and he knew well enough what it was. He could stop pretending to be in love with Varazda now, because he really was.

CHAPTER 10

WHEN DAMISKOS IMAGINED A LASTING LOVE, it had always been in the context of marriage or the army. If you had asked him five years ago what he wanted, he would have said he wanted both. If he had to choose, he would have chosen the wife, as the more respectable option and the one that came with the comforts of a settled home. That was why he had got into the habit of saying that he "preferred women." If he didn't have to choose, if he could have exactly what he wanted, he had always thought he'd want a kind and loyal wife at home, and a lover in the army, so that no matter where he was, there would be someone who was uniquely his, someone with whom he could share a deep companionship of body and soul.

He'd had lovers in the army, on and off, but they had all been taken from him, one way or another, by battle or illness or promotion and transfer to different legions. He had twice almost been married—once in Pheme, a match that fell through when his father's debts were revealed, and once in Zash, at what had been nearly the end of everything. It had been a long time since he thought in terms of having exactly what he wanted.

Varazda wasn't anything that he had ever imagined wanting.

More than that, he didn't even know what loving Varazda could mean. One couldn't marry him, and he wasn't a soldier. What his life in Boukos was like, Damiskos had no idea. Perhaps he already had someone to share it with; perhaps he didn't want anyone.

These thoughts occupied Damiskos in the bath, so that when he emerged, clean and dressed for dinner, he was in something of a fog of misery. He nearly collided with Nione in the corridor outside the bath.

"Oh! I beg your pardon," they both said at the same time.

He looked at her. She was trying to take control of her expression and smile at him, but it was clear she was seething with anger, almost in tears with it.

"What is it?" he asked. "Are you all right?"

She struggled with herself for a moment before unclenching her hands from her skirt and letting out a shaky breath. "It's the students. I *can't stand* them. I want them out of my house. I'm only putting up with them because Eurydemos is family and was disinherited and all that—I'm beginning to think I can't even do that much longer."

"Oh, Nione, I'm so sorry. And—I have to admit I'm … relieved."

She stared at him for a moment, and then her eyes widened. "You thought maybe I'd been seduced by their … their poisonous twaddle?"

"I didn't think you could have changed that much," he said hastily. "But then, I suppose people sometimes do."

"You've changed a lot," she countered, but not unkindly. "You were always serious, but not always sad."

He couldn't think of anything to say to that except, eventually, "You're right."

She gestured him into a room on the other side of the

hallway and closed the door behind them. It was one of the rooms being decorated, empty except for a rough bench spattered in paint and plaster. She dusted this off a little, and they sat down.

"No," she said, "I haven't taken up philosophy, or—or horrible notions about Phemian purity. Blessed Anaxe. Not at all. I just had the bad judgement to allow myself to fall in love with a philosopher's student."

He looked at the patterns sketched on the floor by the mosaicist, curling vegetation around the edge of the room, below the newly painted walls.

"Phaia?" he guessed.

"Yes. You've known that about me all along, haven't you?"

"Yes."

She let out a breath of what sounded like relief. "Oh, Damiskos, I was so afraid you were another one here hoping to marry me. I know you'd make a wonderful husband for someone, but I've never wanted a man, and we would be miserable."

"I thought you might have been afraid of that. I should have said something sooner."

"Oh no, it's too awkward a thing to say, isn't it?"

He didn't disagree. "So what happened with Phaia?"

"Well, she's the real reason I invited the students here. I met her in the city when I visited Eurydemos at the Marble Porches, and she ... she was very charming, and I liked her."

"Of course."

"I thought it would be really enchanting to have her here, with her fellow students, talking philosophy." She shook her head. "It wasn't as I'd imagined it, even in the beginning, and then ... " Her voice trailed off. "And I'm awfully worried about Aristokles, because—Damiskos, you weren't to know this, but he was here on a secret mission."

Damiskos looked up in surprise. "I did know that. I didn't know you knew it. He told you?"

"No, the friend who asked me to invite him explained that it was important state business—to do with Eurydemos's school in Boukos. They suspect his students of being involved in something criminal. I didn't like the idea of inviting someone to spy on my kinsman while he was a guest in my house—it sounds almost blasphemous when I put it like that, and perhaps it was, but by the time the letter with the request arrived … "

She stopped, pushed her hands back over her hair. "Eurydemos and his students had been here a week by then, and were talking about setting up a school in my house, as if they had a right to it, and … I wrote back saying Aristokles could come, and sent it on the postal ship on its return journey, the same day.

"Then of course I couldn't tell the students to leave, because Aristokles had to do his job—but he was behaving so *suspiciously*. I actually had to encourage him to court me, Damiskos, so people would think that was what he was doing here. I didn't actually *tell* him to do it, but I might as well have—the idea certainly came from me—and of course that quickly got out of hand.

"I suppose I had some thought of getting Phaia away from these awful men—which was wrong of me, because she's no more their dupe than I am. She has her own mind and her own conscience, and she's *chosen* her path. She chose to deceive me, too. She's really Helenos's girl."

"Oh, Nione, I'm so sorry."

"I overheard them talking the other night. She probably thinks of me as a stupid old woman only good for getting them a free holiday in the country."

"I'm sorry." It was all he had to say, but it was heartfelt.

They sat in silence for a moment before he reached out and took her hand. He was glad to be able to do it now, to know it would be understood as a gesture of friendship. She squeezed his hand in return.

"And now Aristokles has gone missing," she continued, "and his poor servant … I am glad you bought him, Damiskos, for his sake, but please tell me you mean to free him. It isn't a love affair if one person owns the other."

"Ah," said Damiskos. "About that."

He told her everything he knew, and then they went to dinner with the students who had, quite possibly, murdered Aristokles and hidden his body, who had certainly killed men in Boukos, and who might intend harm to Varazda as well. They pretended that all was well and everyone was enjoying a lovely house party with a heavy emphasis on discussions of the Ideal Republic.

What else could they do? Nione had a houseful of mostly female slaves who could not be asked to subdue and imprison a group of dangerous young men. Of the few able-bodied male slaves in her household, several were away in the Tentines. There seemed nothing to do but rely on the veneer of civility that everyone was still preserving. Damiskos thought that aside from times when he had been held captive or in terrible pain, he might never have passed a worse evening.

Everything that the students said sounded fatuous, even grotesque, as if their words came to him eerily distorted. They were discussing slavery now, debating the views of the radicals in the city who wanted to abolish it. The argument was between two of the new students, who would allow that the radicals might be morally right, though in practice their ideas would never work, and everyone else, who thought that slavery was a natural human institution which could not morally be abolished.

Damiskos had taken it for granted that everyone thought slavery was an evil, and that the only argument was between people who thought it a necessary evil and those who didn't. At any other time he thought he would have been shocked to learn there were people who could argue it was a moral good, not an evil at all. But after what he had already heard about Eurydemos's students, it didn't even surprise him much.

He felt duty-bound to stay at dinner with Nione, now that she knew who she was harbouring under her roof, but fortunately she did not want to linger over dinner herself, and he was able to excuse himself as soon as she quit the dining room.

He went to his room for his sword and hurried to the slaves' courtyard. He found Varazda sitting on a bench with his arm around the shoulders of one of Nione's women, who was drying her eyes. She looked up guiltily as Damiskos approached, but Varazda gave her arm a squeeze.

"It's all right, he's harmless."

The woman gave a watery laugh. "He's your new master, isn't he?"

"That's right," said Varazda dryly. "And he's a good one." He looked up at Damiskos. "One of the students has been giving Dria trouble."

"It's was nothing, really," Dria murmured, with a miserable face that belied the statement. "I only wish I'd been braver and not given in and told him what he wanted to know—we've all heard how he tried to attack you."

"So you were scared," said Varazda. "Of course. I'd've been too. Well. I *was*."

He had a different way of talking to women, Damiskos thought, his mannerisms subtly more feminine, his voice a little bit different. Damiskos wondered if he did it on purpose or if it was just something he slipped into naturally.

Dria's roommate arrived in the courtyard with a bottle and cups from the kitchen. With thanks and more apologies to Varazda, the two women retreated to their room.

"It was Gelon, in case you were wondering," said

Varazda, "and what he wanted to know was where my bedroom is."

"Daughters of Night."

"Mm. I thought I'd better not switch rooms, or someone else might get stabbed in the night."

"Right." For a moment he thought to suggest his own room. But there was only one bed ... he would have to offer to sleep on the floor, or ...

They climbed the stairs and arrived at Varazda's door.

Damiskos said, "Shall I take first watch, or will you?"

"Oh, First Spear. Only you would miss the opportunity to say 'We'd better not sleep much tonight, ha ha'—in favour of setting up a watch rota."

Damiskos drew himself up sternly. "Under the circumstances, I would find it unacceptably crass to make that kind of remark. So I will take that as a compliment."

"How do you know it wasn't meant as one?" He gave Damiskos a hurt look.

"I—I'm sorry."

"I am teasing you, Damiskos. But I can stop. At least," he amended, "I can try to stop." He opened the door and held it for Damiskos to enter.

Damiskos smiled. "No. No, I'm not offended. I'm s—" He stopped himself from saying "sorry" again. "I'm on edge, that's all."

That wasn't all, really; there was also the fact that he wanted to unpin Varazda's hair and bury his face in it, kiss Varazda's white throat, maybe push Varazda against a wall with his hands on Varazda's tiny waist and slide his palms down to feel the shape of Varazda's firm ass through his trousers ...

"You're not the only one."

"What?"

"The only one on edge," Varazda said patiently.

"No. Oh. No, I suppose I'm not. This must be intolerable for you. I mean, with your, your colleague missing and … "

He wasn't sure what to say, and his eye fell on the spare bed, which was still without a mattress. His heart sank a little; he really hadn't wanted to sleep on the bare cords. Though if they were going to sleep in shifts, then presumably he could … they could both …

… the pillow and the sheets would smell of Varazda's perfume …

"I didn't forget about the extra mattress, in case you were wondering," Varazda said. "Rhea said she would find one and have it brought up after she was finished her evening duties."

"Ah."

"Here, sit."

He cleared space on his own bed, pulled the cover across, and sat himself, perched on the edge, his long legs stretched out. Damiskos sat beside him, leaning back on his hands. The day had left him tired.

They sat in silence for a few moments. Damiskos studied Varazda's profile, the clean, smooth lines of it, the slightly aquiline nose, the elegant arch of eyebrow.

When you looked closely, you could see his lineage written in the bones of his face. Damiskos had seen countless faces like it—some marked with scars, some weatherbeaten and lined with age—on the battlefields and in the noblemen's strongholds of the Deshan Coast. That wasn't the part of Zash that he had loved, and its haughty tribesmen were not the people he had liked best, but he had respected them, as one had to respect worthy enemies. It was strange to be reminded of them when he looked at Varazda. And it was strange that he hadn't been reminded of them sooner.

"Aristokles is probably dead," Varazda said, "and I … If he is, I feel responsible. He was afraid he was in danger—afraid we both were—and I dismissed his fear instead of doing anything to insure it was unfounded."

"You thought the only danger was to yourself."

Varazda nodded. "That's no excuse."

"You ... you're fond of him, I guess." In spite of everything, he still found himself returning to this. He still wanted to know.

"What? No, not at all. He's been nothing but a nuisance. That doesn't mean I wanted him *killed*."

"No, no. Of course not. Was he just here to give you an excuse to come to Laothalia?"

Varazda nodded. "He was planning to visit Pheme and had a useful connection that could get him invited to Laothalia. He was strong-armed into the mission by a cousin on the Basileon. He was never comfortable with it, didn't really know what the mission was about except that it's dangerous ... " Varazda sighed. "You see why I feel guilty."

"Yes." He managed to sit there there for a minute or two with a sympathetic look on his face before he said, "So if Aristokles was never really your master ... "

"What was I? In Zash I was a dancer in the king's household at Gudul—a provincial palace in the north, you probably don't know it. When the permanent embassy in Boukos was established, seven years ago, His Radiancy sent slaves and furniture from each of his palaces to outfit it, and I was one of the articles sent from Gudul. It was me and a bed and some wall-hangings."

As if he had been a thing, this beautiful person. And those goat-fuckers in the dining room could argue that slavery was a part of the natural order and essential to good government.

Varazda went on, "Then on the first anniversary of the establishment of the embassy, all of the household was freed, as part of a birthday celebration. There were only three eunuchs in the household at that time, and we thought that the manumission wouldn't include us, because as you know, in Zash, we could not have been freed. But"—he shrugged—

"in Boukos we could, and we were. So. I have been a Boukossian citizen six years now, and I am a free eunuch—one of three, as far as I know, in the world."

"That's wonderful," said Damiskos earnestly. "I'm—I'm delighted for you. I should have said that a long time ago."

Varazda waved a hand dismissively, but he also smiled. "I really did not give you an opportunity, did I?"

CHAPTER 11

"So what do you do now," said Damiskos, "when you're not—I mean, back in Boukos, what do you do?"

"Dance, mostly." Varazda smiled. "In all the best households. I'm terribly in demand. Of course they all know who I am—I don't pretend to be anyone's property—but you'd be surprised how much people take you for granted, no matter how fashionable or famous you are, when you're the entertainment."

"And you spy on them?" Damiskos couldn't keep the delight out of his voice.

"It sounds so *vulgar*, when you put it like that," said Varazda affectedly. Damiskos snorted. "I can't tell you what I really do, First Spear—you are a foreign citizen, you work for the Phemian army. I've already told you more than I should. But you have got the general idea."

"And ... it's satisfying work? You enjoy it?"

"Enormously. It pays well, too. I own my house and support my family in reasonable style."

"Wonderful," Damiskos said warmly, instead of, "Family? How ... What ... *Family?*"

Varazda looked at him for a moment. "Let me show you something," he said finally.

He rummaged in his luggage and brought out something wrapped in a cloth. He unwrapped it and held out a large, flat shell with a miniature painting on the inside: a half-length portrait of a smiling little girl with dark brown skin and black hair in two stubby braids.

"She's beautiful," said Damiskos, smiling up from the portrait at Varazda.

"She's my daughter."

Damiskos looked back down at the picture. "What's her name?"

"Remi. She's three."

There was a long silence. Damiskos realized Varazda was waiting for him to ask something—"How did you get her?" or "What happened to her real parents?"—and hoping that he wouldn't. But giving him lots of time, just to make sure.

"Thank you for showing me," Damiskos said.

Varazda wrapped the picture up and replaced it in his luggage. "What about you?" he said ambiguously.

"I don't have any children."

"You're married, though?"

"No. No, I can't afford to marry. Not that there's any woman sitting around waiting for me to be able to afford it."

"I see." He looked faintly surprised, but whether by the lack of a wife or because he had assumed Damiskos made a decent salary, Damiskos wasn't sure.

After a moment, Varazda said, "The other people in my household are—I call them family, but we've no official relation, we're technically friends who live together. Yazata keeps house for us, and Tash is studying to be a sculptor. They're the other two eunuchs who were freed at the same time I was."

"I see."

"I don't have a … I mean, under Boukossian law, I think

probably I could marry, but it's not something I ever plan on doing, and I don't have a lover." He cleared his throat delicately. "Not that that's relevant."

It struck Damiskos as being extremely relevant; or rather, the fact that Varazda had thought to mention it just now, in a strangely hesitant way that was very different from his usual manner, that seemed monumentally relevant.

"I enjoyed myself last night," Damiskos said.

Varazda went still. The comfortable mood of a moment ago was gone. Damiskos almost swore aloud at his own stupidity.

"Did you."

"Well, the parts that were enjoyable. I enjoyed watching you dance—I enjoyed that a great deal. And after … I mean, the business with the students was touch and go and pretty ghastly, but even still, I … I wished that we had been properly alone in that hut."

"Oh. You got over your disgust, did you? Enough to enjoy yourself?"

"Disgust? What?"

"That might not have been the word you used. Perhaps it was 'horror.'"

"What … " He had been so sure he knew where this was going, but now he was lost again. He tried to remember when he had said anything like "horror" the night before. "Oh! Immortal gods—do you mean what I said about Shahaz's father's business? Of course that filled me with horror, it's—it's a horrible thing, and to discover that the family I was proposing to join made their money from such a thing? 'Horror' was the right word—'disgust' would have done too. But I wasn't trying to suggest that I was horrified by *you*—or disgusted by eunuchs in general. That wasn't what I meant at all."

"No?" Varazda gave him a wary look. "What *did* you mean? By telling me that."

"I meant ... I meant that I felt angry on your behalf. I was *trying* to be sympathetic."

"Oh," said Varazda tonelessly.

"But look—it was misjudged, I can see that now, and I'm sorry. And I'm not—not looking for an apology from you so that I can feel good about myself. If my sympathy isn't of any use to you, then it isn't, and that's how it is. But it isn't disgust, I promise you that."

"I suppose I knew that." He relaxed visibly, though not completely.

"Well. I'm sure I could have expressed it better. It isn't even pity, really. It was in the beginning, I admit, but then I got to know you, and I don't think of you as an object of pity any longer. Didn't, even before I found out that you're free and have a family and a beautiful daughter."

Varazda smiled slightly. He was leaning back against the wall now, one leg drawn up and tucked under the other knee, looking at Damiskos thoughtfully.

"You also said you prefer women. I have to assume you don't usually spar with them, though."

"I'm not pretending you're a woman, if that's what you're asking."

"What are you pretending I am?"

Damiskos shook his head and found himself saying, rather to his own surprise, "Not a damned difficult bastard. It isn't easy."

Varazda gave a boyish shout of laughter. "Oh, all right. Well played."

"Look. I did say I prefer women. It wasn't a lie. It was an exaggeration, but that was because I was trying to put you at ease. You were about to pass out from nerves. I was trying to be sympathetic. Again."

"That was before the other time."

"Shut up."

Varazda made a little mime of one of the parries that

Damiskos had taught him that afternoon. Damiskos laughed. Then he fell silent, and they looked at one another for a long, charged moment.

"You're beautiful, Varazda. You take my breath away. Everything about you. I don't expect—You don't owe me anything for thinking that. My own preferences ... my preferences are—were—formed by my experience, and I have been with both men and women, but never with anyone like you. Perhaps it took me a while to get used to how well I like that. Perhaps it took me longer than it should have."

"I like how seriously you take everything, Damiskos."

"I'm not—I mean, I do know how to enjoy myself. I think."

Varazda smiled. "I said I like it."

"Yes, you did."

"I enjoyed myself last night, too."

"Ah," said Damiskos. "Did you?"

"Yes. In spite of everything."

"I'm glad. I was afraid ... I wondered what had been done to you, that you are capable of ... that you're *capable*, and you know all these different, ah, techniques, but you don't *like* it. I know that isn't any of my business."

"I was a slave, Damiskos. We don't get to say no."

"Right."

"It wasn't any one thing. It was just years of not getting to say no—not getting to say yes, either, when I might have wanted to. Part of what freedom meant to me was freedom from that whole *area*." He waved a hand dismissively.

"I am so sorry, Varazda. The situation I helped to place you in last night ... I can only beg your forgiveness." And he had thought he had been doing the right thing by playing along.

"I don't think I'm quite bringing my point across. There ... are ... things I have wanted to say yes to."

"Oh, I see." Another laden silence. "Such as?"

"I like kissing. Sometimes."

"Last night?"

"Yes."

Damiskos leaned forward to look at him. The gold stud in his nose glinted in the lamplight.

"I've been trying to remember," Varazda said, with a self-conscious lightness, "whether I had ever kissed a man without a beard before last night. I don't think I had."

"I have a beard," said Damiskos, rubbing his jaw.

"You have stubble—I meant a *beard*." He made an explanatory gesture, wiggling his hennaed fingers.

Damiskos laughed. "Right. And so—what did you think?"

"Haven't we covered that already?" Varazda's voice was soft, and he was looking down at his hands in his lap. "I liked it. I was turned on. That … as you may have gathered … doesn't happen all that easily."

It obviously cost him so much to talk about this, and Damiskos didn't know if he was ashamed to have desires at all, or that his desires were not equal to an intact man's, or what. He wondered if Varazda was even sure what bothered him.

Rather boldly, Damiskos said, "Want to see if we can make it happen again?"

Varazda looked up in surprise. "What—right now?"

"Yes, of course right now! Immortal gods. We're sitting on your *bed*, talking about how beautiful you are and whether or not you like sex—it's surprising I even needed to say anything."

"I am literally a eunuch, First Spear."

After that they were both laughing, Varazda giggling helplessly at his own joke, and the mood had shifted again. Varazda reached out and slid his fingers into Damiskos's hair, taking a gentle handful, and leaned in and kissed him, as gracefully as he had done in the doorway in front of Helenos years ago, or whenever it had been.

The first kiss became a whole series of kisses, gentle and uncomplicated. For Damiskos it was like kissing someone he'd known for years. Warm and intimate and comfortable. Varazda drew back and looked at him for a moment, his lips red, his expression open and affectionate.

"That's your yes?" said Damiskos.

"Very much so."

They moved together again, a little awkwardly this time. There was some fumbling and a near-collision before they sorted out what they wanted; Damiskos pulled Varazda onto his lap, and Varazda settled himself carefully astride Damiskos's thighs, bracing his hands against the wall by the bed. Damiskos took Varazda's face between his hands and kissed him again.

Varazda shifted his hips, moving closer, and Damiskos moaned.

"Sorry," Varazda murmured against his lips.

"Uh? Sorry for what?"

"I don't know—was that the wrong thing, or not enough of the right thing?"

He had rubbed up against Damiskos's cock, and Damiskos would certainly have liked much more of that, any time.

"You're out of practice, huh?" he said. "With your lilies and your pomegranates and whatever."

"Shut up."

Damiskos laughed. His fingers burrowed into Varazda's hair, and the kiss that followed was messy and urgent.

"Show me what else you like," Damiskos gasped when they finally drew apart.

Varazda reached up and pulled out one of the ivory combs that held his hair up. Damiskos caught his other hand and moved it away so he could release the second comb himself. Varazda's hair tumbled down, and he shook it out. Damiskos sifted it through his hands and stroked it back from Varazda's face. It was soft and thick, slightly wavy even when it hadn't been braided, and absolutely black. Varazda closed his eyes under the slow caress. He made a little noise like a sigh.

Damiskos wanted to go to the king's palace in Gudul, wherever that was, and seek out the godsforsaken fuckers who had given Varazda such a distaste for sex that he had spent years avoiding something he obviously enjoyed. He'd throw them out a window.

He brushed his thumb over the gold flower stud in Varazda's nose. He remembered thinking that Varazda's master must have made him wear it, not knowing what it signified except an exotic decadence. But Varazda was free and had chosen how to decorate himself.

Varazda opened his eyes and put up a hand to touch Damiskos's face. He ran his fingers through the short curls of Damiskos's hair and down the back of his neck. Damiskos turned his face into Varazda's palm with its delicate tracery of henna flowers, and something about the gesture must have amused Varazda, because he laughed softly as he drew his thumb over Damiskos's lips and lightly along the stubble on his jaw.

"What do you like?" Varazda asked.

"Oh, well … " He slid his hands down to Varazda's waist. "All the usual stuff."

"That covers a lot of territory."

"It does, yes. Can I undress you?"

Varazda looked down at his clothes. "Mm. Can you?"

"Yeah, I can."

He reached up to the buttons that held Varazda's coat closed at the shoulder, flicked them out of their button-loops with his thumb. Varazda shrugged out of his coat. Damiskos reached around to unwind Varazda's sash, then moved his hands to the ties fastening Varazda's trousers.

"You've done this before."

"Not like you're thinking. I've worn Zashian clothes before."

"Really?" Damiskos thought Varazda was talking because he was nervous, trying to be arch and not quite succeeding.

"When I was on leave in Rataxa. Grew my beard too, for a while, but I wasn't convinced it suited me."

"No." He traced the line of Damiskos's jaw again. "I like you with the stubble."

He leaned in and kissed Damiskos, just as the ties came undone. The loose fabric slipped down, and Damiskos ran his hands over firm, smooth thighs. Varazda was bracing himself on the wall again, his face hidden against Damiskos's neck. Damiskos explored slowly, still with that feeling of ease and familiarity, although nothing about this was truly familiar. He'd never needed to take quite so much care with anyone he'd taken to bed—and maybe he didn't precisely need to now, but it felt good to do it.

He kept one hand on Varazda's thigh and moved the other one up under the hem of the long, Zashian-style shirt. He wasn't entirely sure what he was going to find, but it seemed important not to betray surprise. His thumb brushed against wiry curls of hair, which he hadn't expected, but he rubbed into it as if he had. Varazda made a slight, appreciative noise. Damiskos curled his hand around Varazda's half-awake little cock. That was met with a different noise, a wary intake of breath.

He looked into Varazda's face—what he could see of it from this angle—and loosened his grip.

"Still a yes," Varazda murmured. "Just a—a—yes, very much a yes."

Damiskos moved his hand coaxingly. He was careful not to

let his fingers explore too far, not wanting to touch the place where there would presumably be a scar. Slowly, gratifyingly, he felt Varazda's body respond. His prick plumped in Damiskos's hand and grew properly stiff as they kissed again, slowly. He moved his hips, muscles trembling. Damiskos abandoned caution and stroked faster and harder. Varazda moaned in earnest. Damiskos wanted to give him something more; this was very basic, schoolboy stuff, and he knew he was capable of better.

He took Varazda's trim waist between his hands, palms stroking up over the curve of his hips. He paused.

Varazda's eyes popped open. "Still saying yes." He sounded a little breathless.

"You don't even know what I was about to do."

"I have a general idea. And I'm saying yes. To whatever it is."

"You'll have to tell me its proper name afterward."

Damiskos scooted him back a little, preparatory to laying him down. This time there was no awkward tangling and bumping. Varazda swung his leg back over Damiskos and slid down sinuously onto the bed, shedding his trousers fully somewhere in the process. When Damiskos moved over him, in the moment before his bad leg gave out and tipped him forward, he found himself effortlessly caught, Varazda's hand against his shoulder, bracing him with a strength like steel.

Damiskos looked into Varazda's eyes, and the smile that momentarily lit Varazda's face—soft, intimate, just a little wry—had nothing to do with sex. Except that it made Damiskos want him with the heat of a building on fire.

Varazda's shirt had ridden up, exposing his small, neat erection, flushed against his pale skin. His legs were magnificent: long and lean and white. Damiskos stroked down his right calf and ran his fingers under an anklet of red glass beads. He spread Varazda's thighs wider and slid down, moving onto his side to take the weight off his right knee.

He had to prop himself on one elbow, which left him

with only one free hand. He slid it under one cheek of Varazda's ass and felt it tense.

"Still a yes?"

"I think so."

He licked from the base to the tip of Varazda's cock, circled with his tongue, and took the whole thing easily into his mouth.

He'd never gone down on anyone who wasn't a lover of long standing, whose preferences and peculiarities he had known beforehand. For him it was too much of an abandonment of dignity for a casual encounter, and the enjoyment of it was all in appreciating the pleasure you were giving the other fellow, which hardly mattered if you didn't care about him. He knew he was going to enjoy this with Varazda, even before he felt the muscles jump in Varazda's thighs and heard the soft, sobbing gasp that was the first sound Varazda made.

Varazda made a lot of sounds, more than Damiskos had expected, little half-swallowed exclamations in Zashian, in the dialect of the Deshan Coast, nothing Damiskos could understand. His prick was velvety soft and tasted good. Damiskos sucked him gently, slow but not teasing. Varazda's body moved under him, pressing up into his mouth, matching his rhythm, graceful as always.

Damiskos was painfully hard, but he didn't care. He couldn't remember ever having enjoyed giving head this much. He felt Varazda's fingers in his hair, tugging slightly. It felt possessive; he liked it.

Varazda was saying something in Zashian, and Damiskos realized it was intended for him. The Deshan accent was too thick for him to understand. He would tease Varazda about that afterward.

Then he realized what Varazda was probably trying to tell him, and so he wasn't completely surprised a moment later when Varazda came in his mouth.

When he pushed up onto his hands, he saw that Varazda

had actually covered his mouth to mute his final, abandoned shout. It had still been more than audible.

Damiskos licked his lips. "Didn't know the Pseuchaian for 'I'm about to come,' did you?"

Varazda shook his head. He drew his hand away from his lips. His cheeks were flushed, and he looked slightly dazed, almost drunk. It made him astonishingly beautiful.

"Your Deshan accent is really cute, too, but I can't understand a word you say."

Varazda responded with something that probably meant, "May a dog shit in your ancestors' holy place," because that was the sort of thing Deshan warlords said to one another.

Teasing had been the right move, Damiskos thought. They were only friends, after all—had only known each other for a few days. Varazda probably did not want this to get out of hand. He might have revealed more of himself than he meant to, and Damiskos didn't want him to regret it.

Varazda had collected himself sufficiently to sit up. He pulled down his shirt and tucked his legs under him. Damiskos sat back on the bed, and Varazda's hands slipped in under his tunic and touched him through the thin fabric of his loincloth.

Damiskos made a noise much less beautiful than any of Varazda's. Varazda pulled the loincloth down and away, and both of his long-fingered hands explored Damiskos's achingly hard cock, cupped his balls, moved between his thighs.

Still a yes, unmistakably. He wasn't performing; this wasn't anything out of *The Three Gardens*. He handled Damiskos's cock like it was something he wanted. Damiskos leaned back on his hands, letting his head fall back with a moan.

Varazda pulled aside the skirt of Damiskos's tunic and started to move down, in a graceful slither. Damiskos pushed himself up to catch Varazda's shoulders and stopped him.

"Just use your hands, darling. I want you to kiss me again."

What had he just said?

Varazda looked up, frozen for a moment, a wonderful little smile curving his lips. He came back up in another slither, hooked one arm around Damiskos's neck, and brought their mouths together in a hot, deep kiss while his other hand deftly worked Damiskos's cock. He teased with long, light strokes, his fingers supple as the petals of flowers, his grip tightening as he sped up, until finally it was fast and firm, and Damiskos clutched him and came in wave after wave of sensation poised on a knife-edge between pleasure and pain.

He sagged back, breathless, and found himself gathered in and hugged against Varazda's chest, his forehead on Varazda's shoulder. They remained like that, Damiskos breathing in the scent of Varazda's hair, until an interior voice suggested he should pull himself together before Varazda started thinking him clingy. He felt pretty clingy just then.

He straightened up, wincing when he saw what a mess he had made of Varazda's shirt. Varazda had been looking at him with a kind of soft, thoughtful expression, but his smile brightened.

"I should clean up, shouldn't I?" He disengaged from Damiskos and got up from the bed in a beautiful unfolding of white limbs. "Such a messy business."

In more ways than one, Damiskos thought. He was glad Varazda was taking this brisk, friendly line now, because of course it was the right line to take, and he would do his best to keep in step.

He could think of literally nothing to say.

Varazda was pouring water into a basin and tidying himself up. He retrieved a pair of pyjama pants from the chair beside the bed, stepped into them, tied them, and only then pulled off his shirt, which he dumped in a heap on the same chair.

"You're a slob," Damiskos observed, looking at the shirt instead of at Varazda's bare chest and lovely, muscular arms.

Varazda gave an exaggerated sigh, picked up the shirt, and draped it over the back of the chair.

"You're not wrong," he said. He dipped another of his patterned handkerchiefs in the basin, wrung it out, and brought it over to offer it to Damiskos.

He sat on the bed beside Damiskos and watched Damiskos wipe himself off, with an interest that was surprisingly flattering. If Damiskos hadn't been as wrung out as the handkerchief himself, he thought he would have got hard again, just from the touch of his own hand through the cloth and the weight of Varazda's gaze on him.

Finished, he pulled down his tunic, and Varazda took the cloth back and hung it up, very daintily, on the rim of the basin, smoothing it out and straightening it several times. Damiskos snorted and rolled his eyes.

"I'll take first watch," said Varazda cheerfully. "I'm feeling quite full of energy." He bounced slightly on his feet to prove it. "I'll go down now and round up that mattress for you. No, don't get up."

He retrieved his shoes from under his bed, tossed on his pyjama shirt without buttoning it, and bounced out of the room, hair flying and hips swaying.

CHAPTER 12

DAMISKOS WOKE IN THE DARK, jerked awake by a flurry of noise: the crash of the door hitting the bed on the opposite side of the room as it swung open; running feet outside. He pushed himself up, blinking blearily around the room. He'd been sleeping in an awkward position, face-down on top of the rumpled coverlet, with his tunic on and still belted.

Moonlight from the open door showed the other bed in the room still made—halfheartedly—and empty. He caught a whiff of smoke as if a lamp had recently been extinguished. He rolled out of bed and went to the door.

Varazda was coming up the stairs to the gallery, barefoot and pyjama-clad, with Damiskos's short sword in his hand.

"Didn't catch him," he whispered when he reached the top of the stairs. "Not that I know what I'd have done if I had." He handed the sword ruefully back to Damiskos. "It wasn't Gelon, though. It was one of the others. Which is worrying, because it means it's not just Gelon having it in for me personally. They all think I'm a threat. My cover, as we say in the business, appears to be blown."

"That's bad."

Varazda nodded. "I scared him off, whoever he was,

which means either they'll leave us alone for the rest of the night—or they'll send more than one next time."

"I'll take the watch now."

"Good." Varazda yawned elegantly. "I was going to wake you shortly anyway."

They were back in the room by this time, but the door was still open, and Damiskos saw what he'd missed when he'd been jolted awake.

"Terza's head, did I fall asleep in your bed?"

"Mm-hm. When I struggled back upstairs with the extra mattress, you were passed out there with the lamp still burning. I didn't disturb you."

"Gods. I'm sorry."

"Oh, it's fine. The other bed is just as comfortable. I left the light burning too—I'm not sure I'd have been able to keep awake in the dark. I just blew it out when I heard noises from outside, so they'd think I was asleep. I can light it for you again if you want."

"No, I'm going to sit outside on the gallery. They know we know what they're up to now—we don't need to worry about the element of surprise."

"Can I have my bed back, then?"

"Please."

He collapsed gracefully onto it, pulling the covers around himself, and pressed his face into the pillow, drawing a deep breath.

"Mmmm. Smells like soldier."

"I'm sorry," said Damiskos stiffly.

One dark eye looked up at him from the pillow. "I don't know if you've worked this out, First Spear," came Varazda's muffled voice, "but I *fancy* soldiers."

Varazda took the last watch of the night, and he was out on the gallery, leaning on the railing, when Damiskos woke with the first light of morning. He yawned hugely as Damiskos came out to stand beside him.

There had been no more nocturnal visitors, and now the slave quarters were busy with early risers going about their tasks in the thin dawn light.

"Can you go back to bed?" Damiskos asked. "You look as if you need it."

Varazda rubbed his eyes. "Yes, I think I might. I'm not good for much else."

"A two-man watch is hard," said Damiskos, giving in to a yawn himself. "At least we don't have to march anywhere this morning."

"Ugh."

They remained standing there for a moment, leaning on the railing side by side.

"Last night—the earlier part—was very enjoyable," Damiskos said finally.

"I'm afraid my contribution was rudimentary," said Varazda, making a wry face. "I'm … I have been accustomed to being given orders, and I may not have done very well without them."

"No! No, it was … " *It was you*, Damiskos wanted to say. That was what mattered. "It was great. The whole thing."

Varazda nodded. "It was. If we get a chance to do it again, I'd like that."

Damiskos didn't reply at first, afraid that anything he said would sound too eager. There was an awkward pause. Varazda yawned again and turned toward his bedroom door. Damiskos finally thought of something to say.

"If I had a copy of *The Three Gardens*, I'd study it for you." That didn't have the lightness that he had been striving for.

Varazda looked back. "It's only a few pages from the

Honeysuckle Garden that truly appeal to me, First Spear. And, I must say, you've got Training the Vine down *quite* well already."

Damiskos toiled down the stairs from the gallery, greeting the few women whose names he knew as he passed them, and returning the rather knowing smiles of several others. It was a little odd to think that he now legitimately had something to be embarrassed about. They might well have heard him and Varazda last night; goodness knows, Varazda especially had been making enough noise. But even the knowingest looks of the slaves were friendly.

It was still too early for any of the guests or their host to be up. Damiskos returned to his room, put his sword, along with his hunting bow, away carefully at the back of an upper shelf in his closet, took a clean tunic, and went to the bath. He still smelled of sex and Varazda's perfume.

Clean and dressed, he made his way through the quiet house to the garden, assured Rhea when she asked that he didn't need anything, and then as an afterthought asked her to tell the mistress, when she was awake, that he had gone down for a walk on the beach.

He took his time climbing down the track to the beach, thinking that he should have swallowed his pride and asked Rhea if there was such a thing as a walking-stick in the house. Reaching level ground, he strolled at an easy pace. The sunrise was at his back, casting long shadows out over the white sand. He passed the fish-sauce factory and rounded the spit of land into the sheltered cove with the beach houses.

He was looking for something that he hoped very much not to find, but as soon as the sheltered beach came into view, he knew that he had. The body lay at the fullest point of the beach's gentle curve, half in and half out of the surf, a dark, wet heap.

Damiskos made his way over to it, grasped the sodden tunic, and turned the body over to be sure it was Aristokles. It was. He had been in the water some time; the corpse was bloated and ugly, but it was quite recognizable.

Nobody could claim that he had died by drowning. The front of his tunic was torn in several places, the blood washed away by the water but the stab wounds still visible beneath. A frayed rope trailed from one of his ankles; evidently the weight used to sink him had come loose, letting his body bob to the surface.

Damiskos stood looking grimly down at the corpse for several minutes before he roused himself to action.

He had to get the body out of the surf and find Nione and Varazda. He bent and grabbed the wet clothing again, and heaved the corpse up so he could grasp it under the armpits and drag it along the beach. It was awkward work; Aristokles had been a big man, Damiskos's height, and with wet clothes he was very heavy. Damiskos's knee was protesting by the time he reached the beach hut—the same one where he and Varazda had put on their show for the students on Hapikon Eve—and rolled the body onto the dry stone floor. He collapsed onto one of the benches and rubbed the throbbing joint.

He remembered Varazda catching him the night before, bolstering his weak side as Damiskos bent over him on the bed. He remembered the sword fight earlier in the afternoon, the way Varazda had given ground only in slow steps, refusing to dart around and put Damiskos at a disadvantage. It hadn't struck him before how much courage it must have taken to do that, to resist the urge to flee from a stronger, more experienced opponent.

Gods, what was he going to do when Varazda went back to Boukos? He would miss him like fury.

A shadow fell across the threshold of the beach hut, across Aristokles's body on the floor. Damiskos looked up. Helenos was standing in the doorway.

He must have been down on the beach already when Damiskos was dragging the body. Perhaps he had followed Damiskos down.

"Damiskos from the Quartermaster's Office," he said, his voice as calm and uninflected as usual. "And … is it Aristokles? How awkward."

Damiskos got to his feet, regretting that he had left his sword in his bedroom, and wishing once again that he'd asked Rhea for a walking stick. In a pinch, a good stick served as a pretty effective weapon.

Helenos came into the hut, stepping around Aristokles's body, and Damiskos saw he was not alone; Gelon and Phaia stood on the threshold behind him.

"Ugh!" said Phaia, pointing in at the body. She turned to look at Gelon. "I thought you got rid of him."

"You stupid cow," Helenos barked, his tone suddenly so violent that Damiskos was genuinely shocked.

"What?" Phaia rounded on him, obviously not as surprised herself. She gestured at Damiskos. "He obviously knows everything."

"*Now* he does," said Helenos, looking at Damiskos, calm restored to his voice. "The question is, what is he going to do about it."

"Not really your question to ask, is it?" said Damiskos. "I'll do whatever I see fit. Of course if you want to tell me truthfully how this happened"—he pointed to Aristokles's body—"it could influence my decision."

Helenos gave him a pained look, like a reasonable man reluctantly tolerating someone else's unreasonableness. "We know that your friend here was working for the Boukossian government," he said. "He told Phaia so, in the course of bragging about his own importance. Apparently the Boukossians harbour unfounded suspicions about Master Eurydemos."

"Rubbish," said Damiskos. "They know that you and your cronies started a riot and killed men in Boukos."

Helenos's eyebrows rose. "Is that what he told you?" He poked Aristokles with his foot.

"He didn't know which of you was the ringleader," Damiskos embroidered. "I worked that part out for myself."

"You didn't, by any chance, hear it from Aristokles's—pardon me—from *your* eunuch?"

"Him? I doubt he knows anything about it."

Helenos frowned. "Giontes says last night when he went to the eunuch's room, the Sasian chased him off with a sword."

"Yeah? I'm surprised Giontes was willing to admit to that."

"Where did the eunuch get the sword?"

"You saw him dance the other night. He's got swords."

"It was a Phemian sword."

"Oh. Why didn't you say? That was probably mine."

"What was he doing with it?"

"Chasing Giontes, apparently."

"Were you in the eunuch's room?"

"Yes, of course. I thought we'd maybe have some privacy out there. I'm sleeping with him, remember?"

"But you're not."

Damiskos spread his hands hopelessly. "I don't know what to tell you. That is what I was doing in his room last night. Look, you saw him kiss me on Xereus's Day, you saw us making out in here on Hapikon night. Last night, we were in his bedroom making love. I don't know what's so hard to fathom about all that. Do you think that because I was a soldier, if I'm not fucking somebody up against a wall half an hour after meeting him, it means I'm not interested?"

Helenos was giving him the look of distaste that he had been hoping for. It was really very satisfying.

"I tell you who I feel sorry for," Damiskos added, looking at Phaia, "is you. His idea of seduction seems pretty piss-poor."

"That's enough!" Helenos snarled. "You have no idea what I've done for her."

"You mean trying to clean up her mess after she murdered Aristokles Phoskos?"

"You see," said Phaia, "I told you he knew."

"What?" said Gelon, sounding affronted. "You didn't kill him—I did. All she did," he added to Damiskos, "was lure him to the garden for me."

Helenos pinched the bridge of his nose and made an exasperated noise.

"Oh," said Phaia lazily. "Look."

Damiskos turned to see the rest of the students standing in the open front of the beach hut.

He took a step back, but Aristokles's body was behind him, and he couldn't move any further without tripping over it. The students stood shoulder-to-shoulder in the wide entrance, their stance casual, their faces sneering. They were unarmed, but then so was Damiskos. They were tall, athletic young men, soft compared to Damiskos, but there were five of them, plus Gelon, Helenos, and Phaia behind him, and none of them were lame.

He opted to pretend he didn't notice any attempted threat, and simply shouldered his way through the line of students. They were too surprised to stop him, and he knocked one of them down and was walking quickly away from the beach hut when he heard Helenos's voice behind him: "Stop him, you clowns."

Damiskos took that as permission to fight. He swung at the first student to catch up to him, hitting him in the stomach. The student staggered, but he was a big fellow and did not fall. Damiskos grabbed him by the hair and the front of his tunic, and pushed him backward into the man coming up behind him, and they both went over together.

The third student was the one with the broken nose. He didn't give Damiskos time to get in a blow before he kicked him, with devastating accuracy, in the right knee.

His leg buckled under him in an explosion of pain, and he landed on his side in the sand. He managed to pull the broken-nosed student down to join him, and they grappled inelegantly. By that time the rest had arrived, and the two he had felled earlier were getting up, and at another irritable order from Helenos, they gave up all pretence of fighting fairly and simply piled onto him.

He was winded, kicked in the head, spots dancing before his eyes, his knee a red-hot agony. Four of the students hauled him up from the sand between them, grasping his wrists and ankles, and began carrying him across the beach.

They dumped him down on a warm wooden surface that he guessed from the smell was one of the docks outside the fish-sauce factory. Most of them sat on him again—the only effective way they had of containing him—while one of them went into the empty factory.

Why was the factory empty? It clearly was; he could tell from the stillness all around them. But shouldn't the fishermen, the ones who weren't celebrating Hapikon, still be there, receiving extra pay while the slaves were on holiday?

The student who had gone inside—the broken-nose fellow again—returned with a coil of rope. Damiskos felt his stomach clench with nausea.

They rolled him over, and he fought again, was kicked and sat on, had his shoulders nearly dislocated, and finally his hands were bound behind him. And he was back in

Abadoka's stronghold on the Deshan Coast, naked and shivering and bloody, with Abadoka's torturer standing over him. It was the last time he'd had his hands tied behind his back.

"The fight's gone out of him," he heard a woman's voice say, with a mocking laugh.

In Abadoka's stronghold, the fight had never gone out of him. He had struggled against his bonds, attacked the jailers every chance he got, snarled obscenities at Abadoka and his men even when he was too far gone to be sure what language he was swearing in. But that was five years ago, and he'd been a different man. He lay slumped on the warm wood of the dock, trying to stop shaking.

He couldn't go through it again. It couldn't happen again. It couldn't. It couldn't. It couldn't.

"Let's drown him in a vat of fish sauce," a voice suggested. Others laughed and murmured agreement.

"We don't need any more corpses," someone snapped coldly. "It's bad enough that you had to kill all those people in Boukos."

"They were Sasians—the world is better without them."

There was some more discussion after that which Damiskos's mind was racing too frantically to follow. In the end they dragged him inside the factory, pushed him head-first into an empty fermenting tank in the floor, and dragged a heavy stone slab over it.

He was left in thick darkness. The fall had stunned him, and a fiery pain in his right shoulder suggested it might really be dislocated now. He lay huddled, half upside-down in the tank, with no room to move in any direction. And the smell. The overwhelming, sickening stench of fish left to rot in the sun for weeks. The stone under his cheek was slimy with it; the walls pressing in around him had soaked it in for years.

He couldn't breathe properly, couldn't move, could barely think. He focussed all his remaining strength on not throwing up, because some shred of memory told him that if he did, he might choke on it.

Time passed. He knew where he was now, knew that this was going to be different. It was not happening again. But still memories of the Deshan Coast washed over him. He knelt in front of Abadoka, hands tied, two guards holding him down because that was the only way he would stay on his knees.

"They are going to think you are my man one way or another, Damiskos Son of Philion. Why not make it so in truth, and gain the benefits?"

He hadn't known what that meant until later.

His shoulder hurt, but it was not dislocated. There was a faint line of grey around the rim of the tank where the stone slab did not fit tightly. He couldn't move enough to put his good shoulder to it, but he could kick it with his sound leg.

It wasn't enough to move the slab, and on the third try his shoulder slipped in the slime on the bottom of the tank, and he cracked his head against the side. He clenched his teeth and breathed shallowly until the pain faded.

He wasn't going to get out that way. Better to conserve his energy until he heard the fishermen returning to the factory, when they would hear him and let him out.

If Helenos and his followers had chosen this place to leave him, they must have some reason to think the fishermen were not coming back.

Time passed. The arm he was lying on was becoming numb, which was an improvement over the throbbing of earlier. Every so often he would imagine he was getting used to the smell, and then he would take an incautious breath, and another wave of nausea would hit him. Tears ran out of the corners of his eyes.

At first he thought he was imagining the change in the air, the hint of a new smell. But it grew slowly stronger, and he knew it was real. It was smoke.

CHAPTER 13

HE RESUMED STRUGGLING IN EARNEST, bracing his numb shoulder against the edge of the tank and kicking at the lid as hard as he could. He managed to shift it a fraction, so he kept at it, pausing between kicks to gather his strength and make each one count. It didn't do much good; his position in the tank was too awkward, his lame leg too weak. He coughed and whimpered with frustration.

He was *not* going to die upside down in a fish-sauce tank. Except it seemed like he probably was.

Then he heard a voice—a voice he would have known anywhere—still distant, but calling his name.

"Here!" he shouted. "In here!" He kicked the stone slab again, trying to make as much noise as possible. He had his boots on, so this worked fairly well.

"Damiskos?" Louder this time.

"In! Here!" He broke off to cough violently, choking on smoke and the miasma of fish-sauce.

"Holy God."

There was an agonizing pause, and Damiskos wondered what kind of hell-scape of smoke and flame Varazda was having to traverse to get to him, pictured him collapsing on the factory floor, overcome, wanted to shout at him to save himself—and then there was the scrape of stone from above him.

He imagined Varazda's beautiful hands and slender arms struggling with the heavy slab, and only realized how hard he was biting his lip when he tasted blood. But in fact it didn't take Varazda long to move the stone, and there he was, leaning down over the hole where Damiskos was wedged, eyes wide above the wet cloth that he had tied over the lower half of his face. Smoke billowed behind him.

He lay on his stomach and reached down to grab Damiskos under the armpits, which he was only able to do by slithering half over the lip of the tank, until Damiskos was convinced he was going to fall in too. But he didn't; somehow he managed to brace himself so that he could haul Damiskos up, and dragged and manoeuvred him out of the tank onto the floor of the factory.

Varazda produced another wet cloth, one of his ubiquitous handkerchiefs, and held it over Damiskos's nose and mouth. Together they made their way, shuffling awkwardly on their knees, with Varazda half-pulling Damiskos most of the way, across the room to the door, under the worst of the smoke.

Wordlessly, Varazda tugged the rope off Damiskos's wrists, and they both filled foul-smelling buckets from the pier with sea water and forged back inside.

The fire was not the inferno that Damiskos had imagined. It had produced enough smoke to fill the factory and billow impressively out the door, but the flames were confined to a pile of oily rags and crates under the window. They were easily doused. It looked as though someone had started the fire by throwing a lit lamp in the window.

Damiskos focussed numbly on these details, and Varazda had to take his arm and draw him coughing out of the smoky building once more.

Outside again, Varazda hauled Damiskos across the dock and down the steps onto the sand. He didn't stop until they had walked right out into the shallow surf, where he let Damiskos sink down to sit in the water, and knelt with him, pulling the wet cloth—it was his sash, Damiskos noted irrelevantly—down from his face.

Then he leaned forward, taking Damiskos's face between his hands, and kissed him once, hard.

Damiskos collapsed against him as if his bones had all suddenly dissolved. He realized distantly that he was crying —sobbing—in Varazda's arms, and he couldn't stop. The amazing thing was that Varazda didn't seem embarrassed or even surprised.

"You're all right," he kept saying calmly. "You're all right. This isn't then. This is different. I'm here."

Varazda somehow, miraculously, understood.

It was such a relief that Damiskos felt he might choke on his tears. He buried his face in his hands. Varazda scooped up water to wet Damiskos's hair, gently scrubbing through it with his fingers. It felt so good.

"I'm here," he repeated. "This is not then."

"No," Damiskos managed. "I know. Thank you."

He wiped his eyes, splashed water on his face, wiped them again, and finally managed to sit up. "Thank—"

Varazda held up his hands. "Please. It's what one does."

"So is saying 'Thank you,'" said Damiskos.

"Right. So … what happened?"

It took an effort to remember the starting-point of the story. "I found Aristokles's body."

Varazda nodded. "I saw him in one of the beach huts when I was looking for you."

"I'm sorry."

"Me too.

"Gelon killed him—Phaia helped. From what I can make

164

out, he told her he was an agent of the Boukossian government to try to impress her with his importance."

Varazda groaned. "That's the sort of thing he would have done."

"So she and Gelon killed him, and the rest of the students have been trying to cover it up. What made you come looking for me?"

Varazda shrugged. "Someone said you had come down to walk on the beach, but you'd been gone a long while, and I had seen the students go down and come back. I was worried. Shall we get out of the water, and you can tell me the rest?"

"Good. Yes. I will."

"Er, you might care to take off your clothes first. You smell a little *fishy*."

"Divine Terza, that's an understatement."

Varazda helped him undress, tossed his tunic and boots back up onto the shore for him, and helped him wade further into the water to rinse himself off. By this time Damiskos was beginning to feel more like himself. In fact, he was starting to feel more like himself than he had felt in a long time.

He got to his feet, streaming water, but for a moment Varazda did not. Damiskos looked down at him. He was kneeling in water up to his waist, still fully dressed, looking up at Damiskos, who was naked but for his wet loincloth. Just looking at him.

It wasn't a lascivious look. It was appreciative, but it was a little detached, almost wistful. It didn't seem like the kind of look you would normally give a man you had slept with the night before. Damiskos didn't know what it meant.

He held out a hand to help Varazda up, and Varazda accepted it and rose gracefully. His sodden trousers clung to his legs as they splashed up onto the beach. He pulled off his shoes and tried to wring some of the water out of his clothes.

They walked up the beach, away from the smoky, fishy smell of the factory. Damiskos was limping so badly that he did not refuse when Varazda offered him a shoulder to lean on.

"Did they put you in there to kill you?" Varazda asked.

Damiskos stopped to think. "Helenos said he didn't want any more bodies. He wasn't happy about the Zashians in Boukos being killed—perhaps he felt it reflected badly on the school, I don't know. The others think any dead Zashian is a blow struck for their cause, but Helenos focusses on the big picture, which I suppose is hundreds and thousands of dead Zashians. The others wanted to drown me, but Helenos wouldn't let them. I don't remember if they discussed what they were going to do with me. I was … "

Varazda put a hand lightly on his arm. "Don't go back there if you don't want to."

"I … Thanks. I don't think I was really *there* at the time, so I can't … But they dumped me in that tank, and I was there for … " He looked up at the sky. It had been early morning when he came out here, and the sun was past the zenith now; it was mid-afternoon. It hadn't just *felt* like hours inside the fish-sauce tank. "Hours. Hours before somebody set that fire—it hadn't been burning long when you found me. One of the students must have come back and set it. They must have thought the fishermen weren't coming back."

"They know they're not. The fishermen are up at the villa, demanding extra pay for working while the Opos-worshippers are on holiday. It was the students' idea. I heard them talking about it on Hapikon Eve."

"Terza's balls." Too late, the oath struck him as tactless. "Oh—sorry."

Varazda shrugged expansively. "Presumably he has them. I've never heard that he didn't."

Damiskos felt a strong urge suddenly to hug him. He resisted because it didn't seem the time or place, and he wouldn't have wanted it to be misinterpreted. Or correctly interpreted, maybe.

"Anyway," said Varazda, "it wasn't the students who set the fire—it was the fishermen. They were threatening to do it —to let the place burn unless their wages were increased."

"Huh. Clearly a bluff. That fire wasn't going to burn the place down."

"Might have damaged the merchandise, though. Does fish sauce burn?"

"I couldn't say. I don't want to think about fish sauce right now."

"Right. Sorry."

Damiskos's attention had been caught by figures on the path down from the villa. It was a number of Nione's slaves, six or eight of them, led by the steward, Aradne, hurrying down the path with shovels and buckets in hand.

"They must have taken the fishermen seriously," Damiskos said. "Good for them." He wasn't sure about the other women, but Aradne he thought might be capable of putting out a burning building all by herself.

"Planning to sit here and watch while the mistress's factory burns?" Aradne demanded as the group of women approached.

"It's not burning any more, actually," Varazda replied brightly.

"We put it out," Damiskos added.

The steward gave him an impatient look. "That is not smoke coming from a fire that has been *put out*."

Damiskos and Varazda looked back at the factory. There was indeed still smoke rolling out of the window.

"Let me guess," said Aradne, "you just threw a couple of jars of water over it and called it done. I suppose you're sure there's no one inside?"

"There's no one inside *now*," Damiskos clarified. "Varazda got me out."

Aradne cast him a look which suggested that getting trapped inside fish-sauce factories without his clothes was about the level of competence she would have expected of him, and pushed a bucket into his hands.

The fire was *mostly* out. It was smouldering more than it had been when Damiskos and Varazda left it, but Aradne admitted that it probably wouldn't have rebuilt into a serious blaze. The women, who were well-muscled slaves from the vineyard, made short work of dousing the pile of debris thoroughly and spreading out the charred remains with their shovels.

Their job finished, they came back outside and lounged in the sand. Damiskos lay flat on his back, one hand tucked under his head. Varazda dropped down elegantly beside him and spent a minute taking his hair down, shaking it out, and combing it through with his fingers, then putting it up again. Damiskos watched him with a kind of stupefied fascination. His whole body hurt, and he was beginning to feel hungry.

"Why don't you put your head in my lap and sleep for a bit?" Varazda rearranged his legs in the sand and patted his thigh indicatively.

It was a lovely thought. He could even have done it without embarrassment; everyone here already thought he was Varazda's master. It was his own stubbornness that kept him from succumbing to the temptation.

"I'm all right," he said, sitting up and doing his best to look it.

Varazda tipped his head to one side and gave him a sceptical look, but he did not try to argue.

"How," said Damiskos suddenly, "how did you know what to say? Earlier. 'This is not then.'"

Varazda looked surprised. "Did I say that? It just slipped out, I guess. I'm so used to comforting friends whose memories have got the better of them. I grew up in a household of eunuchs. Everyone I knew had things that would sneak up on them like that and set them off. Stick around long enough and you'll find out what mine are, I suppose."

Damiskos didn't know what to say. "I'd like that," would have sounded ghoulish, though in a way it was true. He didn't like to think of Varazda feeling the helpless panic that had gripped him when the students had tied his hands behind his back, but if it was a thing that happened, he absolutely wanted to be there to do what he could to help.

They were all still sitting in the sand when Nione and the rest of the women of the household, some with children in their arms or holding their hands, came down the cliff path to the beach.

Nione gathered up her skirt and ran from the base of the path to where the women were clustered. Her braids had come down and swung wildly about her shoulders as she ran. Her gown was torn at one shoulder, the clasp dangling from the frayed fabric. Damiskos, suddenly alert again, raked his eyes over the rest of the women. Some of them were crying. The ones with children were clutching them protectively, their expressions fiercely focussed. A few were carrying objects—a rolling pin, a broom, the lid of a basket—that they had either brought away in their haste or perhaps grabbed to defend themselves.

"Something's happened up at the villa," Damiskos said unnecessarily.

"There you are!" Nione cried, reaching out to Aradne with obvious relief. Damiskos thought she looked as if she wanted to hug the steward but didn't quite dare.

"We have things under control here, ma'am," said Aradne. "The fire was small and didn't really pose a danger to the building."

Nione looked as though she wasn't really taking all this

in. The other women reached the bottom of the stairs behind her. More than one child was wailing.

"Wait," said Aradne. "What's happened?"

It took Nione a moment to collect herself, but she replied calmly enough. "The students have taken over our house."

"Terza's—" Damiskos censored himself with an effort.

Varazda said something under his breath in Zashian about goats and ancestral tombs.

"Taken over the house," Aradne repeated. "What does that mean?"

"They have Eurydemos locked in his room," Nione said, her voice shaking a little, "and they were going to do the same to me. I didn't know where you were—you hadn't told me where you were going."

"I was in the vineyard, and you always tell me I don't need to inform you every time I'm leaving the house," Aradne retorted. "Why are they locking people in their rooms?"

"I don't know. I gathered up as many of the girls as I could find and got out. It was Tyra who warned me, but I don't know where she is now. I looked for her, but there was no time. I had to get everyone else out. Everyone who would come—the men insisted on standing their ground, to help us get away."

"There's been fighting?" said Damiskos.

Nione nodded. "Two men have been killed. Gelon stabbed Tionikos, and one of the fishermen pushed Demos down the stairs. Neither of them had a weapon." She spoke bitterly.

"I wish I had been there," said Aradne.

"I'm glad you weren't."

Damiskos turned to Varazda. "Let's get everyone inside the warehouse," he said. "Sit them down and pass around wine."

"Good thought."

To Aradne he said, "You know these women. I'll take my lead from you. I think the first thing to do is keep everyone calm."

"Uh. Yes." She wasn't looking particularly calm herself. "That is very important."

Varazda began helping gently to lead the women and children toward the shelter of the warehouse, where Aradne brought out an amphora of the villa's best wine, and they handed around cups of it. Someone else went to the cove with the beach houses, where there was a freshwater spring, and brought back water to drink as well.

By speaking to Nione and several other women, Damiskos pieced together an account of what had happened at the house. Nione had decided to tell Eurydemos what his students were accused of doing in Boukos, and Eurydemos had then rashly confronted Helenos and the others about it. That was what had pushed them into action.

They had shut Eurydemos in his room, gone looking for the mistress of the house, encountered resistance from some of the slaves, and violence had broken out. Nione, warned by Tyra of the students' intentions, had been able to get away with most of her women—all her women, in fact, once the ones who had already been down on the beach were accounted for. She downplayed her own role, of course, but from what the others said, it was clear she had placed herself in considerable danger—been seized and threatened with a weapon and nearly pushed down the stairs herself—in making sure as many of her slaves as possible could flee the house. She bitterly regretted that she had not been able to save all of them.

The fishermen were still up at the house, being whipped into a frenzy by the students. Some of the household men had been suborned, either with threats or rhetoric. Looting seemed imminent, if not already in progress.

"I think I have a good grasp of the situation now,"

Damiskos said to Varazda after summarizing all this. "Except for one thing. The documents the students stole from the Zashian embassy. When you told me about it before, you were pretending to be Aristokles's servant, and I took it for granted you didn't know what the documents were. But you were never Aristokles's servant."

Varazda nodded. "And in fact I know all about it. Yes."

CHAPTER 14

"Varazda has told you that Eurydemos's students planned and carried out an assassination in Boukos," said Damiskos.

Nione nodded. Aradne shook her head but did not look surprised. They stood together with Damiskos and Varazda on the beach outside the warehouse, having left the rest of the women inside. Damiskos had almost forgotten to be tired; the old, familiar feeling of pushing himself past his body's limits to plan the next phase of the campaign returned to him, and it felt something like joy.

"The murdered man was a diplomat from Zash, carrying details of troop deployment and fortifications on the Deshan Coast," Damiskos said. "Those documents were stolen after his death."

Aradne gave a low whistle. "That sounds bad. I take it that's bad."

"Yes," said Varazda, "it is bad."

"The Deshan Coast is a mess," Damiskos explained. "There's been a tenuous peace for the last couple of years, but it's been heating up again recently."

"But it's civil war there, isn't it?" said Nione. "It's Zashians against Zashians."

"It is *now*," said Damiskos. "But for anyone who wanted Pheme to go to war with Zash again, it would be an ideal spot to strike—the power of the king is already weak in the region."

"But no one wants Pheme to go to war with Zash again," Aradne protested. "Do they?"

"Plenty of people do. Helenos has told me himself he thinks the republic needs war to be great, or some nonsense, and there are men in the military—men in high places—who would agree with him. I don't know that any of them would do business with murderous philosophy students hawking state secrets, but I wouldn't rule it out.

"I had a feeling, when I put the pieces together, that Helenos must have some information like this. In fact, it's more dangerous than I've explained. Officially, Zash keeps no secrets from us on the Deshan Coast, because we're *there*—we have legions permanently stationed in the colonies and collaborating with the Zashian crown in the region.

"But of course the king of Zash does have secrets—so do we. Whatever's in these documents, there is bound to be *something* we don't already know, something politicians and power-hungry officers in the legions can point to and claim Zash has been lying to us and breaking the peace of the colonies. It'll be all the pretext they need to start another war."

"That's why," Varazda added, "it doesn't matter whether the king of Zash knows about the theft or not—it won't help just to rearrange the troops so the documents are no longer accurate. That's not the real danger. So we persuaded the embassy staff to delay reporting the theft until we'd tried to recover the documents."

"You mean you're lying to your king?" Aradne looked impressed.

"No, because he's not my king. I'm a Boukossian citizen. I don't work for the embassy—I'm here on behalf of the Basileon of Boukos."

"And you've looked for these documents?" said Nione.

Varazda nodded. "But I was only able to search Eurydemos's and Phaia's belongings thoroughly—and fruitlessly, I'm afraid. Helenos and Gelon share a room and have an extraordinary amount of luggage. I hadn't been able to go through it all before Aristokles went missing. I think the documents could still be there."

"Right," said Damiskos. He stood with his hands on his hips for a moment. He had put his clothes back on, damp as they were. "So. Holding the beach is a strong position. We have fresh water and plenty of food. We can afford to wait for the men to come back from the Tentines and strengthen our hand further. Or for the fishermen to quarrel with the students and come down to retrieve their boats—which, honestly, I might have expected to happen before now. It's also a question how many of the male slaves they can count on to assist them—we know they've coopted a few of them, but we don't know what's happened to the rest.

"Helenos, who's currently in charge, is not as bloodthirsty as his colleagues. He wouldn't let them kill me when they had the chance, and I don't think he was pleased with Gelon and Phaia killing Aristokles. That works in our favour. Our other advantage is that he's likely, given the way he see the world, to underestimate us because we're a bunch of women, slaves, a cripple, a Sasian, degenerates—all the rest of it."

Aradne snorted.

"Our disadvantages," Damiskos went on. "We outnumber them, but we do lack able-bodied men, weapons, and experience—whereas we know that at least some of them are capable of planning and executing assassinations and spur-of-the-moment murders. We have children to protect.

They have hostages. Eurydemos, certainly, Tyra probably, likely some of the household men. That weakens our position, because obviously we don't want any hostages harmed."

"Obviously," said Aradne.

"We're also weakened by the fact that we don't know what the students' endgame is or what plans they may already have in place. On the beach we're vulnerable from the sea, which could be a problem if they've got more reinforcements on the way. That's a possibility we have to consider. The other possibility we have to consider—and I think this one is much more likely—is that they'll realize we can afford to wait them out, and they'll try some sort of preemptive strike before the factory-workers come back. And right now, we'd be vulnerable to that. I think we can expect an exploratory party pretty soon, probably with an offer of some kind—*we'll let you back into your house if you do such-and-such for us*—I'm not sure what it will be because I'm not sure exactly what their aims are. But when we refuse it—which we'll do—they may lose interest in bargaining pretty quickly."

"Right," said Aradne. "So what do you think we should do."

"I think we should fortify our position on the beach."

Nione blinked at him. "What does that mean, exactly? You don't mean build, build defensive … um, defences … do you?"

"I do, actually. With your approval. It's your household, which makes you the ranking officer here."

She gave a startled laugh. "Oh dear, no. I defer to you."

"Well. I think we should dig a trench around the beach huts, extending back to the spring. Then what you do is, you build a rampart with the dirt you've dug out—sand, in this case, which isn't ideal, but we'll make it work—and erect a wall of stakes on top of that. There's plenty of branches in the brush around here that will work beautifully for stakes, we've got the shovels you brought down to fight the fire, and the women from the vineyard will be familiar with this type of work. It shouldn't take more than a few hours, given our workforce and the size of the area we're dealing with.

"Then when we're done with the ditch and rampart, we stockpile whatever projectiles we can find, gather more brush to close up the beach houses and provide better cover—that should be plenty of work for the day. The most important thing is to look like we're doing something and aren't scared —the second most important thing is to do something, to keep from getting scared."

"I see," said Aradne.

"Will you make a speech to tell the women?" Nione asked Damiskos.

"I think it would be better if you did. I'll brief everyone on the plan afterward, but I do feel it's best for you to maintain your authority as mistress of the house."

"Hm." She looked uncertain. "Best for me, or best for the women?"

"Best for everyone." He smiled wryly at her. "Don't worry —I'll have your back."

"I appreciate that." She returned the smile.

Nione and Aradne went back into the warehouse to gather up the women, and for a moment Damiskos and Varazda were left alone on the beach.

"That was magnificent," Varazda said.

"What was?"

"All of it. 'These are our weaknesses, and we're going to build a rampart, here's how it will all go.' That whole display of *competence*. It was marvellous."

Damiskos shrugged self-consciously. He really hadn't given it much thought; it had all just come so naturally, the analysis and the strategy following in orderly fashion. He was feeling like *himself*.

"Easy as breathing."

"I know. It's your element. It's what you do the way I dance."

Damiskos glanced at him and away, and he heard Varazda draw in a breath, and then felt his touch, feather-light, as Varazda slipped an arm around his waist.

"I'm sorry, that was thoughtless of me. No one has taken the dancing away from me."

"Did you learn to dance in the king's household at Gudul?" Damiskos asked after a moment, an easy change of subject. Varazda's arm was still around his waist.

"No. The sword dance was my clan's. I learned it in my father's house before I was gelded. I didn't use real swords then, just wooden ones. I learned other dances at Gudul, but I always practiced my family's dance, even when no one wanted me to perform it. Of course in Boukos they love it, and I dance it all the time now."

"I'm glad," said Damiskos. "That you got to keep something of your own."

Damiskos had been right in thinking that Nione's slaves would make short work of trenching and fortifying the small area around the beach huts. The women from the vineyards took care of the digging while the rest went into the brush, with a couple of small hatchets from the factory, to cut branches to Damiskos's specifications, which they brought back to the beach and began planting in the top of the rampart as soon as a section was finished. Some of the older children helped and were quite adept at weaving the branches together to create a denser barrier. The thing began to take shape and look businesslike very quickly. Varazda worked with the diggers, stripped to the waist, with his hair in a single braid, teasing and trading banter with them in the easy way that Damiskos had already seen him do.

Once work was well underway and Damiskos was no longer needed to give orders, he and Aradne went back to the factory site, where they found a handcart and began loading it up with supplies to ferry back to their camp.

"Remind me why we're not making our base here," said Aradne, as she hefted a jar of olives into the cart. "Where the food is, and where there's walls that aren't half fallen down."

"Fresh water at the other location, direct access to the sea here could be a liability, we're less visible from the villa there, and, frankly, the other location's more comfortable. This place stinks."

"Hah. Yes, good points."

Their cart loaded, they did a thorough search of the three buildings, looking for anything that could be used as a tool or a weapon.

"I remember you," Aradne remarked as they exited the factory. "At first I didn't, I thought you were another one of these men come to badger the mistress about marrying. But you were her friend from back in the Maidens' House."

"That's right. I remember you too. Was it your idea or Nione's to have so many women in the household?" He thought he could ask that now; he also thought he knew the answer.

"Bit of both, I suppose," said Aradne after a moment. "I never really gave it any thought."

He'd been right. "You were used to it, I guess."

"I guess. Though now you mention it, I think some of the men feel … odd about it. Being so outnumbered. As if we're trying to make some kind of empire of women here, and they don't belong. Wouldn't be surprised if a few of them have made common cause with those gods-cursed students. Well. Fuck 'em if they have."

"Just what I was thinking."

They collected the loaded cart, gathered up a few other items, and trudged back over the sand to the sheltered cove.

The fortifications were more than half finished, the ditch fully dug, some of the diggers resting in the sand near the waterline, while the children played in the shallows.

"They've made even better progress than I expected," said Damiskos approvingly. "They're hard workers."

"They are," said Aradne. "And they like the mistress. They have good lives—for slaves. But they're still slaves."

"You think she should free them." It was a radical idea, but there were people doing it, philosophers in the city arguing that everyone should do it.

Aradne gave him a sharp look. "I didn't say that. Never mind what I think."

Varazda came strolling out to meet them, his shirt on again but unbuttoned, a little boy in a dirt-smeared tunic following him, chatting cheerfully.

"We've finished digging," Varazda reported.

"So I see," said Damiskos.

"He was impressed," Aradne added. "Thinks you'd all make good soldiers."

Varazda laughed. "What do you think, Chari?" He looked down at the boy, who had wrapped one arm around his leg.

"I don't think we can be soldiers," said Chari, wide-eyed and serious. "I'm little, and everybody else is girls."

Varazda ruffled the boy's hair. "It doesn't necessarily signify, Chari. Remember that."

"So what do we do now?" Aradne asked. "Do we have a plan?"

"I do, actually," said Varazda. "At least, I have the rudimentary beginning of a plan."

"The postal ship comes on Moon's Day morning?" Damiskos clarified, as they sat in the sand discussing the plan. Around them, the fortifications were finished, and the women and children were making a meal of food they had brought over from the warehouse. "And it's Seventh Day today. So we should set the signal tomorrow night."

"Unless the postal ship is early," said Aradne.

"Is that likely?"

She shrugged. "It was early last week. It arrived on the morning of Hesperion's."

"That was because Aristokles and I were travelling on it," Varazda said, "and we wanted to get here as quickly as possible."

Damiskos nodded. "Right. So we wait until tomorrow night. If you agree." He looked to Nione.

She looked startled for a moment, forgetting again that she was in charge. Then she nodded. "Yes. It's a good plan."

They had finished their meal by the time the emissary from the villa showed up. It was Gelon. He came swaggering down the beach, knife prominently displayed in his belt, and tried unsuccessfully to look nonchalant as he approached the women's ditch-and-rampart defence system. They saw him coming from a long way off, and all the children and the household girls were inside the barrier by the time he arrived, leaving a small group outside to meet him.

He stopped a judicious distance away and jerked his chin at the fortifications.

"What's *that* supposed to be?"

No one answered him. After a moment, Nione took a step forward and said, "Have you something to say to us, Gelon?"

"Yes, ma'am. Helenos says you should come back to the house."

"Tell Helenos I will do that when he and his fellow students leave. They are no longer welcome in my home."

"How's that?" Gelon feigned exaggerated shock. "You wouldn't offend against the laws of hospitality, would you?"

Nione narrowed her eyes at him. "You laid violent hands on my servants and my guests. Tionikos and Demos are *dead*. So is Aristokles Phoskos. You have no claim on anyone's hospitality." Her voice rang with a priestly note in the last words, as if she pronounced a solemn malediction.

Gelon looked at her for a moment with a sour expression. "Fine. If that's how you want it to be. We've got things that we want. We've got the upper hand now, and this is going to go the way Helenos says it's going to go."

"We will see about that," said Nione.

"We want the use of your villa for our headquarters. We'll let you live in it so long as you don't interfere with our work. Or you can give the villa to Eurydemos and go back to Pheme. We'll let Damiskos from the Quartermaster's Office escort you back. Out of harm's way." He looked at Damiskos. "Sorry about the fire and everything. Not our idea. Some of the idiot fishermen took matters into their own hands."

Damiskos frowned at him.

"And my women?" said Nione. "What about them?"

"Take them with you." He waved a hand contemptuously. "We don't want them. They're mostly foreign-born and wouldn't make good wives for free Phemians. We do want the Sasian eunuch, though."

"I'm not sure he would make a good wife for a free Phemian either," said Damiskos, deadpan.

Gelon huffed an angry breath through his nose. "That's not why we want him."

"You don't get him." Aradne spoke up. "You don't get any of this. We're taking our house back."

"I'm not here to negotiate with *you*, you—"

Nione cut him off. "You spoke of using my house for your work. What is the 'work' that you imagine you are going to do here? It isn't just discussing philosophy, I realize that."

"It's the work of restoring Phemian purity," Gelon

replied, predictably. "Helenos has a vision. And this is a strategic location."

"Outside of the city and beyond the reach of its laws," Damiskos supplied. "Or so you can tell yourselves. But within easy reach of both Pheme and Boukos by sea. You can play at being a little republic of your own, distributing state secrets and stirring up wars in the name of Phemian greatness."

Gelon gave him a prim look. "When we restore Pheme to its former glory, you'll wish you had been on our side from the beginning."

"I doubt it."

"So … " Gelon looked around, stumped for a moment. "What is it to be?"

"I believe they've already told you," said Varazda. "Nione Kukara is not going to give you her villa, I'm not going to marry you, and First Spear Damiskos is not going to run errands to Pheme for you. Perhaps you had better go in and tell Helenos."

"I am *not* here to negotiate with *you*," Gelon repeated peevishly. "Look, Damiskos from the Quartermaster's Office, we're willing to let you go if you'll take Nione back to Pheme with you now. Just come up to the house, get your horse and so on … "

It was not an unreasonable gambit. If they let Damiskos go now, they had no reason to think he would come back, and at least they'd be rid of him. It wasn't a stretch to imagine that he'd be eager to escort Nione to safety.

Or they might have a trap prepared for him up at the house. That seemed equally likely.

"Not interested," Damiskos said shortly.

"Look, there's no trick. You just … go back to Pheme— get your things and go back to Pheme, take her with you, she's safe, you're fine—right?"

"Yes, I understand what you want. The answer is no. I'm staying here."

Gelon glowered at him. "You're making a stupid mistake."

"Nevertheless."

A bit more glowering, then Gelon sneered openly. "I've heard the Quartermaster's Office is a dumping-ground for officers who have been reduced in rank but not turned off. Everyone knows it."

Damiskos said nothing.

Gelon was getting red in the face now. "What did you do to get sent there, First Spear of the First Koryphos?"

"Second Koryphos. There's no First Koryphos. School-children know that."

"What was it, then?" Gelon all but snarled. "Rape too many women in Sasia? Or boys—I bet it was boys, the Sasians hate that kind of thing. Or you like to pretend to, don't you?" he spat at Varazda. "Really you like it, you degenerate sons of—"

"You shut up," Aradne burst out in a voice like melodious thunder. "You shut your filthy, gods-cursed mouth, go back to whoever the godsdamn fuck you answer to, and tell him we're staying where we are until you all clear out of our house. You heard us. Nobody's leaving at your say-so. Now fuck off."

Gelon raked his eye over the four of them, standing abreast, then turned abruptly, hitched up his trailing mantle, and scurried back across the beach.

"Sorry for the language, ma'am," said Aradne gruffly.

"Oh, not at all, dear."

Aradne turned to Damiskos. "It was some political bull-shit, wasn't it? The reason you were reduced in rank."

He looked at her for a moment. It was a rather nice compliment, in a way. "I wasn't reduced in rank. I was honourably discharged on account of injury—I don't know if you've noticed, but I'm lame."

She looked embarrassed. "Right. I apologize."

"Not at all." He went on, to smooth over the awkwardness. "I, er, I went back to work for the Quartermaster's Office instead of drawing a pension because I wanted to be useful. It *is* a dumping-ground for disgraced officers, and someone told me they were in need of good men. And the pay is slightly better—the Second Koryphos may be a famous legion, but the pay is terrible and the pensions are worse. The joke is that you're not meant to retire—you're meant to die in battle or be promoted on to commander."

CHAPTER 15

THE REST of the students arrived as the last sliver of the sun disappeared into the sea, striding in a ragged line in silence down the beach. They stood around outside the women's defences, dark shapes with here and there the glint of moonlight on knife blades. The effect was sinister, and Damiskos was pleased to find the women remained calm behind their barricade.

"Let them come within range, and then we'll hurl a few stones," he instructed in an undertone.

The order was relayed in whispers. The children and some of the household women were in the southern hut, some already asleep. The rest of the party was sitting in the sand behind their defensive perimeter. They had lit a fire to cook fish for dinner, but it had died to embers by this time, and everyone had been yawning before the students arrived.

The women sat in quiet readiness. The students had stopped at a cautious distance. From inside the southern hut, a baby gave a gurgling chuckle, an eerily ordinary noise. Damiskos smiled to himself, and caught Varazda's eye on him.

"You're not worried," Varazda whispered in Zashian.

Damiskos wasn't sure what to say. It was true he wasn't worried. What he felt was exhilaration, but that wasn't what he would have expected anyone else to feel.

"There is danger," he whispered back finally, answering the question he thought Varazda was really asking. "They're armed and angry, they have killed before, and we have already refused an offer of amnesty. But we're well fortified, and I don't think they're here to attack, just to intimidate."

"You're not intimidated."

"Not at all, no."

Varazda smiled, tense and beautiful in the shadows. "It's the thought of those children being in danger … "

Damiskos thought of the painted shell with the picture of the little girl, and felt heartless.

"We'll protect them," he said firmly.

"I know."

The minutes crept by, and the students stood around on the beach, not coming any closer. Damiskos could not spot Helenos in the dark, but assumed he was there. This was an organized action, planned beforehand, not a spur-of-the-moment thing with shuffling and discussion. It bore Helenos's stamp, if Damiskos had judged him right. It was just a matter of waiting them out.

Aradne moved quietly among the women, speaking a reassuring word here and there, and after watching her for a moment, Nione got up and followed her lead. The low murmur of voices was comforting. There was even a soft laugh from time to time. Inside the hut, the baby gurgled again, and one of the women began singing to it.

Damiskos was just wondering whether he should offer some gesture of comfort to Varazda, and what it should be, when Varazda reached out in the dark and slipped his cool, slender hand into Damiskos's. Damiskos gave it a squeeze, and Varazda moved to nestle lightly against his side.

It felt so good to be trusted with this, to have Varazda

turn to him, however subtly, for reassurance. To be able to give it.

"They don't have any projectile weapons," Damiskos whispered, because he could offer more practical forms of reassurance than hand-holding. "Any slings or bows."

"No," Varazda agreed. "You're right. There aren't any up at the villa."

"There aren't. How did you know that?"

"I made Aristokles try to put together a hunting party to get everyone out of the house on the second day we were here. It didn't work. Apparently no one in the household hunts, and none of the guests brought their own bows."

After a moment, in the interest of complete honesty, Damiskos said, "I did, but I hid it at the back of my closet along with my sword."

"I doubt they'd be able to string it if they found it," said Varazda. He ran his fingertips delicately up the muscles of Damiskos's upper arm. Damiskos tried to suppress a shiver.

By this time the students, who had probably expected screaming and pandemonium to greet their appearance on the beach, had begun to get restless. A buzz of disagreement arose, from which Damiskos could separate out the voice of Gelon, and the voice of Helenos telling Gelon to shut up.

If they were going to approach the perimeter, Damiskos thought, they would do it soon. He looked up at the roof of the nearest beach hut, judging whether there was enough light for the tactic he had envisioned earlier in the day.

"You're thinking of getting up on the roof to throw stones down on them?" said Varazda.

"I, ah. I couldn't do it myself." Gods. That was hard to admit. And he'd thought he was used to it by now. "The roof is too steep, I'd … "

Varazda squeezed his hand, surprisingly hard. "I didn't mean that—I meant are you thinking of sending someone.

Because you could send me. I'm a terrific shot. I used to hunt deer in the king's park at Gudul."

"Of course you did." Damiskos smiled at the image that flashed into his mind of his beautiful Varazda riding through the dappled woodland of northern Zash with a bow in his hand. Not *his* Varazda. Not his, he reminded himself sternly.

They crept over to the corner of the hut, Damiskos gave Varazda a boost, and Varazda slithered easily up onto the tiles of the roof. Damiskos handed him up a supply of the stones they had gathered earlier, tied in a sling made of one of the women's shawls.

Presently, as Damiskos had expected, the students shuffled closer, and Helenos took a step forward as if about to speak. Varazda whipped a stone at his head. Helenos dodged by a hairsbreadth and jumped back. The women laughed. One of them whistled. They got to their feet, their own collections of stones at the ready.

Varazda was silhouetted against the sky, arm drawn back to hurl another stone, and Damiskos, exhilaration gone and actually feeling a little sick to his stomach, prayed that he had been right about the students having no bows.

Helenos, who was no longer in control of his troops, gave no order, but the students charged anyway, half-heartedly and with abysmal discipline. The women and Varazda launched a barrage of stones. Howls of shock and pain met the onslaught, and the students beat a ragged, piecemeal retreat. Some of them simply kept running along the beach, a couple lay down in the sand, clutching injured body parts, and the rest stood at a safe distance and had a shouted argument about what to do next. In the end, they gathered up their wounded and slunk away to the villa.

Damiskos woke with a feeling that he'd forgotten something. The tree-covered slopes beyond Laothalia stood out black against the slowly lightening sky. Varazda was sleeping in the sand nearby. The women were asleep in the beach hut, or in the sand outside its entrance, rolled up in their mantles.

Damiskos realized that he had fallen asleep where he sat after the students departed, before he had set up a watch rota —and of course he hadn't kept watch himself. He would have earned well-deserved lashes if he had neglected his duty like that in the army, no matter how tired he had been. Of course, in the army he never had neglected his duty like that.

Looking around, he saw he was not the only one awake. A young woman, one of the vineyard workers, sat on the other side of the remains of the fire, with her mantle drawn tight around her shoulders.

"Can't sleep?" he asked quietly, when she had seen that he was awake.

"Oh, no, sir," she said shyly. "I'm keeping watch. We've been doing it all night, taking turns, you know. Pharastes suggested it, but he said really it was your idea. Aradne said it was a good one."

"Ah," said Damiskos, unable to suppress a smile. And it's been quiet, has it?"

She nodded. "But I'm scared all the same, sir. If any of those men come back … " She shivered.

"Would it help if I sat up with you?" said Damiskos.

"Yes, sir. But only if you're not too tired."

"Not at all," he said truthfully. "I feel quite wide awake."

The girl didn't seem to want conversation, so he sat on his side of the fire pit, silently keeping her company while the sky behind the mountains grew brighter. He watched Varazda sleeping, his face half-hidden between the crook of his arm and the tangle of his long hair. He had an endearing way of sleeping, unguarded and somehow untidy, hair in his face, limbs sprawled carelessly.

Damiskos wondered what he looked like in *his* sleep, and whether Varazda had spent any time looking at him in the firelight the night before. Probably not; Varazda had probably been too busy organizing the watch and claiming that it was Damiskos's idea.

The sun peeked out from a cleft in the mountains, gold light spilled across the beach, and Aradne joined them at the cold fire pit. She gave Damiskos a nod of greeting.

"All quiet, Kore?" she asked the girl who had been on watch.

"Yes, ma'am."

"Right. Well, you're … relieved." She glanced at Damiskos. "That is the term, isn't it."

"Relieved? Yes."

Varazda woke up, rolling onto his back and rubbing his eyes and stretching gorgeously. He pushed his hair out of his face and sat up. He was as grubby as the rest of them, his face smudged with soot, one sleeve of his shirt torn at the shoulder, the dark fabric of his trousers stained with salt water.

"Good morning," he said rather muzzily, squinting around at his companions at the fire pit.

"Good morning," said Damiskos, trying to keep his tone brisk and soldierly.

"Morning," said Aradne, doing a much better job of what he had been trying for.

Varazda looked up at the sun rising behind the mountains as if trying to decide what time it was.

"I'm not usually up this early," he remarked.

Kore laughed, then bit her lip. "You're not … Somebody told me you're not really a slave?"

"Not any more. Even when I was, I didn't have to get up early, as a rule."

Aradne, to Damiskos's surprise, did not snort derisively at that. She nodded with a thoughtful expression, as if this information had told her something significant about

Varazda. Damiskos realized what it was: that a slave who didn't have to rise early, especially one who looked like Varazda, was probably being used by somebody for sex.

"It sounds nice," said Kore innocently.

She got up then and went into one of the beach huts, where there were sounds of the babies and children waking. For the moment, Damiskos, Varazda, and Aradne were left alone at the fire pit.

"What's going on with you two?" Aradne asked abruptly.

"What do you mean?" Damiskos countered.

"Are you a couple."

"No," said Varazda, decisively, before the last syllable was quite out of her mouth. "We've been pretending to be so that Damiskos had an excuse to keep an eye on me, ever since my supposed master—may God give him peace—went missing."

"Right," said Aradne. "I wondered. Good man," she added to Damiskos. "Thoughtful of you."

Damiskos smiled, because this formidable woman's approval actually did mean something to him, but he couldn't really feel it just then. He was too winded by Varazda's "no," the speed and obvious sincerity of it, the way his lovely eyes had widened a little to emphasize its definitiveness. Varazda hadn't actually laughed or said, "My God, never!" but Damiskos couldn't help thinking it might have been easier if he had. At least then it might have been possible to feel angry about it rather than just stupidly bludgeoned.

It promised to be a long day. There was little that they could do, but they must remain on their guard against another incursion from the villa, and keeping up morale would be crucial. Damiskos advised Nione to tell the women that they could go out onto the beach so long as they remained ready to run back into the fortifications at the first sign of any approach. The sight-lines along the beach toward the villa were excellent, but Damiskos arranged sentries all the same. He set another group to watch for anyone approaching from the steep wooded hillside above the beach huts, though it was unlikely anyone could get down that way. They gathered up the stones they had thrown the night before and made neat piles of them before sitting down to breakfast.

"Everyone wants to bathe," Aradne told Damiskos. "Do you think it's all right?"

"So long as they go out a few at a time and keep an eye out for trouble. I'll, er, make myself scarce in the meantime. To give them some privacy."

"Good man. Suppose Pharastes can stay, though. Somebody said he's a whatyoucall, a eunuch?"

"Uh, yes, that's right."

"Huh. So that's your thing. You like eunuchs."

"What? No. Not—not as such."

"But you like him. Don't try to lie—I saw it. You *flinched* when I asked whether you were a couple and he said 'no.'"

"Did I?"

"You did. I don't think he noticed, though." After a moment she clapped Damiskos on the shoulder and said, "Poor bastard. I was sorry to do that to you. Wouldn't have said anything if I'd known."

He took himself down the beach to the other side of the factory, only noticing after he had set off that Varazda had followed him. He hoped it wasn't with an eye to any kind of sex, because he felt like he had been ridden over by a cavalry unit and its baggage train, and his hair and tunic, cursorily washed in the ocean, still smelled faintly of fish sauce. Besides, he was still smarting from that "no."

Then it occurred to him that Varazda was doing the same thing he was doing—leaving the women alone to bathe— because Varazda had spent the last seven years in Boukos living as a man, and probably no longer thought of himself as entitled into women's private spaces.

Damiskos stopped, feeling mortified, to let Varazda catch up to him.

"Wait for me!" Varazda said cheerily as he did catch up. "Did you think I was going to bathe with the women?"

Terza's head. This was presumably part of why Varazda had been recruited as a spy. Nothing escaped him.

"I thought you might," Damiskos admitted. "I'm sure they're better company. I'm very sorry. I shouldn't have assumed."

Varazda shrugged. "As these assumptions go, that's not a bad one."

They continued walking at an easy pace. Damiskos thought for a moment, then said, "You mean because I know you're not interested in gawking at naked women—"

"And don't hold it against me … "

"Far from it. Works out in my favour, really. So all I was assuming was that you might take advantage of your, um … status … to stay on that end of the beach with the rest of our party instead of trudging down to this end with me. And that's not particularly insulting. Whereas if we'd been going to, say, the Civil Palace in Pheme, where only men are allowed in, and I assumed you would stay outside, that would be insulting."

"Honestly? Yes, I'd probably take offence at that, but as to whether I would intend going in or not in the first place? It depends on the day, or the mood I'm in, or who I'm with. I never really think of myself as a man, but most of the time I'm quite happy for other people to think of me that way."

"I see."

Varazda gave him an arch look. "Do you?"

"Look, I'm giving it an effort, you insufferable fellow. I don't know what more you want."

That got another unguardedly boyish laugh out of

Varazda. Damiskos had never been much for teasing his lovers—wouldn't even have said it was something he felt comfortable doing—but as with everything, Varazda was an exception.

They rounded the corner of the factory and came to an open stretch of beach from which they could see the steps up to the villa but not the beach houses or the water where the women would be bathing. Damiskos craned his neck and squinted against the sun to satisfy himself that there was no sign of movement on the stairs or the cliff above.

"I don't think I've ever bathed with anyone I've slept with before," Varazda remarked. "Is there any etiquette about it?"

Damiskos considered that for a moment. They stood at the water's edge.

"There is, but only when other men are present and you don't want everyone to know what you've been up to. We're the only ones here. I wouldn't worry about it."

"Hm. What does that mean?"

"Oh. Uh. Not having to worry about where to look, I guess. Though honestly, Varazda, I'm such a wreck after yesterday—please don't be insulted if I don't, you know, show any obvious interest. It isn't you, it's—"

"Dami, please! No explanation necessary."

"No. Thanks."

Varazda toed off his shoes, unknotted his sash, and let the whole length of fabric fall to the sand. Hooking his thumbs under the hem of his shirt, he drew it fluidly off and dropped it on top of the sash. He unfastened his trousers, let them fall, and stepped out of the pooled fabric. He didn't do any of it seductively, but the grace with which he did everything was always seductive. He stepped into the water and stood a moment, shaking out his hair and pulling it forward over his shoulder. He half turned, looking back at Damiskos, and his smile was like the one that had glowed in his eyes the other night when he caught Damiskos to keep him from collapsing

195

on the bed. He held out a hand, hennaed palm up, in uncomplicated invitation.

Naked in daylight, Varazda was beautiful in a way that made Damiskos feel, in spite of what he'd just said, that he should look away. He felt as if he had seen something he did not deserve, was not worthy to see: a vision of translucently white skin, and that tiny waist flaring into the supple curves of hips and rear. Damiskos's desire in that moment seemed separate from his body, a Varazda-shaped hole in his soul.

When Damiskos was a boy, he had for a time been infatuated with a female acrobat who belonged to the household of one of his father's friends. Varazda was built rather like her: long, lean muscles on a delicate, feminine frame. It struck Damiskos that this was a body Varazda had worked hard to reclaim, to shape for himself, after it had been so precisely mutilated. Varazda's beauty was his own possession, not something created or nurtured for the satisfaction of Damiskos's particular tastes.

Having hesitated long enough to make everything awkward, Damiskos briskly unbuckled his belt, shed his tunic, loincloth, and sandals, and splashed out into the water past Varazda, catching his beautiful outstretched hand and pulling him along in his wake. Varazda came laughing in mock-protest.

They waded out until the water was deep enough to swim, and Varazda disappeared under the calm surface in a flash of white limbs. Damiskos, who'd never been much of a swimmer, returned to lie in the shallows, letting the warm water lap over him.

It was not entirely pleasant. The smell of charred wood and cloth mixed with the scent of fish sauce in the air, a pungent reminder of their situation, trapped on the beach while the students occupied the villa. He tried to work out what might be going on in the villa just then, much the way he used to try to predict what was happening inside a besieged stronghold, the better to devise his own strategy.

"I think I know what their next move will be," he said when Varazda walked up out of the water, lovely as a sea-nymph, hair dripping in a dark rope over his shoulder.

"Oh yes?"

Varazda sank to his knees and arranged himself, nymph-like, with his legs tucked to one side and his wrists crossed gently over his lap. He glanced down and seemed to realize what he had done, then self-consciously uncrossed them.

Damiskos looked up into his eyes and could see the tension in him, like a faint echo of his nerves at the beach house on Hapikon Eve. That had been such a short time ago, and yet Damiskos understood so much better now what was going through Varazda's mind. Understood, but still couldn't quite have put into words. Perhaps that was just as well.

He remembered he had been about to say something.

"I think they'll try persuasion or threats again before they try violence. I think we want to make a show of force—be prepared, in fact, to drive them off again—but also to give them hope that we'll give in if they just wait a little longer."

"You mean stockpiling weapons and when they show up, bickering amongst ourselves and wringing our hands."

Damiskos grinned. "Exactly."

The water lay shallow over Varazda's thighs, over his prick nestled between them, over his long, beautiful hands, masculine in size but with their feminine decoration.

"I'd have a hard time being discreet, if we were in a public bath," said Damiskos.

Varazda's eyes went wide and startled.

"Not to change the subject," said Damiskos.

"No, no. We weren't talking about anything important, after all."

"I just wanted to mention it."

"Thank you." Varazda smiled, relaxing a little. "I am quite sure I couldn't manage it myself."

"Manage what?"

"To be discreet." His cheeks coloured slightly.

Damiskos laughed aloud. "I'm quite sure you *could*."

Varazda gave him a curious look. "Is that modesty, First Spear, or a compliment to my dissembling ability?"

"I don't know ... both?"

"Fair. I will take the compliment, but I reject the modesty as unwarranted."

Damiskos snorted, but he couldn't help feeling a little glow of pleasure. He still had a soldier's body, hard with muscle, marked with the scars of battle, curly dark hair on his chest and belly and legs because it was the fashion in the colonial legions not to depilate. He pretended not to be proud of what he had left of his physique, but the truth was he worked hard on it.

Varazda looked as if he wanted to say more but didn't know what. Damiskos imagined picking up one of Varazda's hands and laying it on his own chest, drawing it down over his pectoral muscles to his abdomen, inviting Varazda to explore if he wanted to. Damiskos thought he did want to.

Varazda moved briskly, getting his feet under him. "I've had a thought too. Something that might slow them down a little when they do come to hector us again."

He stood and held out a hand to help Damiskos up. Damiskos took it and was pulled smoothly upright, though it couldn't be said that Varazda made it look easy.

"It's not exactly light," said Varazda, looking him up and down ostentatiously. "All ... *that*."

"We can't all be water-nymphs."

Varazda shouted with laughter, in that way that was becoming delightfully familiar to Damiskos.

"Perhaps," Varazda said as they were dressing on the

shore, "later we'll find another chance to be alone, some-where where it doesn't smell like burnt fish sauce."

"That would be great," said Damiskos. "We should—if we can—we should do that."

He knew he was going to think about that for the rest of the day.

CHAPTER 16

VARAZDA'S PLAN was to booby-trap the stairs from the villa with jars of fish sauce. By the time they had hauled a sufficient number of full jars halfway up the narrow stairs and piled them precariously on the steps, it had been long enough that Damiskos thought they could safely rejoin the women.

Nione met them outside the fortifications. "I want to have a funeral for Aristokles," she said without preamble.

"Yes, of course," said Damiskos. "Wait. You mean right now?"

She nodded. "You said yourself it was important to keep up morale."

"You want to have a funeral to keep up morale."

"Yes, I realize it sounds absurd," said Nione patiently. "But it isn't good for morale to have him lying in the beach hut uncremated. And it is impious."

That was undeniably true. And Damiskos had gone out of his way to try to convince Nione that she was the ranking officer.

He nodded curtly. "We will make it work."

The women of Nione's household knew exactly what to

do, and were amazingly calm about doing it. Nione had clearly been right to think that preparing for the funeral of a man none of them had liked much would take their minds off their situation. They had already seen to the washing and laying out of Aristokles's body, and gave Damiskos quizzical looks when he was surprised to learn this. Now a small party set off to walk to Laokia to ask for the local pyre-maker. The village would be deserted, as most of its residents had gone to the Tentines for Hapikon, but the pyre-maker was not an Oposite and so should still be there.

The rest of the party, while not on sentry duty, began gathering firewood. Nione went into the empty beach hut to say some preliminary prayers. Once her mistress was gone, Aradne said that she knew how to build a pyre and that they needn't wait for the pyre-maker from the village. She directed the others to pile the wood and deflected questions about where she had learned how to do this.

They waited for the pyre-maker anyway, because she would bring with her the necessary spices for the fire. Aristokles's body was brought out, wrapped in a couple of the household women's mantles that had been sacrificed to make a shroud. Nione emerged and did not ask how Aradne came to know how to build a pyre.

The women who had gone to the village returned in a cart, with the pyre-maker and her tools, along with some supplies: bread, cheese, fruit, and blankets. The pyre-maker looked at Aradne's amateur effort and seemed impressed.

Nione, as a former Maiden of the Sacred Loom and priest of Anaxe, led the funeral. The women joined in the choruses of lamentation around the pyre, singing as strongly and respectfully as if Aristokles had been a member of their household or a departed friend. Varazda joined in. He took the torch from the pyre-maker and lit the kindling to start the fire. He said something in Zashian after the pyre was lit that sounded like a short prayer; Damiskos was not close enough to hear.

No doubt there were people in Boukos who would have given Aristokles a more impressive funeral, where there would have been more weeping—genuine and feigned—and fewer of the guests would have been wearing grubby, soot-stained clothing. But Damiskos did not think that anyone could have asked for a more respectful ceremony than the one they performed on the beach that afternoon.

There was no sign of the students. Varazda went back to the stairs to check on their booby-trap and reported that several of the jars had been knocked over and broken, but the others were still in place. It suggested that someone had come down, tripped over them, and given up rather than attempting to clear the rest away. That fit with Damiskos's theory that the students would send another emissary before returning in force.

While Aristokles's pyre burned brightly in the late afternoon sun, the women prepared a funeral meal with olives and wine from the villa's warehouse, bread and cheese and apples from the village, and fresh fish from the bay.

"It's too bad you don't have your lute here, Midina," Nione said to the Gylphian musician from her household.

"I am worrying about it," Midina admitted. "They will break it, you think, the crazy men?"

"I don't know," said Nione with a sigh. "Can anyone remember whether music was supposed to be good or bad in the Ideal Republic?"

No one could.

"I would like to hear you play again, sir, the Zashian music," Midina said to Damiskos.

"Yes," said Nione. "He's very good, isn't he, Pharastes?"

"He is," said Varazda.

"I remember when you were a boy you used to sing, too," said Nione. "Do you still?"

"Well, I—I can, yes."

"Oh, sing for us!" exclaimed Rhea.

"Sing us something in Sasian," Nione suggested.

"I—I—My pronunciation will offend Varazda's ears, but … "

"He can cope," said one of the other women. "He'll laugh at you. But he does it with *love*—don't you, Phari?"

Varazda flashed her a grin. This was a level of awkwardness that Damiskos felt quite unequal to dealing with. The household women—who apparently had taken to calling Varazda by a jaunty nickname—still thought that the two of them were a couple, while Aradne knew that they were not but that Damiskos wished they were. The gods only knew what Nione thought was going on at this point.

"This is a song from Rataxa," Damiskos found himself saying. "It's a very famous one. The words are by Zash's most esteemed poet."

He sang. In spite of his modesty, he knew he was a good singer. Playing and singing came easily to him, and he could lose himself blissfully in the music. He didn't lose himself now. He heard the words as he sang them, as if he was hearing them for the first time. He would have kicked himself for choosing this song, except that it seemed somehow inevitable.

It was a song of unrequited love, of yearning for a beloved who was distant and yet nearby, who gave joy and sorrow in equal measure. Damiskos had learned to sing it in Rataxa, with the style and accent of the region, courtly and elegant—but he was neither of those things, and he sang it with an inflection of his own, transposing it into something different. For him it had always been about his love for Zash, complexly tinted as it was by a centuries-old enmity and the fragile peace of the colonies on the Deshan Coast. It was still about that, partly.

He finished singing and risked a look at Varazda, who was watching him with uncomplicated pleasure. Plainly he did not think Damiskos had been singing about him.

Everyone complimented Damiskos, and then someone said, "You sing one for us, Phari!"

"Absolutely not! I'm a dancer. I don't sing. Definitely not like *that*."

They pestered him until Aradne spoke over everyone to say, "Leave him alone. I'll sing."

There was cheering at that. By coincidence, Aradne sang a Phemian song with a similar theme to Damiskos's. She too gave it a unique inflection, making the words of longing sound almost belligerent, like a challenge: why don't you love me? haven't you got the guts?

After that, other members of the party were persuaded to sing. The little boy, Chari, was a talented singer, with a clear, piping voice. They sang all together, popular songs that everyone knew, clapping in time. One of Varazda's friends convinced him to sing a duet with her, and everyone berated him afterward for saying he couldn't sing, and told him his voice was lovely. It was, Damiskos thought: light and precise and obviously trained. But his singing lacked the passion of his dancing. It was a little remote, almost cold. Damiskos would bet it was something he had learned to do in the king's household at Gudul.

When the sun had gone down completely and the women and children were all settling down inside the barricaded beach houses, Damiskos and Varazda slipped out the gate. Aradne set in place the barbed hurdle that blocked it after them and nodded a soldierly farewell.

They walked up the beach toward a path cut through the brush halfway around the sheltered cove. It led up through the terraced vineyard to the front of the house, bypassing the cliff stairs at the back of the garden. The path was not very well maintained, and it was slow going pushing through the shrubs and plants that crowded its edges. They walked single-file with Varazda in front.

He looked back at Damiskos as they reached the gate in the stone wall bordering the lowest terrace of the vineyard.

"I wish we were sneaking away for something more enjoyable than breaking into Nione's house," Varazda whispered.

Damiskos gave him an exaggerated frown which he hoped would be readable in the moonlight. "I don't know what you mean. We have a duty to do."

"I, uh … " He looked momentarily stricken. Then he melted into laughter. "Bastard," he hissed.

The gate was stuck, the latch pinned in place with tendrils of vine. Varazda grasped the top rung of the gate, drew his legs up, and was over in one neat motion. He turned and was probably about to reach out to help Damiskos, but vaulting a gate was something Damiskos could still do. He braced one hand on the top rung and swung himself easily over, landing on his good leg.

"I've practiced that," he admitted.

Then he found himself backed against the gate, Varazda's slim arms trapping him on either side, Varazda's dark eyes soft in the moonlight. Varazda paused.

"May I?"

"Please."

Varazda leaned in and kissed him, very gently, his body swaying forward against Damiskos in a seductive motion that was just the way he always moved. Damiskos leaned back against the gate, boneless and melting, catching Varazda's upper arms as Varazda's hands came up to cradle his face, and

Varazda's tongue stroked over his. As gentle as the kiss was, it was also full of command. Damiskos surrendered to it whole-heartedly, resisting the urge to take control, relishing the fact that Varazda wanted this enough to venture to take it. When Varazda stepped back, Damiskos let him go—regretfully but without fuss.

"The situation seemed to call for that," said Varazda lightly. He shrugged, touching the back of his fingers to his lips. "A moonlit vineyard, and you so ... so *you*. Besides, I have been wanting to do that all day."

Damiskos drew in a deep breath and let it out. "You could go on doing it all night, as far as I'm concerned."

"If we did not have a mission in hand. Come. I've distracted you—distracted myself. I should know better."

He held out a hand, and after a moment's stunned hesitation, Damiskos took it, and they walked along the corridor of grapevines together, hand in hand, as if it were a normal thing.

Damiskos wished he could achieve the same kind of cool-ness about all this that Varazda evidently had. Just enjoy the time they had together rather than yearning preemptively for more before they had even parted. He resolved to try harder.

They traversed the length of the first terrace and reached the stairs in the stone retaining wall leading up to the second level. The flights of stairs after that were all slightly offset, zigzagging up the hillside. They were short flights with shallow stone steps, easy enough for Damiskos to climb, especially since Varazda casually gestured for him to go first so that he could set the pace.

Divine Terza. Had he ever, in the last five years, met anyone so effortlessly considerate? Or was it just that he appreciated Varazda's consideration more because it came in such a beautiful package?

No, he reminded himself sternly. That was exactly the sort of thought he had to expel from his mind. Varazda was a very decent fellow, certainly. No need to make too much of it.

As they climbed to the topmost terrace, they went over the details of their plan. The general idea was that they would get into the house and raise the signal for the postal ship from Boukos, due tomorrow, so that it would stop at Laothalia on its way down the coast. The signal was a nondescript flag flown from a pole on the villa's squat tower; it was unlikely the students would notice that it had been raised.

That much was straightforward; Nione had described the location of the flag, and Aradne had even drawn them a map of the house. After that, they would have to improvise a little. They would take up the search for the stolen documents where Varazda had left off, but they wouldn't know until they got into the house how they might best go about that. It all depended on where the students were when they went in.

There had been some negotiation about who should go back into the house. Varazda had been very prepared to do it by himself, but both Damiskos and Aradne had been adamant that he should take one of them along. Damiskos had been on the point of suggesting they draw straws, because he could see that in some ways Aradne, who knew the house and the servants, might be more useful than he, when she had folded her arms across her chest and said, "You'd better go, Damiskos. Neither of us can move fast, but you know how to use a sword—that might come in handy. I'll stay here and guard the camp." So it was decided.

"So," said Varazda as they climbed one of the flights of stairs in the moonlit vineyard. "Plan of attack. I say we go in over the kitchen garden wall—it's low and out of the way. We can check the kitchen for any knives the students may have overlooked. Then across the yard to my room, in case my swords are still there."

Which they might well be, if the students, like Damiskos, assumed that the weapons were purely decorative.

"Take the picture of your daughter, too," Damiskos suggested. "You don't want to leave that behind if you have to sail for Boukos in a hurry."

Varazda smiled. "No, I won't forget that."

They had not spoken about what would happen once Varazda had finished his business at the villa, successfully or not. But obviously it would involve him returning to Boukos, perhaps on the very postal ship they were now going to signal. There was really nothing to talk about.

"Then we'll go to my room," Damiskos went on, "get my sword and my bow. Maybe a clean tunic, too, while we're there."

"I wouldn't discourage that."

"Then upstairs to the tower to set the signal. You can go up while I stand guard. Then on to the students' rooms, same procedure. If it turns out they're not drinking or arguing about virtue in the garden, contrary to expectations, we'll play it by ear."

They had reached the topmost terrace. Damiskos stopped here, and Varazda looked at him questioningly.

"I was just thinking. We should probably have gone over this earlier, but there are a few hand signals we might want to have sorted out before we go in. So we can communicate if we can't risk speaking aloud. Here, I'll show you the ones I think we're most likely to need. This is for 'stop,' obviously." He held up a hand, palm-out. "And for 'come.'" He beckoned with his whole hand. "This is for 'message received.'" He held up his hand with fingers and thumb pinched together. Varazda imitated, beautiful hennaed fingertips held together.

"Uh. If you're ahead of me and you see someone coming and want to alert me, you do this." Damiskos made a rolling motion with his hand. Varazda copied it elegantly. "Then hold out the appropriate number of fingers to tell me how many enemies—well, how many philosophy students or fishermen or whatever—there are." He demonstrated. "You'd probably be doing this while facing away from me, so you'd just hold your hand out to the side."

"Had we better have signals to distinguish philosophy students from fishermen, or indeed from household slaves?"

"Yes, good thought. The one I showed you normally means 'enemy combatant.' We'll say for our purposes that's just the students." He made a different gesture, twirling one finger instead of his whole hand. "That's for 'civilians.' Should we consider the fishermen civilians? We don't really know where they stand."

"How about this for them?" Varazda made a delicately undulating, fishy motion with his fingers. He grinned.

Damiskos snorted. "I'm not sure I can make my hand do that, but sure."

He demonstrated a few more—danger, listen, switch places, look—and then he began to get the impression that Varazda was humouring him, and said, "We'll, that's probably enough for our purposes."

"Probably," said Varazda with a smile. "It was well thought of. Where did you use these, in the army?"

"Reconnaissance work. Scouting near enemy lines and that sort of thing. Sometimes silence is crucial."

"Indeed it is. Listen, First Spear, I wanted to say something. I wouldn't have asked you to come with me, but I'm very glad to have you along. I wouldn't want you to think otherwise. I have done *roughly* this sort of thing before—sneaking about someone else's house looking for something —but the stakes have never been quite so high for me. I've never been in a situation where if I were caught—and I hasten to add I never *have* been caught—but if I had been, I could always have passed off what I was doing as being lost, looking for the privy, admiring the view from the upstairs bedroom, or what have you. That's very much not the case here. I'd be much more nervous about this if you weren't coming with me."

"You've no need to be nervous. You will do fine. I've seen clearly that you can defend yourself."

It was the sort of thing he would have said to a new recruit on the eve of battle, and it came out of his mouth, in exactly the tone he would have used then, before he stopped to think whether it was appropriate now.

Varazda smiled with a little shrug, the most unsoldierly thing imaginable. "Nevertheless."

CHAPTER 17

THE WALL of the kitchen garden was higher than the vine-yard gate, but Damiskos was still able to boost himself up and vault over without too much difficulty. Varazda, of course, went over with a sinuous slither as if he vaulted higher walls every day.

The garden was deserted, the barred windows of the kitchen dark. They picked their way down between rows of onions and rosemary bushes to the back door of the kitchen. It was latched from the inside, as they had rather expected. They went around the building to the side, ducking behind another, lower wall that fronted the garden. On the other side Damiskos could see the roof of the well in the yard. He heard nothing, and it was dark.

Varazda turned to signal that he would look over the wall, using the gestures Damiskos had taught him. He crept along a little and peered over the top of the wall. He held out a hand, ready to signal for Damiskos to follow or stay put, but instead he curled his hand in a dancerly, flowerlike gesture. Damiskos gave an inaudible snort. Varazda glanced back, grinning, and then beckoned for Damiskos to follow, and flowed over the wall.

Their first stop was the kitchen, which they entered by the unlocked door off the yard. It was a mess, with broken vessels on the floor and the tables, food spilling out of containers, unraked ashes on the stove. Most of the knives had been taken, leaving only a couple of rather blunt cleavers and three small fruit knives. Damiskos bundled these up in a towel and tucked them into his belt, and they left the kitchen.

They crossed the dark yard without incident and reached the gate leading into the yard shared by the stables and the slave quarters. Here there were signs of life. Light glowed in a couple of downstairs windows of the slaves' building, and when they slipped cautiously over the wall into the yard they could hear a murmur of voices coming from the lit room.

Varazda had explained the layout of the slave quarters to Damiskos earlier. The men were all housed downstairs, in double rooms, the women upstairs along the gallery. Downstairs was also a common room, a dining hall, and the slave baths. The light and voices were clearly coming from one of those.

Varazda leaned close to Damiskos to whisper in his ear. "Do you want to go listen under one of those windows while I go upstairs? See what you can find out?"

Damiskos nodded crisply and gave the signal for Varazda to move out toward the staircase. Varazda made a comical face at him, and Damiskos allowed himself another soft huff of laughter. All very unprofessional. He should be ashamed of himself.

He watched Varazda move off toward the stairs, visible only because Damiskos was straining his eyes to follow him. He really was very good at this, catlike and cautious, pressing himself into the shadows and moving smoothly and swiftly. He would have been fine alone, just as Damiskos had said. But it still pleased Damiskos absurdly that Varazda was glad to have him along.

He waited until Varazda was halfway up the stairs before moving toward the lit windows, hugging the wall, crossing quickly past the main door. When he reached the far side, he dropped to sit the ground and scooted himself along with his hands, a totally undignified performance that was the best he could do since he couldn't crouch properly anymore. He positioned himself under one of the windows, back to the wall, where he could hear the voices from inside reasonably clearly.

The windows must have belonged to the dining room, because he could hear sounds of eating, spoons chinking against bowls, voices muffled by mouthfuls of food, cups clunking on the table. It sounded like half a dozen men, no more than that. He recognized the voice of the boy Niko among the rest.

"Going to make a raid on the kitchen tomorrow morning, I don't care," Niko was saying. "What are they going to do to me if they catch me, anyway? Philosophize at me?"

"They could kill you the way they killed Tio and Demi. You are *not* leaving the yard."

"It's not the philosophers I'm worried about," rumbled another man's voice. "It's Sesna and his boys."

There were grunts and murmurs of agreement.

"Well, I'm not afraid of them," Niko blustered, "and I'm going. First thing tomorrow. You'll thank me when I bring back some decent food."

Conversation died down into the sounds of eating and drinking. Damiskos crept back around the building to the gate leading out of the slaves' yard. Sure enough, it was barricaded on this side, a couple of stout beams affixed as makeshift bars.

Varazda appeared at his shoulder, swords under one arm. He had changed into a clean shirt with flowers embroidered around the neck; the buttons were not done up, the shirt fastened only by his sash. He gave Damiskos a questioning look. Damiskos pointed to the bars on the gate.

"They've barricaded themselves in," Damiskos whispered. "I think only some of the men are in here. They're worried about someone named Sesna?"

"Mm. The head porter. A bully, I gather."

"And 'his boys,' they said."

"He has a few flunkies. They're the ones who feel hard-done-by in a house full of women." Varazda shrugged contemptuously. "It's about what you'd expect."

"Should we go in and speak to the men in here? See if they have any intelligence we haven't gathered yet?"

"Yes, I think so. I'll go in, you stay outside with the swords." He handed them over. "I'm not sure we want to show our hand completely until we have to."

Damiskos nodded agreement. "You didn't forget the picture of your daughter, did you? While you were busy frivolously putting on clean clothes?"

Varazda gave him a fond smile and patted the front of his sash, where Zashian men were in the habit of stashing their valuables. "No, First Spear, I didn't forget the picture of my daughter."

He leaned in and kissed Damiskos on the cheek, then he was gone across the dark yard, headed for the door of the slaves' quarters, doing up his buttons as he went. He was inside for only a brief time before he reappeared in the lighted doorway and beckoned for Damiskos to join him. Damiskos came, carrying Varazda's swords, and followed him through the door into the slaves' dining room.

There were only four people at the table; they were just noisy eaters. And Damiskos saw immediately that this was not a useful auxiliary force. There were two old men, stooped and white-haired, a young man who looked to be blind, and Niko.

They were eager to give Damiskos and Varazda their

account of the seizure of the villa, but it was mostly what they had heard already: the fishermen had come in demanding extra pay; the students had locked Eurydemos in his room and drawn knives when the slaves tried to protect their mistress. The mistress had escaped with her women, and the men had stayed behind voluntarily as a diversion

"The mistress wanted to take us four with her," said the blind man. "She would have taken us with her, but we insisted on staying."

"It was noble of you," said Varazda warmly. "But are you four the only ones left in here? What happened to the rest of the men?"

"Sesna and his thugs threw in their lot with the philosophers," said the blind man, scowling. "The others, we think they locked them in the cellars, but we don't know."

"When they didn't come back, we barricaded the gates," Niko explained. "The gate from the yard, and the one on the other side, by the stables. Your horse is all right, by the way, sir. Grandad and I've been looking after her—and the others."

Grandad, whom Damiskos recognized as one of the grooms, grunted something about the boy knowing nothing of horses, which Niko ignored. Damiskos thanked them both sincerely for taking care of Xanthe.

Since they had spent the last day and a half hiding in the slaves' quarters, the men didn't have much more to report. They said the porters had made a couple of attempts to get into the yard, and threatened to get ladders to scale the walls, but since the ladders were actually stored in back of the stables, they hadn't been able to make good on the threat. They had heard the students arguing once or twice, but didn't know what it was about.

Varazda and Damiskos thanked them and explained that they were on their way to get help.

"It's probably best for you to stay here," Varazda said. "So long as you feel safe. If all goes according to plan, the siege should be lifted by tomorrow morning."

"I wouldn't," Damiskos added, looking pointedly at Niko, "risk going out to the kitchen. For instance."

"Did we do the right thing, leaving those men there?" Varazda asked in a whisper as they edged around the walls toward the house door.

Damiskos stopped, the question unexpected. It had been Varazda's decision, but Damiskos didn't think it had been wrong.

"Yes, I think so," he whispered back. "We couldn't bring them with us now, and we need to finish what we came here for. If we're able, on the way back, we could stop and collect them. Or try to—they may not come. They may say they need to stay and take care of the horses or something. Not wanting to abandon their post. They strike me as that type."

"Well, you would know, First Spear. But thank you. I'm glad we agree." He made the "go ahead" gesture.

The windows on the front of the house were small and high up, and opened onto unoccupied bedrooms rather than onto the atrium. As in any traditional Phemian house, no outside windows looked onto the atrium, which was lit and ventilated by its central skylight. They could not risk trying the front door, as they would be going in blind. They had to take a circuitous route, described to them by Aradne, to reach Damiskos's room. They crossed the front of the house and reached a narrow alley beside the kitchen building which opened out at the back into a small paved yard smelling of kitchen garbage and privies.

On their right was the bath complex, a low-roofed annex to the main house, overgrown with vines which trailed on up the house's western wall. The ground-floor windows of the rooms on this side looked out over the top of the tiled bath-house roof. Damiskos's room was one of these, and their plan was to climb up to the window by way of the bath-house. Aradne had said it should be possible, though personally she had never tried it, and that was what they had to go on.

Clouds had half-covered the moon at this point, and it was very dark in the little yard. Varazda stood looking up at the view of roof and wall and windows above them for a moment, then adjusted the swords that he had tucked through his sash, crossed at the back. He reached up, and with a little jump caught hold of the overhanging edge of the bath-house roof and pulled himself lightly up.

He crouched on the tiles of the roof, looking over at Damiskos, and beckoned with one hand: come up.

Damiskos reached up to grasp the roof; he was just slightly taller than Varazda and didn't have to do more than stand on tiptoe to reach it. He kicked off the wall using his good leg, and hauled himself up over the edge onto the tiles. This was not something he had practiced doing since his injury, but he managed it efficiently enough, though he must have looked laboured and ungraceful compared to Varazda. Who was poised ready to help him over the edge if he needed it, but made no comment when he didn't.

There were five ground-floor windows along the length of the bath complex, all close enough to the roof that they would have to slither on their stomachs when passing under them to be sure of not being seen. All were dark except for the second and the fifth, whose shutters were open with light glowing out from within. Faint voices came from the second window, which Damiskos thought belonged to another bedroom.

Crouching by the first window, Varazda pointed down the line and back at Damiskos: which window is yours? Damiskos pointed at the third window, hoping that he remembered Aradne's diagram of the house well enough. It was too dark now to consult it. Varazda nodded and gestured "forward."

He'd really taken to the hand signals, Damiskos thought with amusement. *I must remember to tease him about it later.*

They crawled along the roof close to the wall, moving slowly and carefully for fear of dislodging a loose tile; Aradne had warned them that this roof was in bad repair. It sloped at a gentle angle away from the main house wall, and was easy enough to traverse except for that consideration. They passed under the lit window, pressing themselves as low as possible. None of the voices that Damiskos could hear from below were familiar. It sounded like a game of dice in progress. The fishermen, possibly.

They reached the third, dark window and stopped beneath it. Damiskos levered himself up to push experimentally at the shutters. They were latched from inside. Varazda sat up next to Damiskos, drew one of his swords, and offered it. Damiskos mouthed "Thank you" and used the thin bronze blade to lift the latch and let it drop to the side. He smiled at Varazda in the dark as he returned the sword.

It was odd to be on a night mission—behind enemy lines, so to speak—with a fellow you wanted to kiss all the time.

Damiskos pushed the shutters open and looked into the room. A little faint light slanted in through the window above the door, which opened onto the atrium, and he could see that it was indeed his room. The bed was directly under the window where they sat. He turned and signalled to Varazda that he would go in and Varazda should wait here. Varazda touched his arm to stop him, pointed to himself, and pointed up at the wall of the house.

Damiskos followed the gesture, looking up at the thick trunk of a vine twining up the wall to the second-storey windows. He shook his head.

Varazda raised his eyebrows: why did Damiskos think it was a bad idea?

It wasn't a bad idea; it was a good way of getting into the upstairs rooms, one they hadn't thought of because they hadn't known the vines would make the wall scalable at this point. But it would require them to split up. There was no way Damiskos could make it up that wall, and Varazda had to know that.

Damiskos reached through the window to rap his knuckles on the shutter, and gestured upward. What if the windows above were closed? Varazda laid his hand on the hilt of one of his swords. Shrugged. Yes, he probably could unlatch a window with his sword while hanging one-handed onto a vine, Damiskos thought. He craned his neck to look up at the window above them, the one Varazda could most easily reach from the vine. It did appear to be shuttered, but there was no light showing between the louvres.

Varazda tapped his shoulder and made a complicated but clear series of gestures to indicate that Damiskos should go up through the house and meet him upstairs. It would give Varazda a chance to begin searching the students' rooms before they went to set the signal for the postal ship. Damiskos didn't particularly like it, but he wasn't going to prevent Varazda from taking the most effective route to the second storey just because he himself couldn't manage it. He nodded.

As a compromise for his own peace of mind, he lay on the roof waiting while Varazda climbed nimbly up the vine, braced himself with one foot on the window ledge, drew his sword to flick the latch open, and pushed the shutters noise-lessly inward. He slid the sword neatly back through his sash, caught the top of the window to swing himself fully over from the vine to the windowsill, and crouching there, poised as a cat, looked down at Damiskos, and blew him a kiss.

A moment later, Damiskos had collected himself enough

to swing over the edge of his own window and drop down onto his bed.

The room had been cursorily turned over; his portable shrine lay on the floor, the ashes of the last burnt offering spilled over the tiles. His saddlebags had been dragged out of his closet and opened, but they had not found either his sword or his hunting bow, hidden at the very back of the top shelf.

He tucked the shrine and its statue into the bag along with the bow, quiver, and the bundle of kitchen knives, tied the bags shut, and buckled on his sword belt. Then he got up on the bed again to heft the saddlebags out the window, letting them down gently onto the roof outside.

Getting down from the bed, he crossed quietly to the room door and listened at it for a cautious interval. There were no sounds from the atrium, not even faint rustles or soft footfalls. He remembered that sounds from outside had been clearly audible in this room, no doubt because of the connecting window. He eased the door open and slipped out into the empty atrium.

There were no lights burning here, but the door to the room where he thought he had heard the fishermen stood open, and lamplight spilled out. It lay between him and the foot of the stairs, but the atrium beyond was deeply shadowed. He pulled the door gently closed behind him and started around the long way, creeping close to the walls to stay in the darkness as much as possible.

He passed the open archway of the anteroom to the library, which he thought was where they had seen the second light burning from outside, but here he could hear no voices, and the inner door was closed. He paused at the opening to the passage out into the garden, looking cautiously around the corner. There was no one in the portico, so he ventured a quick detour down the passage. Hiding behind a column, he looked out into the garden.

Torches flickered in the summer dining room, and he could see students lounging on the couches and hear raised voices. Someone was pouring wine, but whether it was one of the turncoat porters or someone else, he had no idea.

He slunk back the way he had come. Through the half-open folding doors of the winter dining room he could see a chaos of uncleared dishes and broken wine-cups. There were articles of clothing on the floor in the atrium, and a statue had been toppled from its pedestal and lay in pieces on the tiles. The pool in the middle of the atrium smelled faintly of urine.

He reached the bottom of the stairs without incident, but someone had broken some crockery on the first few steps, and he barely avoided stepping on the fragments in the dark. He felt around for a clear space on the step with the toe of one boot, and unluckily a number of shards fell off the edge of the step to the floor with loud chinks.

"What was that?" demanded someone in the lit room beside the stairs.

"A cat or something," said another voice, blurred with drink. "Aw, come on, leave it!"

"If it's one of those students creeping about, though … " A third voice. "I don't trust any of 'em."

"Or the damn slaves getting out of the cellar. I told you we should've cut and run a long time ago."

There was more cursing and unintelligible, raised voices. This time Damiskos was sure there were at least five of them. He had retreated around the corner into the passage leading to the front door, hand on the pommel of his sword, but no one emerged from the room, and presently they seemed to have gone back to their game of dice. He crept out again. Armed, he liked his chances against five fishermen well enough, but they were civilians; they would have to mount a very determined attack before he would think himself justified in killing any of them, and he would prefer it didn't come to that.

The stairs had a railing with an upper and lower rail on their open side. He grasped the hand-rail, stepped up onto the lower rail, and managed to pull himself clumsily up past the crockery-strewn steps. After that the rest of the flight was easy.

He reached the gallery at the top that ran around three sides of the atrium, giving access to the upstairs bedrooms. Looking down, he established which room was directly above his, and went to its door. He wished they had thought to arrange some signal so that he wouldn't have to surprise Varazda, but at this point it couldn't be helped. He eased the door open a crack, relieved to find it wasn't locked, and looked in.

The room was a fantastic mess, with clothes, books, and dirty dishes on the floor, and two large sea chests under the window. Varazda was up to his elbows in one of them. Damiskos tapped lightly on the door to get his attention, and he looked round, wide-eyed and wary, before his face broke into a smile. He held up one hand, and in the moonlight from the window Damiskos could see the bundle of small, tightly-rolled parchment scrolls that he held.

CHAPTER 18

"THOSE ARE THE DOCUMENTS?" Damiskos whispered. He had been picturing something larger, somehow, more impressive-looking.

Varazda nodded. "It was as I suspected—there was a false bottom in one of the chests, and they were in there. I didn't have time to pry it up when I was searching before. And I was trying to keep them from noticing their things had been searched, which made it take longer."

Damiskos looked around at the clutter on the floor. "You've given up on that, I see."

Varazda made a face that Damiskos thought he might have learned from his three-year-old daughter. He tucked the small scrolls away in his sash and gathered up an armload of debris from the floor to dump it back in the open chest.

"What? That's what it was like when I came in." He closed the chest, closed and latched the shutters, and gestured to Damiskos: let's go.

Finally they turned to their principal reason for entering the villa: the raising of the signal flag from the tower in the north-east corner. They made their way around the gallery, still moving stealthily although Damiskos at least was convinced that the second storey of the villa was more or less empty. Varazda, walking in front, indulged in a couple more elegant, improvised hand signals, and Damiskos nudged him playfully in the small of the back, making him look round with an innocent shrug.

Damiskos had met men in the army who genuinely enjoyed danger, who were at their happiest when facing the enemy with the odds against them. He wasn't really one of them himself, and he felt sure Varazda wasn't at all. This heady mood of joking and teasing between them was something else, something specific that Damiskos couldn't quite name. It might have threatened to be distracting, but instead he felt his instincts sharp and ready, his senses keen.

They found the narrow door in the corner of the gallery that led up to the tower. Varazda indicated that he would go up, and Damiskos nodded. He positioned himself behind the half-open door, where he could command a view of the gallery in either direction, and see part of the atrium below, without being too obviously visible himself. Varazda padded off up the stairs.

He hadn't been gone more than a minute—not long enough to have found the signal flag and raised it—when he came flying back down the stairs and out the door. He beckoned Damiskos to follow him as he ran down the east side of the gallery, scanning the doors and picking one halfway along. He pushed at it, hard, but it was locked.

Damiskos didn't know what this was about, but he didn't need to. He stepped past Varazda to put his shoulder to the door and shoved sharply. The lock gave with a splintering crack, and the door swung open.

The room was lamplit, and Tyra was sitting on the bed with a comb in her hand, her hair loose over her shoulder. She froze, wild-eyed, and let out a startled scream.

"Shit!" Varazda cried. "I'm so sorry! I got the wrong door." He grabbed Damiskos's arm. "It must be that one."

He pointed to their left along the gallery. "It's Eurydemos—he's hanging out the window. Can you—"

"On it." Damiskos made for the left-hand door while Varazda apologized again to Tyra.

It took Damiskos two tries to break down Eurydemos's door, which must have had a stronger lock than Tyra's. Charging inside, he saw that the bed, a delicate piece of furniture, had been pulled diagonal under the window and lifted at one corner by a torn sheet tied around its leg and stretching taut over the windowsill. He squeezed past the bed to assess the situation outside the window.

Eurydemos was dangling at the end of the hopelessly short length of sheet, holding on with one hand, legs thrashing feebly, tangled in his trailing mantle. He had evidently been trying to get to the top of a window below and to the right of his room, but he dangled several feet away from it, far enough above the rocky ground sloping away from the villa's wall to be seriously hurt if he fell. The sheer, bone-headed idiocy of the man. Damiskos gritted his teeth.

"What was that?" he heard the fishermen calling from below. "Somebody screamed."

Damiskos gave a tug on the sheet to get Eurydemos's attention. "I'm going to pull you up," he hissed. "Grab on with your other hand and turn toward the wall."

The philosopher stared up at him with a mulish expression, and for a moment Damiskos was afraid he was going to let go and drop rather than allow himself to be pulled back into captivity. He wouldn't be killed by the fall; he'd just break a limb or two, and then they'd have to deal with that, and oh, immortal gods.

"We're going to get you out," Damiskos said firmly, trying to sound reassuring rather than massively irritated.

Eurydemos grasped the torn sheet with both hands and made a pathetic attempt to twist around to face the wall. Damiskos hauled him up gingerly, wary of overtaxing the already fraying sheet. Eurydemos bumped and scraped against the wall, unable to get his feet out of the coils of his mantle to help his ascent.

What kind of imbecile climbed out a window wearing his mantle?

"I heard a crash," one of the fishermen was saying from the atrium.

"Leave it—it's not our business."

"What if it's the prisoners getting out?"

"They're not our prisoners."

"Do you think *they* know that? What if they attack us?"

Damiskos had just got Eurydemos over the windowsill and into the room when there was another crash, this one from the back of the house, in the portico or the garden, as if something large had fallen and shattered.

"What was *that*?" Eurydemos yelped.

"What was *that*?" the fishermen cried from below. "That was out back! Come on!"

Footsteps slapped on the tiles in the atrium as the fishermen ran toward the garden. Damiskos seized Eurydemos's arm and dragged him, clutching his mantle, out the door into the gallery. At the same time, Varazda emerged with Tyra from an open door at the back of the house, above the portico. Damiskos hurried toward him with Eurydemos in tow.

"Dropped a big vase out the window," Varazda reported breathlessly. "Diversion. You take these two downstairs and out. I'll finish setting the signal and meet you in the kitchen garden."

"Understood."

Varazda took off for the tower stairs again while Damiskos herded his charges toward the stairs to the ground floor. Tyra was eager and quick enough to scurry ahead of him, but Eurydemos had got tangled up in his mantle again, and was staring confusedly after Varazda.

"Move," Damiskos ordered him. "Now."

Somehow he got the philosopher downstairs and out the door before the fishermen came back into the house. The three of them hurried across the dark yard to the kitchen building. They unlatched the back door and went out into the garden.

"Poor Nione," said Tyra. "What they've done to her house!"

"At least she got out safely," Damiskos said. "That's thanks to you."

"I wish I had been able to do more," Tyra said. "I thought I would stay and talk to Kleitos, and between us we would be able to persuade the students not to do anything foolish. They're quite intelligent, really—I thought surely they would listen to reason. But when they found out that I'd warned Nione, they made Kleitos lock me in the bedroom. They said if he didn't, they'd—they'd think of something worse to … "

"Brutes," Damiskos growled, to keep her from trying to finish the sentence. "But no one did hurt you, did they? Aside from scaring you, I mean."

She shook her head. "I think Kleitos was as scared as I was—he's a good man, really."

"They were planning to kill me," Eurydemos announced, sounding a little bit like a small boy who felt he had been ignored by the grown-ups for too long. "They were waiting for the right moment, to make it appear that I killed myself. I heard them discussing it."

Damiskos spent a moment trying to dredge up some sympathy. "Must hurt," he said finally. "Coming from your own students."

"Of course it hurts," said Eurydemos condescendingly. "You can have no idea."

"No," Damiskos agreed. "Never had any of my men mutiny on me."

They waited in the kitchen garden until Damiskos could no longer ignore his unease. Eurydemos fidgeted and kept trying to talk and needing to be shushed. There was no sign of Varazda.

"I'm going back in to look for him," Damiskos said abruptly, cutting short something Eurydemos was starting to say.

"What? Look for who?"

"Varazda." Damiskos gave Eurydemos a sour look. Wasn't the man supposed to be in love with Varazda, to the point of poetry?

"And leave us here? Surely you don't expect us to come with you?"

"If you think it's best," said Tyra quickly, looking embarrassed for Eurydemos.

"He's been gone a long time. I don't know what might be happening in there. But I don't think you should stay here. I'll show you the route down to the beach."

He took them to the bottom of the kitchen garden, explained how to get down through the vineyard to the path to the beach, and helped them over the wall. Tyra thanked him; Eurydemos gave him a baleful look as if Damiskos were abandoning a sacred trust. Damiskos walked briskly back up the garden.

He slipped back in through the now-unlocked kitchen and out into the yard. The house looked dark and still, but he knew that meant nothing. He pushed the front door open cautiously.

Loud, angry voices met his ear immediately.

"Yes, of course!" That was Helenos's voice. "What did you think we were going to do, mount an attack on the kingdom of Sasia ourselves? Of course we're going to sell the documents."

"But if we do that, how are we any better than common thieves?" That was Phaia.

"She's right," someone else cried. "I say, and have always said, that we must keep them for ourselves."

Clearly they had not yet discovered that the documents were gone.

"—the fuck you're doing, and anyway—"

"Don't you tell me I don't fucking know what I'm doing, who was the one who had to haul your ass out of the Sasian embassy when you—"

"Shut up, all of you! Shut up!" That was Phaia again, shouting furiously over the men, who ignored her and went on arguing.

A high level of philosophical discourse there. Damiskos risked edging into the narrow opening of the door to look into the atrium. There was no one visible on the ground floor, and he thought all the voices that he had heard were coming from the gallery. That was why Varazda hadn't come down, then; he was trapped, his route out of the house cut off by the students.

"—got to do something about those goat-buggering fishermen anyway—"

"Of course we are better than common thieves—Our cause is just!"

"Exactly! Our cause is just!" Gelon bawled. "Fuck the Ideal Republic!"

"Shut up, you bleating moron!"

"You leave him alone, Helenos. No one has done more for our cause than Gelon."

"I dispute that!"

Helenos growled, "You two have caused me enough trouble already, killing that Boukossian imbecile when you did. You forced us to move much sooner than I meant to, and this *mess* is the result."

"The Boukossian spy had to die, Helenos. Sometimes I

think you're a coward at heart. You were squeamish about killing those Sasian dogs in Boukos, too."

"You whore! How dare you insult Helenos like that?"

"How dare you call her a whore?"

"You called me a thief!"

"I will make you eat your words!"

By this point all the hells had broken loose in the gallery, with Phaia shrieking and the men shouting. Someone—probably Gelon—evidently had a weapon, and others were trying to confiscate it. It struck Damiskos as a good moment to slip in through the half-open door. Pressing himself to the wall, he crept around the corner into the atrium, ducking back into the shadows on the far side from the action.

No sooner had he done that then the fishermen came back into the house.

"We've decided—" one of them began, then broke off as they looked up and saw the chaos on the gallery.

Two of the male students had succeeded in subduing Phaia—to an extent, though she continued to scream—but Gelon was still at large, and several people, including Helenos, were bleeding. The fishermen started toward the base of the stairs, reconsidered, and stopped, looking at one another desperately.

Something small flashed past Damiskos's peripheral vision to drop to the floor a short distance in front of him. He looked down. A small gold earring winked up at him from the tiles.

He stepped forward and looked up, and Varazda, crouched in the shadows of the gallery above him, gave a little wave. Damiskos couldn't keep a stupid smile off his face. Entirely unprofessional. Of course one could be happy to see that a comrade had come through unharmed, but a curt nod of acknowledgement should be enough; you didn't stand smiling fondly up at the fellow.

Varazda pointed to himself and gestured up, over the

balcony rail, then pointed at Damiskos and made a catching motion. Now Damiskos nodded, but it still couldn't have been called curt. The idea of catching Varazda when he dropped from a railing suggested midnight assignations and romantic fiction more than escape from a reconnaissance mission gone wrong.

Varazda swung himself lithely over the railing, glanced over his shoulder, and let go with a nicely-judged little jump so that he fell clear of the floor of the gallery. Damiskos caught him by the waist and set him lightly on his feet.

Damiskos's senses were full of Varazda for a moment: the scent of his perfume, the soft fabric of his clothes, the muscles of his little waist under Damiskos's palms. The twin swords still tucked through his sash at his back, their bronze blades whispering over the fabric of Damiskos's tunic.

It took him a moment—much longer than it should have—to realize that Varazda had been spotted from the other side of the atrium when he jumped.

"Get the Sasian! Block the door! Don't let him out!" Helenos was leaning over the railing opposite, shouting wildly to the fishermen below.

"To your room?" Varazda suggested, looking across the atrium.

Damiskos nodded.

The fishermen were moving reluctantly toward the entrance; Damiskos was confident he could have ploughed through them, but likely not without injuring or killing one of them.

He strode out into the atrium, drawing his sword, keeping his eye on the fishermen. Behind him, Varazda darted across the room, leaping over the pool in the centre, and drew up short as something fell from the gallery and thudded on the tiles in front of him.

Damiskos glanced over. It was Gelon. He lay stunned on

the atrium floor, and Varazda stood frozen in front of him, looking like he'd come within a hairsbreadth of being hit.

"Move!" Damiskos called. "Leave him!"

Before Varazda had a chance to comply, Gelon had recovered enough to roll over onto his side, clutching his arm and howling in pain. Damiskos whirled around at the sound of footsteps in heavy boots tramping in from the portico.

It was the porter, Sesna, a bald, bronze-skinned man with ropy muscles in his arms, and his cronies, all built much the same way. They were all armed. The underlings had clubs in their belts, but Sesna had a blade, a broad, heavy cutlass of the type equally good for hacking through brush and felling your enemies.

"The Sasian!" Helenos shouted again. "Get! Him! *Now!*"

The porters wheeled toward Varazda. Damiskos changed course, caught his right foot on the lip of the pool, and stumbled. Varazda turned and drew his swords.

Sesna swung at him, artlessly but forcefully, with the cutlass. Varazda parried beautifully with one blade, swung the other in the same direction, stepping to the side, and hit the porter hard across the ribs. It might have been a killing blow if the sword had been sharp.

Damiskos plunged forward in time to catch the raised club of one of the flunkies against his own sword, throwing the man backward to trip over Gelon, still writhing and groaning on the floor.

Sesna was still on his feet, Damiskos saw out of the corner of his eye. Varazda dodged another heavy slice from the cutlass, but missed when he swung at Sesna in his turn.

One of the fishermen splashed up through the pool behind Varazda with a big rope-splicing spike in his fist. Damiskos swung away from the porters to lunge at the fisherman, catching him in the shoulder. He heard the spike clatter onto the tiles of the pool and the man howl in pain, but he had turned his attention back to the porters. One of them was swinging a club at Varazda from the far side. Damiskos shouted a warning, and Varazda dodged. His hair had come down, falling around his face.

Damiskos stepped past him to slash at the wrist of the porter, making him drop his club. There was a crash and a ringing clang as Sesna knocked one of Varazda's swords out of his hand, and it hit the floor.

Damiskos spun, lunged under Sesna's upraised sword arm, and stabbed him in the gut. Jerking his sword free as the man stumbled back, he reached for Varazda, hauling him up by the arm from where he was stooping to retrieve his dropped blade, and ran for the door of his room.

They made it through the door, which Damiskos bolted quickly behind them, across the room, and up onto the bed. The only sounds that followed them were confused shouts and groans from the atrium, no running feet.

Varazda's hands were shaking so badly that it took him two tries to get his swords stowed back in his sash. Damiskos, having sheathed his own sword, grasped the windowsill and pulled himself up and out, then turned and reached back to help Varazda. He could no doubt have made it without help, but he didn't refuse it.

Only after he had pulled Varazda up did Damiskos notice that he had landed on his saddlebags, lying on the roof tiles where he had left them earlier. He slung them over a shoulder, and he and Varazda clattered across the roof to drop down into the little yard beside the kitchen. From here, it was just a matter of vaulting a low wall, and they were in the kitchen garden.

Damiskos was still riding the flood of exhilaration that followed a fight—his first real combat in years—but Varazda had stopped on the far side of the wall and simply folded at the knees, hitting the ground in a barely-controlled fall, and leaned forward to be sick between the rosemary bushes.

Damiskos got awkwardly down onto the ground beside

him. He rummaged in his saddlebags for the half-full flask of the soldiers' drink of water and vinegar that he knew was in there. The sort of bracing words that he might have said to a new recruit after his first engagement almost came out of his mouth. Before they could, it occurred to him that this was not Varazda's first taste of battle. He must have been taken prisoner as a child in one of the complex clan wars of the Deshan Coast. This wasn't about the shock of the unfamiliar, but about memories of the past. Damiskos offered the flask and said nothing.

CHAPTER 19

VARAZDA TOOK a few swallows from the flask and passed it back without comment. He levered himself up to his feet.

"We'd better press on," he said tonelessly.

"Yes."

They picked their way to the bottom of the garden. The clouds were over the moon again, and they both trod on onions and nearly tripped. They got over the wall and back into the vineyard.

Damiskos paused, holding up a hand for Varazda to wait. He listened, straining for any sounds of pursuit. There was nothing.

"I don't think they're following us," he said finally. "But let's lie low in the vineyard for a little so that if they do come after us, we won't be out in the open. And we can take a rest. Let's get down a few terraces, find a hidden corner, and just sit."

He rather expected Varazda to protest, and wasn't going to press the matter if he did. It wasn't as if he thought either of them would have trouble making it back to the camp on the beach; it was all downhill, and he himself was feeling rather energetic. It was just that in Varazda's position—and he'd been in Varazda's position—he would have appreciated a little time to collect himself before seeing other people.

Varazda blew out a breath. "That's a good idea."

They descended four stone stairways and made their way to the far end of the terrace, where the vines ended and the gravelly soil was overgrown with grass and overhung by branches from the encroaching trees, making a sheltered nook. They waited warily in the shadows, still listening for signs of pursuit, but the vineyard was quiet around them.

"I think we're safe," said Damiskos.

He dumped his saddlebags on the ground and sat, leaning back against them and stretching out his lame leg, the other knee bent. He thought about taking off his boots, but there was still the possibility of pursuit from the villa.

Varazda drew the swords out of his sash and set them aside to drop down cross-legged on the grass. He did take off his shoes. He was looking a little steadier, but not his usual self yet. He unwound his sash and bundled it up, knotting it around the scrolls and the shell portrait of his daughter. He looked up at Damiskos, whose gaze he had been quietly avoiding.

"How are you doing?" Damiskos asked.

"Oh. Uh." He raked a hand through his hair. "I'll be all right, I think. Thank you for … " He made a vague gesture. "Everything."

"Of course. Would you like … " He didn't know how to make the offer, didn't even know exactly what he was offering. He held out a hand.

Varazda looked at him for a moment, then seemed to make up his own mind about what the offer meant. He nodded.

He moved to sit in front of Damiskos, leaning back against him. Damiskos wrapped his arms around him, and Varazda sank back into his embrace, his body loosening, relaxing.

"Oh, Dami. *Thank you.*"

Damiskos kissed into the soft, tangled waves of Varazda's hair and tightened his hold. "No trouble at all."

They sat like that for a long while. The clouds slid away from the moon again, silvering the vines with their heavy bunches of grapes. A pleasant breeze moved across the terrace. Still there were no sounds from the villa. Varazda's body was a warm weight against Damiskos's chest, one wrist lying across Damiskos's thigh, wholly at ease now. Damiskos could feel him breathing, softly and evenly, and wondered whether he was asleep.

"Do you mind if I call you Dami?"

Apparently he wasn't asleep.

"You can call me anything you like. First Spear, Dami, whatever."

Varazda laughed slightly. He did sound a little sleepy. "I don't have any nicknames myself—just so you know."

"Yes, you do. I heard the girls down on the beach calling you Phari."

"Oh, well. They just made that up. Nobody calls me that at home. Anyway, I like that you can pronounce my real name."

"Me too."

They sat still a moment longer.

"This is … this is nice," said Varazda finally. He sounded … Damiskos couldn't quite place it at first. A little embarrassed? "I feel much better. Actually, I feel a little … "

He shifted in Damiskos's arms, arching his back slightly, his hand trailing featherlight over Damiskos's thigh.

Oh.

"That's normal, actually," Damiskos said softly, lips brushing over Varazda's hair. "You get a sort of rush in battle, and then when it's over—if you're not completely exhausted —it's got to go somewhere."

"And that's where it goes?"

"Often."

"Mm. I don't think it's that at all. I think it's just *you*."

Damiskos laughed. "Sure."

He was hard as a rock himself—had been since before he invited Varazda into his arms—but he hadn't expected any relief. Truthfully, he wasn't even bothered by that. It was all about what Varazda wanted in that moment. But if what Varazda wanted was … well.

He gathered up the hem of Varazda's shirt in one hand, pulling it up, and with the other stroked firmly over Varazda's flat, tight stomach, letting his fingertips dip down under the upper edge of Varazda's trousers.

Varazda gave a sobbing gasp, a beautiful sound that shot through Damiskos like a pang of hunger. One lovely hennaed hand curled in Damiskos's hair, the other clutched at his thigh. Damiskos went on stroking, slow and warm and simple, pushing his fingers a little further under the fabric of Varazda's trousers, until they brushed the curls of hair that went straight across, like a woman's.

He wanted to find every place where Varazda liked to be touched. He had always imagined himself a reasonably good lover, patient and attentive when he needed to be. He wanted to be better than he had ever been before, to find things to do to Varazda that Varazda hadn't even known he wanted.

He slid his left hand over Varazda's belly, lifting his right hand away to unfasten the buttons of his shirt. This left him free to explore the smooth planes of Varazda's chest, silver-white in the moonlight. He let his hands roam above and below, over slim pectoral muscles and tight nipples, up over Varazda's white, exposed throat, down to trace the subtle V that delineated his abdomen. And here, improbably, was that calm joy that Damiskos had felt eluding him earlier: sinking into this moment, giving pleasure like a gift.

Varazda was much quieter than the first time, almost withdrawn in his pleasure, eyes closed, biting his lower lip.

But the soft sounds he did make were enough to convince Damiskos that he was enjoying everything so far.

"Will you sit up for me so I can take your shirt off?" Damiskos whispered presently. "If you'd like that, I mean."

Varazda rolled forward pliantly, sweeping his hair out of the way. Damiskos peeled his shirt back over marble-white shoulders and down lithe, lightly muscled arms, exposing the beautifully tapering lines of his back. He ran his fingers gently in under Varazda's hair, lifting it, and kissed the back of his neck lightly. That won him a shiver, so he carried on, skimming his lips over Varazda's shoulder, the curve of his ear, darting out his tongue. That made Varazda giggle, so he did it again.

With another lover, Damiskos might have offered compliments at this point—he was not poetic, but he could articulate some simple praise of a beautiful body. But he didn't think Varazda wanted compliments, or words at all, really.

He pulled Varazda back to lie against him as before. He slipped his hand all the way down into the front of Varazda's trousers, where he found Varazda already hard, his hips thrusting up in a little wriggle to rub his cock against Damiskos's palm.

There was a special pleasure in touching under clothing —Damiskos had learned that in Zash, where everyone wore so much *more* clothing—so he took his time again, teasing Varazda with light touches, fingers stroking the crease between thigh and crotch, lips soft on the side of his neck.

"Aren't you … " Apparently Varazda couldn't stand it any longer. "If you want to … "

"I'm fine," said Damiskos truthfully. "What do *you* want?"

Varazda rested his hand on Damiskos's through the fabric of his trousers, stilling his fingers on a silky thigh. He was leaning back against Damiskos's shoulder again. He seemed to give the question some thought.

"I'd like to feel you naked against me," he said finally. He pressed his face into Damiskos's neck, and Damiskos could feel the blush warming his cheeks.

"I'd like that too."

Varazda unfastened his trousers and shimmied neatly out of them. He twisted around to unbuckle Damiskos's belt.

Damiskos wished he had taken his boots off after all. Even with Varazda helping, it was a much more awkward and less alluring process getting him out of his clothes than it had been for Varazda to get out of his.

Varazda didn't seem to mind. He settled in Damiskos's arms again, rubbing his cheek a little tentatively against the hair on Damiskos's chest. Damiskos stroked the curve of his hip, circling his thumb around the soft hollow created by the muscles of his flank. Varazda's fingers moved over the inside of Damiskos's thigh.

"You probably need ... " Varazda began, trailing a finger lightly up the hot length of Damiskos's cock.

Damiskos couldn't help catching his breath sharply, but he whispered back, "I don't need anything that doesn't make you happy."

Varazda didn't seem to know what to say to that, and somehow Damiskos liked that, liked that he didn't resort to an easy answer—"I'm sure I'd like anything you'd like," or "It would make *me* happy to make *you* happy"—when it wouldn't have been true.

"Here, I've an idea," Damiskos said. "I like this a lot, and you might too."

He wrapped his arms around Varazda, gently gathering him up and moving him down to lie on his side, still with Damiskos at his back. Then Damiskos reached around into his saddlebag for the oil that he used on his sword belt and his horse's harness. He poured a little into his palm.

"Tell me if you don't like it, all right?"

"Mm," said Varazda noncommittally. He lay with his head pillowed on his arm, trustingly not watching what Damiskos was doing.

Damiskos parted Varazda's white thighs and rubbed his oiled hand between them, anointing the soft skin above and below, his touch intimate and careful. He could feel Varazda tense, but without pulling away or making a sound. He carefully avoided letting his fingers touch the firm curve of Varazda's ass. Withdrawing his hand, he lay down again on his side, bringing their bodies together, holding Varazda for a long, comfortable moment before he rubbed the tip of his cock against the slicked crease between Varazda's legs.

Pleasure flooded him like strong drink, fiery and sweet; he felt drunk, dazed with it. He felt as if his body would fly apart, disintegrate, unless he clasped Varazda tighter.

Varazda reached around to spread his fingers on Damiskos's hip, pulling him in closer, and Damiskos sank into silky heat, pressing deeper, his body flexing against the warm alabaster of Varazda's. Belatedly, he remembered to put his hand down to envelope Varazda's cock in his slick palm. Varazda cried out, pushing back and moving against him in tight undulations, the muscles of his thighs gripping Damiskos's cock and grinding it against the sensitive skin of the place where Varazda's legs met. Damiskos buried his face in the side of Varazda's neck and groaned.

He felt fused with Varazda, twined like the strands of steel in a sword-blade. They moved together, slow and hot, held in a kind of tension for as long as they could manage, luxuriating in the simplicity and the aching insufficiency of their union. At last Damiskos came in a long moment like a shower of sparks. Varazda's body arched and tensed against his as he came too.

They lay panting, loosely clasped together, for a languid

minute before rolling apart. Varazda turned his head to look at Damiskos. His face was flushed.

"Do you really like that?" he asked. "That type of … whatever you call that."

"Love it. Why?"

Varazda thought for a moment. "It's so easy. Not painful. Doesn't taste bad."

"It's also easier on my leg, to lie side-by-side like that."

"I guess it would be."

Varazda was silent for another moment, looking up at the sky, then he pushed up onto one elbow, looking down at Damiskos. His hair fell down to caress Damiskos's shoulder.

"I'm sorry—" he began gently.

"That you're not being more romantic?" Damiskos finished for him. Keep it light, he reminded himself. "I *had* noticed that."

Varazda's face stilled briefly, then he smiled. "It was utterly lovely, Dami. It almost … " He ran a hand down over his own thigh. "Almost made me feel like a woman."

"Is that good?" From Varazda's expression, it looked like it was.

"Sometimes. Yes."

"Interesting."

Damiskos reached up and brushed his fingertips over the gold flower stud, the woman's decoration that Varazda always wore. Varazda kissed softly into his palm.

"Is it odd?" Varazda asked.

"What? That you wear that? No! It suits you. That and the henna, and the way you braid your hair sometimes—it's subtle, I don't know how to describe it."

Varazda had settled beside him, head propped on one hand, the other one spread on Damiskos's chest. "It's a way of making myself feel whole. Balanced. In a way it fills up the space of the manhood I'll never have."

"Oh, I see," said Damiskos, enlightened. "You don't want to be *neither*, so you're *both*."

Varazda smiled. "Something like that. I can pass myself off as an actual woman, too, when I want to—but that's different. That's dressing up. It's fun, but I don't do it often."

"I'd like to see that. I can't quite picture it."

Varazda looked amused.

"I'll tell you a secret," he said. "I think this masculine-feminine thing isn't just because I'm a eunuch. I think I would have been like this—sort of wanting to be both—even if I'd grown up as a whole man. But I might not have known what to do with it."

Damiskos touched the soft curtain of Varazda's hair, trying to think of something light and easy to say in response to that. Because it suddenly made all his longing for an impossible future return in full force. This beautiful person, who dwelt so gracefully in the space between man and woman, who had never been made love to properly and yet was everything Damiskos desired—he wanted to have him, to keep him, to belong to him.

"I see," he said. "Or wait, no—this is where you say, 'Do you really?' and I swear at you."

"We can skip that, if you want." Varazda looked down at Damiskos for a moment. "Dami, you're a serious man. I know that. You don't have to joke when you don't feel like it."

That undid Damiskos completely. He put a hand over his eyes, trying to swallow all the things he wanted to say. But he couldn't. He drew the hand away again.

"What am I going to do when you go back to Boukos and leave me?" The words could have been light, almost joking, but they were not; his voice shook as he spoke, and he knew he sounded anguished.

Varazda went very still, but this time it was not, Damiskos could tell, because he was offended.

"I've never had a love affair," Varazda said finally. "Not even close. I'd never had sex for pleasure before the other night, with you. I ... I'm completely at sea here."

Damiskos didn't know what he'd expected. Maybe some part of him had harboured a hope that if he told Varazda how he felt, Varazda would respond that he felt exactly the same, that Damiskos had unlocked some secret place in his heart and they would somehow be together forever. Or at least, failing that, Varazda would laugh and tell him not to dream, because Varazda had the courage to face reality, the courage Damiskos lacked.

Instead Varazda had just responded honestly. He wasn't in love with Damiskos; he didn't know how to be, didn't know what to do with the fact that Damiskos was in love with him.

"I'm not asking anything of you," Damiskos said. "Don't think that, please."

"No, I understand. There isn't really anything you could ask that I'd say 'yes' to, is there? Ah, God, that sounds harsh, but you know what I mean."

"Yes."

"I like you a lot. If I'm honest, I've liked you since you got here. You're my type, in any number of ways. That's probably why my clever schemes to get myself out of trouble all involved kissing you, much as I told myself that was the last thing I wanted. But ... I do have to go back to Boukos."

"I know. I know. You have a life and a family there. It's your home, your republic. I'm glad you have all that." Tears stung behind his eyes and in his throat.

Varazda smiled rather sadly. "You must have ... What do you have to go back to in Pheme?"

The pressure of the tears eased after a moment. "Uh. Well. My job. It's not a bad job. It's interesting. But I've been doing it almost five years, and I haven't been promoted. There's nowhere to be promoted to, until my commanding officer retires. And I was fucking First Spear of the Second Koryphos. I don't care about the status, but I'm capable of doing more than bargaining for olive oil and fish sauce contracts. I just—I like to feel useful, and at one time I really was." He drew a deep breath and let it out shakily.

He went on: "And there's my family. My little brother's serving in the colonies now, and my parents and I don't see eye-to-eye anymore. I try to keep my distance—to be filial, you know, but not … not be in their lives too much, because it just makes everyone upset.

"I spent my savings outfitting Timiskos—that's my brother—when he went into the legions. Our parents couldn't afford to do it. They could when I enlisted myself, but that was before they lost all their money. Not in any kind of tragedy—they just began living beyond their means. They still do, even though they lost the house and live in a rented place now. I try to help out, but I don't live with them—I couldn't stand it any longer, watching them dig themselves deeper into debt. I had to move out and rent a place by myself. It's one room, all I can afford. I'd like to m-marry— or I thought I did, before I met you—but I haven't got the money." His voice gave out, and he stopped speaking.

"Shit, Dami. What a shambles."

"Oh, no. Other people endure much worse."

"Yes, that's always such a comforting line to take."

"I shouldn't complain of these things to you, Varazda."

"You're not complaining of them, you're just dispassionately listing them. It actually makes it worse."

"I'm sorry. That wasn't what I intended. I meant … you've—you lost so much yourself, and … the strength it must have taken to build the life you have now … "

"That doesn't mean I can't be sympathetic. I think … you've seen a side of me that's not usually much in evidence these days."

"Um … yes."

Varazda laughed. "I don't mean the, um, the sex. I mean the anger. I'm not usually so angry any more. It was having to pretend to be a slave again—which, let me hasten to add, was *my own idea*—that was harder than I would have expected. That's why I was so prickly when we first met. In truth, I'm generally much happier these days."

"I do admire the angry Varazda," Damiskos said, feeling a little shy about it, "but I think … it's mostly the happy one I've fallen in love with."

Varazda gave no response in words, but he leaned over and kissed Damiskos softly.

CHAPTER 20

THEY LAY QUIETLY under the stars on the grassy gravel of their little corner of the vineyard. Soon they would need to get up and return to the women's camp. It was plain no one was coming after them from the villa; the students were probably still too busy fighting among themselves.

Varazda seemed in no hurry to get up and dress, which Damiskos had expected he might be, embarrassed after Damiskos's confession.

"Do you ever think about going back to Zash?" Varazda asked presently. "It sounds as if you were happy there."

"Yes, I was. But no, I don't. Zash was done with me. I miss it, though. Do you?"

"Miss Zash? Of course." He smiled faintly. "I miss the palace at Gudul. I miss my friends there, and riding in the mountains, and trivial things, food that you can't get in Boukos, that kind of thing. And I miss my childhood home, which was burned to the ground, and my mother and brothers, who are long dead. Even if there were a way for me to go back to Zash without losing my freedom—and there isn't—I wouldn't want to. Boukos is home now." After a moment he said, "I guess you could say Zash was done with me too, though in a different way."

Damiskos felt he ought to explain. "What I meant by that … "

"Oh, I know what you meant by it. That is—if you want to tell me about it, I will be happy to listen, but if you don't … I was the son of a Deshan warlord. I know how you get a limp like that. I've seen it done."

Damiskos absorbed that piece of information. Varazda knew, or at least had suspected. Whatever regard he had for Damiskos had included that truth already—for good or ill.

"And that first night, when you arrived here," Varazda added gently, "one of the idiots was talking about Zashian punishments, and I thought I saw something in your face for a moment."

Damiskos linked his fingers behind his head and looked up at the dark sky. "You probably did. But I don't find it all that difficult to talk about. Sometimes I *want* to tell people, because they all assume it's a battlefield injury and that it was all very heroic, and … it wasn't."

"Were you actually enslaved?"

"No. I can't claim to understand what that's like. What happened to me was … It was in the year '93—you'd already have been in Boukos by then."

"Yes."

"That was when I made First Spear. I replaced a man who deserted. This was just after I broke off my engagement—it felt like a consolation prize from the gods, to be honest. But I inherited a mess. We were in the middle of the worst clan fighting the Deshan Coast had seen in decades.

"Most of my first year—my only year—in command we spent dealing with this one warlord, Abadoka. He gave us so much trouble. Burning farms, harassing our allies, breaking treaties for no reason. We had a couple of skirmishes with his men and finally hit him hard enough that he agreed to sit down for a parlay with me. At least … I thought we'd hit him hard enough. It turned out he was nursing a grudge—our former First Spear, the man I'd replaced, had been in Abadoka's pay, and Abadoka didn't understand why I hadn't come to bend the knee to him yet. When I said I didn't plan to, he violated the terms of our truce, slit the throats of the men who had come with me, and took me prisoner.

"He tried a bit of persuasion … You don't need me to tell you about that. I'm reasonably stubborn, so that was a dead end. Then he decided to make an example of me, to show my commander that I'd been his creature and betrayed him. Breaking my legs like a runaway slave was meant as some sort of symbolism."

"Angels of the Almighty. It didn't work at all, did it? Nobody believed you'd been in his pay?"

"No. Everyone knew what kind of a vicious shit Abadoka was. It was a shameful failure on my part—my men were killed, and we lost any advantage we'd had with Abadoka—but I wasn't turned off in disgrace. I was able to retire with honour. I felt it was more than I deserved. I felt … like a jilted lover. As if this country I'd come to love had rejected me. I'd no right to feel that way—it's not my country, I was there as part of a barely-tolerated foreign army, but … " He trailed off hopelessly.

"Oh, Dami. I'm so sorry."

"I'm lucky I can still walk as well as I can. My left knee healed completely—it hardly ever hurts."

Varazda turned on his side again, laying his hand lightly on Damiskos's arm. He made no more contact than that, and Damiskos wondered if that was because he was wary now that he'd realized how attached this man had become who'd slept with him all of twice.

It was true that Damiskos didn't find it difficult to speak about what had happened. In some ways it helped to rehearse it in clear, unemotional terms. The things that would plunge him back into the memories were different: sounds or smells or the feeling of having his hands tied behind his back.

He thought back on some of the things that didn't bother him. He remembered Abadoka's stronghold—the first one, the one they had taken, not the one where he had been held prisoner—with the dark forest of the Vanesh encroaching on two sides. Suddenly something slid into place in his mind.

He pushed himself up to a sitting position. Varazda came with him, startled, hand clasping his arm.

"I just had a thought," Damiskos said. "Were you old enough to remember the capture of Sumuz?"

Varazda let go of his arm and gave him a mystified look. "Sort of. I remember riding past Sumuz with my brothers shortly after it changed hands and seeing red flags flying. But the details I didn't hear about until years later. The subterfuge with the … " He stopped, closed his mouth for a moment, then said, "Dami. You're not thinking what I think you're thinking. Are you?"

"I don't know. What do you think I think I'm thinking?"

"That we could pull off something like the capture of Sumuz at Nione's villa. You *are* thinking that."

"I've actually done something like it before. It was one of the first blows I struck against Abadoka—that's what made me think of it. I took great pleasure in using one of his countrymen's famous tricks against him. The terrain here is different, but that would actually make it easier—and we don't have a legion, which would make it harder—but we're not trying to take a stronghold garrisoned with trained men-at-arms, we're trying to retake a country house from a bunch of fishermen and philosophers. I likely killed their best fighter, and their second-best has a broken arm. They've lost their two high-status hostages, and I'd bet they wouldn't even think to use the slaves as leverage—they put too low a value on slaves' lives themselves to think that they could make worthwhile hostages. I think we could do it."

"Look at you. This is what the poets mean when they say someone has 'a glint in his eye,' isn't it?"

"Probably."

"I think if anyone could pull this off, Dami, it's you."

They dressed, Damiskos in a clean tunic from his luggage, and retraced their steps. When they finally came back, loaded with the items they had returned to pick up, they took the rest of the stairs down through the vineyard and the path to the beach at a leisurely pace. Damiskos felt easier now, almost content. He was glad he had told Varazda how he felt, even if in the long run it wouldn't make any material difference.

Varazda was treating him a little differently—with a touch of a kind of careful affection—but it was a subtle thing.

"When I told Aradne that we are not a couple this morning," Varazda said from behind Damiskos, as they neared the end of the path, "that must have hurt you. I am sorry."

"Oh, that's all right. It is true, after all."

"Not because we want it to be true, though—and I needn't have made it sound as if I did."

The camp was still half-awake when they returned, the children and some of the women asleep inside the beach huts while others sat around a small fire they had built inside the fortifications. Aradne and one of the vineyard workers hurried to open the gate for Damiskos and Varazda to enter, and Nione got to her feet and came around the fire to embrace them both. They set down their bundles and returned her embrace.

"We were worried about you both when you were gone so long," she said.

"We had some difficulty getting out," said Damiskos. "And then we went back for some things."

"We dawdled," said Varazda at the same time. "I'm— we're—sorry."

He shot Damiskos a guilty look, and Damiskos felt like a bad influence.

"Damiskos has had an idea," Varazda went on. "You've got to hear it. It's utterly mad."

"Here's what it is," said Damiskos, when they were all sitting around the fire. "We've set the signal for the postal ship from Boukos, so it should stop here some time tomorrow morning. They may well see that from the villa—it works to our advantage if they do, because I propose we go up and knock at the door and tell them that a band of crack Zashian mercenaries has arrived from Boukos on that ship, has the villa surrounded, and demands their immediate surrender."

"And," said Aradne into the stunned silence that followed, "they'll believe this because … "

"Because when they look out from the signal tower, they'll catch glimpses through the trees of riders in Zashian clothes, they'll see the glint of sun on weapons, they'll hear strange, unintelligible shouts and signals, see foliage swaying as the Zashian forces marshal just out of sight."

"Oh!" Aradne cried, all but bouncing up from the sand with a girlish delight that was equal parts endearing and alarming. "It's a ruse! It's like how they captured that place, Sou … Sou-something, in Sasia."

"Sumuz," Varazda supplied. "How do you know about that?"

"Someone told me the story. Oh, we must do it, Nione. It will be such fun."

"Fun?" Nione repeated, giving Aradne an incredulous look.

"Fun," Aradne repeated. "What did you bring back with you from the house?" she asked, turning back to Damiskos and Varazda.

"Mostly Varazda's clothes," said Damiskos with a grin. "Fortunately he doesn't travel light. We've got some of the grooms on our side as well—we talked to them about the plan."

They had gone back into the slave quarters, ransacked Varazda's room for anything useable, and done some plotting with the four remaining slaves, who had been nearly beside themselves with eagerness to help.

"So do we have your permission, Nione?" Damiskos asked.

"Wait," said Eurydemos, holding up a hand. "What are you proposing to do?"

"We're going to pretend to be Zashian soldiers," said Aradne, as if addressing a child she didn't like very much.

"But surely," said Eurydemos, "it is nothing more than a cowardly trick. Can such a thing be compatible with honour?"

"Is that really of primary importance, Eurydemos?" Nione cut in before either Aradne or Damiskos could answer.

"No, no," the philosopher conceded easily, but with a kind of superior tone that Damiskos found grating. "I merely raise it as an interesting point."

"I'm sure it is," said Nione, "on some level. But as this isn't a philosophical debate, I think we can set that aside."

"Of course, of course," said Eurydemos.

"Actually," said Damiskos, "let's not. Because I have an answer for that question. Honour is a matter of deeds in the world—it isn't something you can make up in your own head. You can't take away my honour by thinking I don't deserve it—that's not how it works.

"Now. I led a manoeuvre very like the capture of Sumuz, in the Zashian year 993, when I was First Spear. I had my company of a hundred, and I was waiting for my subordinates to arrive with their men, but there'd been a rockslide and they couldn't get through the mountain pass to reach us. The stronghold we were intending to besiege was fully garrisoned, and it was only a matter of time before they realized our reinforcements weren't coming and made a sally to attack us.

"I massed most of my men in front of the stronghold, sent a couple of parties through the woods surrounding the other sides, making a lot of noise and hanging helmets on trees and so on—exactly the same strategy as Sumuz. The defenders fell for it, we captured the stronghold with minimal bloodshed, and—" He held up his right wrist, indicating the bronze bracelet of the Second Koryphos. "My honour is intact. It's no more a cowardly trick than feinting in a sword-fight, moving left when you're going to cut right."

"Ah-yah," said Varazda under his breath. It was what Zashians sometimes shouted instead of clapping or whistling. Damiskos flashed him a smile.

Eurydemos nodded serenely, his superior look still in place. Damiskos didn't care; he hadn't really expected to convince the man. He just thought Nione and Aradne and the other women deserved to know that what they were proposing to do was something even the Phemian army wouldn't have thought dishonourable.

"Very well," said Nione. "What do we need to do first?"

"I seem to spend all my time these days listening to you strategize," said Varazda drowsily.

He lay in the sand with his head in Damiskos's lap. They were alone at the nearly extinct campfire now. It was extremely late.

"Getting tired of it, are you?"

"No," said Varazda. "I love it."

He settled himself more comfortably against Damiskos's

thigh and mumbled something about getting up. After a minute or two Damiskos could tell that he was asleep.

Eurydemos, who had gone around behind the beach huts earlier, returned to the fire at that point, hitching up his mantle, dashing Damiskos's hope that he had intended to sleep somewhere else.

"We are exiled out here, I take it?" Eurydemos said as he sat in the sand beside Damiskos.

Damiskos smiled politely, looking down at Varazda in a pointed way that he hoped would cause Eurydemos to be quiet.

It didn't. Eurydemos just looked at Varazda and sighed. "I do envy you, Damiskos. You have achieved what I so desire. But do not worry—I would not dream of asking if you would be willing to share."

"Good," said Damiskos stonily. "Because that would be up to him, really."

Eurydemos looked at him as, Damiskos imagined, he might have looked at a student who had presented an interesting but rather outrageous argument in a debate. For all that his students had abandoned him, Damiskos thought, he really was almost as much of a swine as they were.

Damiskos opened his mouth to say something about letting Varazda sleep, but Eurydemos got in first.

"You know how much I have sacrificed to my desire. If I had been better able to conceal it, I might have kept the respect of my students longer." He sighed. "And yet it is entirely unjust. You understand. Desiring a creature like him, neither woman nor man, that does not make either of us a degenerate. If anything, we have more refined tastes, able to appreciate such rare, fragile loveliness. While others see something contrary to nature, what I see is a product of civilization, a work of art almost. Cruelty is always inherent in the great work of art—the cruelty of deception, the statue that fools the eye into seeing a living form, the tale that beguiles us without being true. Just as he beguiles and deceives, blending the forms of male and female—without the frailties of womankind or the virtues of a man."

"I think you should go sit somewhere else," Damiskos cut him off finally. "If you keep talking, I'm going to punch you in the mouth."

Eurydemos blinked at him, genuinely surprised, but he did get up, with a muttered apology, and took himself away as far as the other side of the fire pit, where he lay down with his back to Damiskos.

Varazda showed no sign of having woken to hear any of that. Damiskos was glad, though it wasn't much of a comfort. Varazda had probably heard things like that before. He was probably used to Pseuchaian men rhapsodizing about his dual nature and how he lacked womanly this and manly that.

What bothered Damiskos was the thought that some of what Eurydemos had said might not be utter bullshit. He was right that Varazda wasn't "contrary to nature." And Varazda *had* been physically shaped for a particular civilization that had a use for people they could classify as not-quite-men. Of course there wasn't anything wrong with finding him attractive; Damiskos didn't think there was anything wrong with finding *anyone* attractive. But what about the rest of it?

Eurydemos was a bloviating asshole who thought Varazda especially desirable. Damiskos found Varazda desirable too. Did that make him an asshole? Was he doing without meaning to what Eurydemos was doing very consciously: thinking of Varazda as a beautiful *thing*?

It bothered him as he tried to fall asleep, and he slept badly, thinking of this every time he woke. Was this the real reason why Varazda couldn't return his love? Because it wasn't love at all, just fetish—a worship of his body as if he were a work of art? He didn't *think* so, but would he know, if it were so? He wasn't a philosopher.

Part of the reason he didn't sleep well was because Varazda was a very restless sleeper. The position Damiskos had tried to adopt when he settled down to sleep himself, curled around Varazda, leaving Varazda's head pillowed on his thigh, meant that every time Varazda flung out an arm or stretched or rolled over in his sleep, one or both of them would wake at the resulting collision. Eventually Varazda got up and went in to sleep with the women, leaving Damiskos with the blanket they had been awkwardly sharing.

CHAPTER 21

Damiskos was woken by a shriek. He bolted upright in the sand to find that it was fully light, and their stronghold was under siege again.

"Don't you tell me what to do, you—you—you harpy!" one of the women wailed behind him.

Another gave an outraged gasp. "*What* did you just call me?"

"Girls, girls!" Nione cried, literally wringing her hands. "Please, you mustn't fight like this."

Damiskos suppressed a grin as he realized what was going on. They were putting into practice his strategy to make the enemy think they were on the verge of mutiny. They were doing it beautifully.

He got to his feet, looking out at the besieging force, which consisted of most of the fishermen, some of the porters, and the broken-nosed student. They were armed with clubs and kitchen knives, but they didn't look particularly eager to approach.

"Silence!" Aradne roared from the doorway of the nearest beach hut. "Inside, all of you! Now! You, soldier, make yourself useful, can't you?"

The women scurried meekly into the huts, stones in their hands and bundled into their skirts. Damiskos joined Aradne in the doorway.

"Sorry about that," she murmured. She had Damiskos's hunting bow in her hand and its quiver slung across her back. "Wanted to make it look good."

"No, not all. I'm impressed."

Varazda stood inside the hut, his swords under one arm. "Morning," he said brightly.

They stepped out of the doorway together, once all the women were inside. Damiskos drew his sword and rolled his shoulders. Varazda swung one of his swords in a couple of lazy arcs, the bronze catching the early-morning sunlight. Aradne lifted the bow and nocked an arrow with convincing form.

"Something you men want?" Damiskos called out.

Two of the fishermen were backing away already.

"By all the gods," the broken-nosed student growled, "I wish we'd drowned you when we had the chance. You're a disgrace to the legions, consorting with barbarians and slaves."

One of the remaining fishermen lost his nerve completely and turned to pelt back along the beach. The porters, to show they were made of tougher stuff, swaggered closer.

"I'm sorry," said Damiskos, "did you come to parlay, or ... Because you don't seem to be doing anything else."

"I'm here to speak to ex-Maiden Nione Kukara."

After a moment, Nione peeked out from among her women, doing a lovely job of appearing cowed and terrified.

The student jerked his chin disdainfully. "Hiding behind your slaves, I see. You've every right. But you're lucky they're loyal. It would be a shame if anything happened to shake that loyalty, wouldn't it? I can't guarantee it, though. The longer you hold out here, the more chance something might happen that you'll regret."

Varazda leaned toward Aradne to whisper something, and she lifted Damiskos's bow, pointing the arrow up, hauled back on the bowstring, and released it, sending the arrow soaring up and tumbling down in a sharp arc on the other side of the barricade, narrowly missing one of the porters.

Their bravado dissipated quickly after that. "Where the fuck did she learn to use a bow?" one of them yelped as they backed away from the stronghold. A couple of women emerged from the beach huts to fling stones, and the men hurried away.

"What was *that* about?" one of the women asked scornfully.

"Just bluster," said Rhea. "That's all they have."

Damiskos turned to the others.

"We need to act right away. I was wrong. They are going to use the male slaves as leverage. That's what he meant about shaking your loyalty. He's thinking you might be induced to switch sides to save your fellow slaves."

A hush, and then a murmur of alarm ran through the group. Some of the male slaves were the fathers of the female slaves' children. Some of them were their sons.

"I will not let that happen," said Nione fiercely. "What do we have to do?"

"All we can do," said Damiskos. "Get everything set up, and pray the postal ship arrives on time."

"Better go out and pick up that arrow," said Aradne, handing Damiskos back his bow and quiver. "Did you know you've only got two good ones in there? The rest are broken."

"I know." He had checked his equipment after arriving at the camp, and guessed that the arrows had been broken in their escape from the villa, when he fell on the saddlebags on the roof. "I don't suppose it would do any good to ask where you learned to shoot?"

"Oh, you know," she said vaguely. "Looking at frescoes

and things. Not that I could hit anything. Pharastes told me what to do just now."

As he retrieved his arrow and helped gather up the thrown rocks from outside the fortifications, Damiskos tried to recollect how he felt about Varazda that morning. He had confessed his love, and it hadn't gone as badly as he had feared—or as well as he had hoped. Varazda had been very *nice* to him afterward, and that might have felt insulting, but it hadn't. And then Eurydemos had sown that horrible seed of doubt in Damiskos's mind, and that was why this morning everything felt slightly off, like a melody played on a badly-tuned lute.

He could not talk to Varazda about this. It would not be fair. What could Varazda say to him? He would have to offer reassurance, no matter what he really felt. Besides, there was unlikely to be an opportunity any time soon. There was work to be done before the postal ship arrived.

And maybe there was no point in trying to discuss his feelings with Varazda anyway, because the term of their acquaintance was drawing to a close. Varazda would go back to Boukos on the postal ship, and that would be the end of it.

The postal ship could arrive any time between dawn and the fifth hour, depending on the conditions of wind and sea and when they left Boukos. The plan was that Varazda and Aradne would go down to meet it and explain what they needed. Meanwhile, the women would be hidden throughout the woodland around the villa, with articles of flashy Zashian clothing—Damiskos had made sure to tease Varazda about this while explaining the plan—and every vaguely weapon-like shiny object they could lay their hands on. Nione and Damiskos would wait by the front of the house for a signal from Varazda, and then would ride through the gates on horses supplied by the grooms and smuggled out through the stable's back entrance. The other horses would be in the woods with the women.

At Varazda's signal, the women would begin making noise in the trees as if they were a troop of soldiers advancing to surround the villa. In the meantime, the sailors from the Boukossian ship—provided they agreed to help—would come up from the shore to make a real barrier on the garden side of the house. Damiskos and Nione would demand the students' surrender, telling them that the house was surrounded. Aradne would go in search of the imprisoned slaves while Varazda waited in the garden with the sailors to take the students into custody and bring them back to Boukos.

The morning was spent assembling imitation weaponry —Varazda offered his swords, and there was fierce competition over who would get to wield one, before Damiskos suggested that Varazda should probably keep them—dividing up Varazda's clothes, and finding lengths of rope to tie in the trees to create the illusion of movement through the branches. Everything else would have to wait until the ship was sighted. And the day was still and hot, the water of the bay glassy. The sun climbed overhead, and there was no sign of the ship.

"Could we do it without the sailors," Aradne wondered, standing with Damiskos by the water's edge, hands on her hips.

He shook his head. "I don't want to risk it."

"We don't know they're even going to help."

"If they won't, Nione can get on board and go to Pheme for help. In a few days the factory workers and the villagers will be back anyway. If it weren't for what that bastard said about shaking the women's loyalty, I'd have said we'd be better off waiting."

"This will work," said Aradne stoutly. "If not today, then tomorrow."

Damiskos turned to look back up at the villa, shading his eyes with his hand. He would have liked to know what was going on inside. How many dead bodies were there by this time, and whose? The fishermen and the porters seemed to have stuck with the students so far. But there had been a clear rift among the students themselves, and it was anyone's guess how that would have played out by now.

Varazda and Nione walked over from the beach huts. Varazda slung an arm casually around Damiskos's shoulders —not exactly a comradely gesture, but not exactly a lover's, either. Nione beamed at them, and Aradne raised an eyebrow but said nothing.

"I think we're finished our preparations," Varazda reported.

"Just in time," said Nione, pointing. "Look."

There it was, a speck on the bright water, moving with the freshening breeze from the Tentines toward the coast of Pheme.

The women of Nione's household went up through the vine-yard to take their places around the house, following the instructions that they had all gone over carefully early that morning. Tyra and a couple of the indoor women stayed behind in the beach huts with the babies and younger children; the older children went with their mothers, serious-faced and intent on their grown-up task. Damiskos, watching them go, felt as confident as he ever had in any soldiers under his command.

Of course the women were not really going into danger, Damiskos reminded himself. Their job in the woods was crucial, but it was only those who were going into the house who faced potential violence. Much depended on the state of affairs inside the house, whether it was complete chaos yet, or whether Helenos had things under some sort of control.

Eurydemos, who had waffled and debated about the morality of their plan all the while they were discussing it last night and this morning, had finally made up his mind to participate and had been on the point of leaving for the woods with the women when he had a change of heart and decided to stay behind after all. Damiskos was privately relieved.

Now Damiskos stood on the jetty with Nione, Aradne, and Varazda, watching the postal ship approach. It would soon be time for him and Nione to go up to the front of the house, as they had planned, but something was worrying him now, something that had only occurred to him within the last few minutes. It was a feeling that was familiar to him, a kind of suspicion that crept up sometimes before a carefully-planned engagement. Listening to it had more than once made the difference between victory and defeat on the battlefield.

The sun was almost directly overhead, flashing off the water, making it difficult to look out at the ship for long. It had approached close enough to the shore now that Damiskos could make out the figures that crowded the deck.

"Are there usually so many passengers on the postal ship?" he asked.

Nione squinted out at the water. "I can't see from this distance. How many would you say?"

"A few dozen," Damiskos guessed. "It's hard to say from here."

Varazda shot him a worried look. Damiskos nodded grimly.

"You're thinking ... " Varazda began.

"I'm wondering if Helenos is expecting reinforcements after all."

"Blessed Anaxe," Nione murmured.

Aradne muttered something much saltier.

"I miscalculated," said Damiskos savagely. "I knew this was a possibility, but I didn't properly take it into account."

He cursed himself inwardly in worse language than Aradne had used. He had been too preoccupied last night with confessing his love for Varazda and then the dreadful fear that it wasn't love at all. He should have done better.

"I thought of it," said Varazda quietly. "Last night. But I thought the women would be safer hidden in the woods, if it did turn out that reinforcements were arriving."

"You're right," said Damiskos.

He'd been on the point of panicking, doubting himself, falling headlong—and there Varazda had been to catch him. Yet again.

CHAPTER 22

"IT MIGHT BE AS WELL for you and Aradne to go back to the beach houses, my lady," Varazda said to Nione. "Keep everyone hidden inside if you can, and be prepared to throw stones again if you can't." He glanced at Damiskos. "Don't you think?"

"Yes, I think that would be best."

Aradne nodded smartly and took Nione's arm. "Let's go, ma'am."

"Of course if it turns out we're wrong and there are no more philosophers on that ship, we'll send word," said Varazda.

Nione let herself be led away by her steward, and Damiskos and Varazda were left alone on the jetty.

"They'll have seen us by now, I expect," said Varazda.

"Yes, I expect so. Though the sun may be in their eyes."

"Let's stroll up the shore and go into the factory as if we're not watching them. It's probably the best we can do in the way of concealment."

They walked back up the jetty and across the sand to the factory. Varazda laid his hand on Damiskos's arm as they walked.

"It's still a good plan," he said. "We'll handle whatever comes."

"Thank you," said Damiskos warmly. "We will."

Varazda gave his arm a squeeze and let his hand fall. They went in the nearer door of the factory and took a position under one of the windows, sitting on the floor with their backs to the wall. Varazda had Damiskos's bow and his quiver with its two arrows as well as his own swords. Judging by how far away the ship still was, there would be a little while to wait.

They sat in silence for a moment. Damiskos thought about the ship approaching and what awaited them up in the villa, and thought this might be their last opportunity to speak privately before all the hells broke loose. There were things he did not want to leave unsaid.

"Varazda," he said, "I regret some of what I said to you last night. I don't want to leave you with the wrong impression."

"All right." Varazda clasped his hands around one knee, looking at Damiskos with his head a little tilted, a pose of listening.

"It seems absurd to say I've enjoyed myself this last week, but I have. Coming to know you has been the best thing to happen to me in years. I wish I had enough poetry in my soul to tell you what a splendid fellow you are—how brave and kind and beautiful. You probably don't need to hear all that, so maybe it's just as well I don't know how to say it. But when I'm around you I feel … as if you cast your light on me. As if I'm a little bit better—a better man, a better person —because of you."

He stopped, feeling self-conscious.

"There wasn't anything wrong with that, as poetry," said Varazda softly.

"But I regret the way I spoke last night," Damiskos repeated. "You haven't broken my heart—you've been more than decent to me. Terza's head—that's not what I mean. You've been generous and patient and magnificent. I will treasure the memory of the time we had together. I wish it could have been longer. But we—we're on different paths in our lives, and you don't have room for me in yours, and that's absolutely fair. You have to go back to your home and your family and spying for your republic, and I have to go back to Pheme and—I suppose—see what I can do to expose the warmongers who would have bought those documents from Helenos."

A rather sad smile flickered over Varazda's lips. "You'll get promoted after all."

"No. I think I'll retire. Draw my pension, such as it is, and look for some other kind of work." He hadn't realized until he said it that this was true, but it was. "I'll make enemies if I take this thing on—I couldn't have much of a career in the army after that. Anyway, I think it's about time I moved on."

"Ah," said Varazda. He looked at Damiskos for a moment with an expression that Damiskos didn't understand. A kind of uncertainty. "Dami … if you're going to quit your job, can you afford to take a proper vacation before looking for a new one?"

"Yes, barely—but yes. You're thinking that I should take some time off to recover from all this."

"No. I was thinking that you could come to Boukos and stay with me."

"Oh." That was all he could manage. He seemed to have lost his power of speech.

"I'd very much like it if you would."

"Yes. I'd like that too."

The world seemed to have gone quiet around them.

"I have room in my life for you, Dami. Of course I do. You'd be a part of my life I never expected to have—I wasn't sitting around waiting for you—but there's room. Honestly,

I'd—I'd promise you more right now, but I do have a family, and you'll have to meet them and they you before I can say, 'Come live with me.' But I've wanted to take you home with me since … I suppose the first time I thought about it was that night you fell asleep in my bed. Last night when you said you didn't know what you'd do without me, I—I panicked, I didn't know what to say. But I wasn't trying to say I could never love you."

"You mean you think you could?"

"That's just what I mean."

Varazda smiled and opened his arms, and Damiskos scooted the short distance across the floor to fold him in a tight embrace. He had to fight to allow himself to feel Varazda's lithe body in his arms, Varazda's hands pressed against his back, without a pang of anticipatory regret. Could this really be only a temporary parting? He couldn't quite believe it yet.

He said into Varazda's hair, "And you don't … don't think that I'm just infatuated with you because of some, some idea of how you're like a *thing*?"

As an explanation, that was quite incoherent, but Varazda seemed to understand.

"Oh, please. Believe me, I know that when I see it. The way you make love to me—you don't think of me as a thing."

Damiskos laughed. "No, I suppose not. Come to think of it."

"You've been 'more than decent' to me too, Dami."

"Someone should have been years ago," said Damiskos with sudden heat. "That is—I'm sure people have been good to you before—"

"But not in quite the way you have."

Damiskos drew back just enough to kiss Varazda, but a slight sound carried across the water made him stop before their lips met. He pushed himself up onto his good knee, letting go of Varazda reluctantly, to look out the window.

"They've dropped anchor."

The ship stood broadside to the shore, some distance out in the bay. They had begun to lower a boat.

"What? Oh. May their mothers all get the mange," Varazda said, in his best court Zashian, so Damiskos could understand it.

Damiskos laughed and laughed, far more than the quaintly coarse insult deserved. Everything he felt for Varazda and had tried to suppress seemed to bubble out of him in laughter. He slid down the wall to sit next to Varazda again.

"I know, I'd forgotten all about them too," Damiskos said when he got himself under control. He wiped his eyes. "But after all, they are only philosophers. It's not as if we're going to be dealing with armed men."

Varazda's eyes widened. "I'm not sure of that."

"Why? Did you see weapons?"

"No, but it's a military ship. Isn't it? I'd have thought that was your area of expertise."

"What? Is it not the postal ship from Boukos?"

Damiskos hauled himself up to look out the window again. It was a smallish, thirty-oar vessel, not a warship, with a red sail and a distinctive prow, a goat's head, the emblem of Boukos.

"Only military ships carry a red sail," Varazda explained.

"I see. It's not a warship. If that's what you were thinking."

"Ah. Well, it has got a red sail."

"It looks more like a large yacht. If it *is* meant to be a warship, the Boukossian navy is in worse shape than I realized."

"Shut up."

"I expect it's an attaché or a commander's personal vessel or something. I do see men in breastplates on board, actually, now that I look. But they're not the ones disembarking. It's a bunch of young men in mantles—I count ten, not including the sailors. Why do these philosophers always insist on keeping their mantles wrapped around themselves all the time? Eurydemos couldn't even take his off to jump out of a window."

"The general Pseuchaian affinity for mantles has always puzzled me. If you cut all that cloth up and sew sleeves in it, it's so much more convenient."

"You don't have to convince me." He let himself down to the floor again.

"All right," said Varazda, "so it's not the postal ship, but it does seem to be disgorging a lot of philosophical types. Enough to make a material difference to our plans?"

Damiskos frowned. "Maybe not. But if we let them get up to the house, the others will know this wasn't the postal ship, and we won't be able to pretend that it brought our crack Zashian troops to surround the villa."

"Right. So what should we do?"

"I'll go out and stall them. I'll pretend to be one of them —they've no reason to think I'm not—and tell them they can't go up to the villa yet because … "

"The slaves have retaken it. You got out before it happened, and you don't know what the situation is now, but you think they'd better let you go back in and scout things out before they come up to the villa."

"Right."

"I'll watch your back." He patted the hunting bow. "Kiss for luck?"

"Divine Terza. Of course." Damiskos leaned in and gave Varazda a soldierly kiss, brisk but passionate, then pushed up to his feet and strode toward the door, leaving Varazda wide-eyed and rather pink-cheeked in his wake.

As Damiskos swung around the corner of the factory, the boat with the new contingent of philosophers had reached the jetty, and the sailors who had rowed it were making it fast to a mooring ring. The young men in mantles began climbing out. Damiskos stood by the factory wall, watching while they still had not noticed him.

He saw swords and knives clumsily concealed under mantles. This group had come prepared for violence.

Damiskos had opened his mouth to hail them when he caught a movement out of the corner of his eye. He looked. Eurydemos was running down the beach from the direction of the hidden cove, his own mantle flopping and flapping around him, heading for the jetty and the boatload of students.

What in Terza's name was he playing at? Damiskos was too far away to intercept him before he reached the jetty.

"Halt!" Damiskos bellowed at a parade-ground volume. "Halt there!"

Eurydemos glanced around wildly and then stumbled on. Damiskos ran to cut across his path, but it was hopeless.

"The gods be thanked!" the philosopher called to the students. "You've come to rescue me!"

For a moment Damiskos faltered. Was it possible Eurydemos was right? *Had* they come to rescue him?

No. They hadn't. They were fumbling their weapons out from under their mantles and coming down the jetty toward Eurydemos.

"Master," one in the lead called out, "the time has come for you to step aside. The old order must give way! Pheme must be restored to greatness, that Boukos may follow in her footsteps."

Eurydemos was on the jetty now, the students halfway down. They had stopped, standing across the width of the jetty, swords and knives out, in stances ranging from "would pass muster in the Sixth Koryphos" to "knows which end of the knife to hold." Eurydemos slowed but continued to walk toward them.

"Boys, what are you saying?" he called.

The students replied with something about purity and barbarians. Damiskos reached the end of the jetty himself and started down it. Eurydemos had stopped finally, within striking distance of the students, but the students had not struck. They were waiting, Damiskos realized, for him to come up behind Eurydemos and take him unawares. They had heard Damiskos shout at Eurydemos and thought he was one of them.

If he could just keep Eurydemos from flinging himself on his students' swords, this might all work in Damiskos's favour.

He came up behind Eurydemos, who was in full flight with some nonsense about virtue, and caught him around the throat with his right arm, drawing his sword left-handed at the same time and flipping it around to grip it loosely. Eurydemos made a startled noise and then turned a baleful glare on Damiskos.

"What are *you* doing *now*?" he demanded, his tone more irritated than alarmed.

"Good work," said the leader of the students, who was the one who wouldn't have disgraced the Sixth Koryphos. "You must understand, Master. On the battlefield of the intellect, as you yourself have said—"

"No, no, no!" Eurydemos interrupted impatiently. "He's not on your side." He twisted around in Damiskos's hold, which was not very secure only because Damiskos hadn't thought it needed to be. "You're not on their side. I cannot allow this subterfuge."

"I see why you think he needs to be replaced," said Damiskos to the students, getting his hand over Eurydemos's mouth, which he should have done sooner.

He didn't know how much of this exchange would be

audible in the factory, and he could only pray that Varazda wouldn't show himself. No one could be confused about whose side *he* was on.

"Who are you, anyway?" one of the students asked with a doubtful frown. "Are you from the Marble Porches? Whose student?"

"*I* was at the Marble Porches," another one spoke up. "I've never seen him."

"I'm not a student," Damiskos answered while Eurydemos struggled uselessly in his grip, making affronted noises. "I'm a soldier. I'm here to talk to Helenos about the documents he stole from the Sasian embassy."

He felt rather clever as he was saying this, but when the words were met by stunned silence, he realized he'd made a tactical error. They hadn't known about the theft.

"Are you calling Helenos Kontiades a thief?" a voice in the back demanded.

"Whose side *are* you on?"

"Your side, of course." Damiskos tried to brazen it out.

"Let him go," said the lead student, gesturing with his sword at Eurydemos. "If you are not trying to protect him from the consequences of his folly and intellectual corruption, let him go."

Ah, what the hell. When you put it like that.

Damiskos let Eurydemos go, and the lead student swung immediately on Damiskos, a powerful, hacking blow. Damiskos parried left-handed, soundly turning the blade aside, and felt the surprise in his opponent's reaction. Here, Damiskos judged, was someone who could really fight, but was accustomed to thinking that his enemy couldn't.

Eurydemos had broken away from the other students, who had made a grab for him, and at last had the sense to turn and pelt back down the jetty. Three students set off after him.

There was a scream and the thud of a falling body.

Damiskos risked a glance down the jetty. One of the pursuing students had fallen, and Damiskos caught of a glimpse of Varazda, framed in the factory door, bow in hand, like a warrior in a Zashian epic.

Damiskos and his opponent traded a series of quick blows. The student was about Damiskos's size, a little heavier, slower with his arm but of course nimbler on his feet. Military trained. It would have been a satisfying bout if Damiskos hadn't had to worry about what was happening behind him.

He heard another shout from down the jetty, and managed to manoeuvre his opponent around so that he could look. Varazda had come between the remaining students and Eurydemos, who stood watching, stunned, as his delicate work of art lacking the whatever-it-was of a man knocked the knife out of one attacker's hand and broke the nose of the other with a blow from his blunt-edged sword.

It was at this point that one of the sword-wielding students decided their leader needed some assistance and stepped forward to stab at Damiskos's open left side. Damiskos dodged. The lead student howled something about honour and fairness but didn't stop attacking Damiskos, and neither did the fellow who was trying to help, who bawled back something about ends justifying means.

The fight became chaotic, a series of fragmentary impressions like lightning flashes. Blood spraying from a slashed wrist, Damiskos's sword punching through a flapping fold of someone's mantle. The students shouting back and forth. There was no space to think about whether to kill or wound or spare lives; they were fighting him in earnest, in blood-drunk elation, eager to kill for their cause, whatever it was. He grabbed viciously at a mantle, bringing its wearer heavily to the ground. He parried and dodged the blows that might have struck home, tried to ignore the ones that wouldn't.

Varazda came running down the jetty, swords in his

hands, to join Damiskos. A couple of the students who hadn't been able to get within striking distance of Damiskos peeled off to meet the barbarian. Their weapons rang against his, and someone—not Varazda—yelped. The sailors had cast off and were rowing hard back toward their ship, and Damiskos could hear the soldiers on board shouting to them, though not what they were saying.

He felled the lead student finally with a low cut across the thigh. The man went down with a howl, and his sword skittered across the stones. Another student lunged after it, grabbed it, and tripped one of his fellows in the process.

Varazda was bleeding. He had taken a cut to his upper right arm; Damiskos had missed the moment when it happened. Locking swords with his new opponent, Damiskos shoved him back so hard that he stumbled and fell off the jetty into the water. Damiskos swung around and caught the blade of Varazda's opponent, knocking it up and away.

He risked a glance at Varazda, but Varazda was already eeling around to his opposite side to batter away at the next oncomer with his blunt swords. If he was favouring his injured arm at all, Damiskos didn't see it.

They fought back to back for what seemed an age, but was really just the length of time it took the sailors to row back to their ship and return with a boatload of soldiers. They couldn't have been said to be holding the jetty, because they were surrounded, but they kept the students busy.

Damiskos slipped in under the next student's defence and ran him through. The man Damiskos had knocked into the water had hauled himself out, but he had lost his sword, and Varazda easily knocked him back in. Another swordsman gave Damiskos a decent fight before Damiskos disarmed him. Varazda kicked a man in the groin and knocked him on the back of the head with the hilt of his sword as he doubled over. Of the ten young men who had piled out of the boat, three were left standing by the time the soldiers arrived on the jetty. Several had gone into the water and dragged themselves or been dragged out; at least two were dead.

"Put up your swords!" the officer leading the small group of men bellowed.

There were six of them, in tooled and gold-chased breast-plates, with red-crested helmets and bronze-studded sword-belts. An honour guard of some sort.

The remaining students, formed up three abreast across the jetty, seemed to think the command directed only at Damiskos and Varazda, and ignored it.

"Get me through to speak to their captain?" Varazda asked breathlessly.

"You're sure?"

Varazda nodded.

It wasn't easy to hack through a line of men—even a line of only three men—without a shield. But he only needed to provide Varazda a ridiculously narrow opening, and Varazda slid through it, ducking hair-raisingly under Damiskos's sword-arm, and stopped short in front of the captain of the honour guard. He raised his hands and let his swords clatter on the stones of the jetty.

An impossibly long moment passed, during which Damiskos dodged and parried by pure instinct, and then the captain of the guard said, "Pharastes the Dancer?" in a disbelieving tone, and time flowed again.

"I knew I recognized you," said Varazda, as cheerfully as if he were paying a social call. "Autarches, isn't it? Who are you escorting?"

Damiskos gave ground by a few steps, deliberately, to draw the enemy away from Varazda, and as a result he did not hear the name, which would have meant nothing to him anyway. But it seemed to mean something to Varazda, and the gist of the ensuing conversation, as far as Damiskos could make it out, was that if the guardsmen wanted to know what Varazda was doing there, they should ask their boss.

The captain dispatched one of his men in the boat, and in the meantime took Varazda's word that the students who remained alive should be disarmed and held under guard. Surrounded and outnumbered, the men gave up their weapons without much further resistance. The guards took Damiskos's sword away too, and he made no protest. Varazda's swords they did not confiscate.

Damiskos found himself gripped by an odd feeling, as if Varazda was receding from him into his own world, the world to which Damiskos did not belong, and the understanding that they had shared just now in the fish-sauce factory, that had seemed to unmake and remake Damiskos's world, that was receding too.

He wanted to get to Varazda now, to touch him, see how he was; he remembered the bad reaction Varazda had the night before after they tangled with the porters in the villa. What they had just been through here was much worse. He wanted to check that Varazda's arm wasn't too badly injured. But he couldn't get close to Varazda. As far as the guards were concerned, Damiskos was another suspicious, ex-military-looking character—in fact, the one who had struck the first blow and the only one who had killed anyone (the man Varazda had shot was badly wounded in the shoulder but not dead). Damiskos hung back, trying to look as cooperative as possible. The least he could do for Varazda now was not cause trouble.

One of the guardsmen was looking at Varazda's injury and wrapping a makeshift bandage around his arm. The blood had soaked all down his sleeve. He would probably need stitches.

The other injured men were being attended to as well. The captain of the guard addressed the unhurt men.

"What was this all about? You told us when you

boarded our ship in Boukos that you were philosophers. This isn't what philosophers usually do, is it? And what would possess you to fight Pharastes? He's a—um —dancer."

The man whose nose Varazda had broken moaned at this addition of insult to injury.

"We are philosophers," one of the students announced grandly—or with an attempt at grandeur. It fell a little flat because his mantle was tangled around his knees, his hands tied behind his back, and he was dripping seawater on the jetty. "Ordinarily we do battle with ideas, not with blades. But we are no strangers to warfare."

The captain of the guard gave him a pained look.

One of the other students spoke up, his tone patronizing. "The old man you saw running toward us when we landed? He used to be a great philosopher, but he has gone soft. Seduced by barbarian immorality. He needs to make way for the younger generation."

"Ask Helenos," said another student. "He's the one who gathered us all to the cause when he was last in Boukos. He promised us places in his new school, here in his villa, away from the corruption of the cities. Here we will work toward restoring—"

"Yes, yes," the captain cut him off, "the greatness of Pheme. One of your mates told us all about it on the ship. We thought that meant lying on couches and talking about things, not attacking people with knives."

So Helenos had set all this up before leaving Boukos: two successive waves of reinforcements, the first students from Pheme, the second new recruits from Boukos. He couldn't have known precisely what use he was going to put them to, but he had briefed them well enough that they knew to attack Eurydemos on sight.

"The thing is," Varazda said in a tired, colourless voice, "the villa doesn't belong to Helenos."

The captain of the guard raised his eyebrows. "That's awkward. Puts rather a different face on things."

Varazda glanced around at Damiskos, and then his gaze flicked up, sharply, past Damiskos. He pointed discreetly, using one of the hand signals Damiskos had taught him. *One enemy combatant that way.*

Damiskos turned and looked up. One of the students stood on the cliff's edge at the back of the garden, looking down on the scene.

CHAPTER 23

"THEY KNOW we've taken out their reinforcements, so our position may actually be strengthened," Damiskos explained as he, Nione, Aradne, and Varazda hurried across the beach. "But we do need to get up there quickly, before they begin making other plans."

Specifically, before they did anything to hurt the male slaves, but Damiskos was not going to say that out loud. Part of the secret to effective command was knowing when projecting calm was more important than impressing the troops with a sense of life-and-death urgency.

He didn't feel particularly calm himself. They had lost valuable time waiting for the men of the honour guard to receive word from their employer. When it came, it had been, "Give Pharastes everything he needs and invite him aboard the ship," but Varazda had politely declined the invitation, saying he still had more work to do on shore. Damiskos kept glancing across at him now, worrying about him but trying not to show it.

Varazda looked sick and white, but he was setting the pace as they walked back to the stairs, staring straight ahead of him and saying little to the others. Holding on by the skin of his teeth, if Damiskos had to guess. Damiskos wanted desperately to hold him, even just his hand as they walked, but doubted it would be welcome. When you were in that state, sometimes you just needed to keep going or risk collapsing in a heap.

"But we're not taking the soldiers with us," said Aradne, rather out of breath from their brisk trot across the beach.

It was hard to tell with her, but Damiskos thought this was a question. "They're an honour guard for a Boukossian diplomat, and he wants them to stay with the ship. Which is fair since he now has several prisoners on his hands. They couldn't spare any of the sailors either. It's all right. We think whoever came to the end of the garden only saw the aftermath of our engagement, not the actual fighting. With luck it shouldn't be difficult to convince them that there were more of us fighting than just me and Varazda."

"And that the rest are surrounding the villa now." Aradne nodded.

"Please don't let her try to sneak in to rescue the other slaves," Nione addressed Damiskos.

She was labouring along in the sand in impractical sandals, holding up her skirt with both hands, looking almost as unwell as Varazda. She had looked scared enough by what she had witnessed of the fight on the jetty—and what had been reported by the hyperventilating Eurydemos when he stumbled back into the fortifications—that Damiskos had considered leaving her behind, but her authority as owner of the villa really was necessary for the coming confrontation. Besides, she seemed to have guessed what was in his mind, because she had said, "Don't you dare think of leaving me behind."

"It is not for me to say," said Damiskos now, "but I would strongly discourage it. That was a feasible plan only when we had the element of surprise—we've lost that now. I think," he added to Aradne, "that you would be more useful now at your mistress's side."

"Yes," Nione put in, probably wishing she had led with that line. "I need you with me."

"Of course," said Aradne, obviously not pleased. "Whatever you say, ma'am."

"This is where we part ways," said Varazda, turning to address the others. He was to take the vineyard path up to signal the women in the woods.

"Very good," said Damiskos crisply.

He didn't like to see Varazda going off on his own in his current state, injured and exhausted and fragile. He reminded himself that Varazda was not, as far as they knew, going into mortal danger. Once he made it up through the vineyard, he would signal the women and then make his way around to the stable to help bring the horses out. With any luck, he would not encounter any hostiles. He should be fine.

Damiskos had already made up his mind that there would be no embracing, lest it make Varazda break down. Instead he held out a hand as he would to a fellow soldier. Varazda grasped it hard for a moment, the grip of his slender fingers almost fierce. Then he took off at a run across the sand, left hand clasping his injured arm.

Damiskos, Aradne, and Nione reached the top of the stairs and took a moment to collect themselves. Damiskos was beginning to come down from the exhilaration of the fight and to feel sore and tired. Aradne was out of breath and clutching her side after the long climb, and Nione had to stop to remove a stone from her sandal. All in all, it was not an impressive entry into the garden.

The whole contingent of students, fishermen, and porters

were there to meet them. At least, they were not standing awaiting them, but they were all gathered near the central fountain in the garden, arguing.

Gelon was there, with his arm in a sling, and Phaia was sitting on a bench, hollow-eyed and tragic-looking. Evidently they had decided to throw in their lot with Helenos after all. Damiskos didn't like that much; they were both volatile, not to say crazy, and having them added to the mix could not be good.

There were fewer of the porters than Damiskos remembered from the fight in the atrium, and more were missing than just the one man he had killed. That might mean that some of them were guarding the male slaves, prepared to use them for leverage as needed.

One of the fishermen was the first to notice Damiskos and the two women approaching. He pointed and shouted to get the others' attention. Damiskos gestured to his companions to stop, a safe distance away, on one of the quartz-gravelled garden paths.

He stood with his hand on the hilt of his sword. There was blood on his tunic, none of it his. He knew that he looked grim. He looked to Aradne.

"It's time for this little game to end!" she bellowed. She had a magnificent voice for bellowing.

The men stared at her. A few laughed.

"Surrender yourselves now, and you may leave alive," Aradne continued. "Give us any more trouble, and you'll suffer the fate of your friends who just arrived from Boukos. Half of them are prisoners—the other half are dead." That was an exaggeration, but Damiskos approved of it.

"You expect us to believe that?" one of the porters blustered.

"It's true," someone else said. "I saw what happened. There was blood all over the place."

"Quiet, everyone!" That was Helenos. He stepped

forward from the crowd, hands tucked casually into his mantle. "This is an unfortunate business," he said coolly, looking at Damiskos rather than Nione or Aradne. "You have killed some men, and I don't doubt you are very skilled. But can you take on all of us? Is that really what you propose?"

"Are you talking to me?" said Damiskos blandly. "Because I didn't speak to you."

Helenos was actually momentarily stymied by that. He gave Damiskos an ugly look, then transferred it grudgingly to Aradne.

"Well, slave?" His voice dripped contempt. "You seem to speak for both your mistress and this pitiful excuse for a soldier. I'm surprised you didn't bring the Sasian gelding along to complete the picture. Which of you is going to kill us all, then? You, maybe? Smother us with your—"

"Since you ask," said Nione loudly, stepping forward from beside her steward, "it is the men who are now in the forest surrounding my villa who will kill you if you do not surrender to us."

There was a pause. She had spoken in a ringing voice, angrier than Damiskos had ever seen her and yet totally in control of herself. No one could have failed to hear her; no one could have failed to take her seriously.

"The *what*?" said Helenos finally.

And on cue, the rustling of leaves in the trees around the edge of the garden. The men glanced wildly around. Branches swayed. Sunlight flashed on something that might have been a spearpoint. (It was a marlinspike tied to the end of a wooden spoon.) A figure in Zashian clothes could be seen moving behind the screen of foliage, then another, and another.

The women must have moved back to surround only the garden, Damiskos thought, since all the men were clustered here. It had been a shrewd variation of the plan. The woods looked menacingly full of figures.

A horse neighed and stamped on one side. Hoofbeats sounded from the yard at the front of the house, echoing oddly so that it was hard to say how many animals were making them. Low shouts in—well, in gibberish, but it might have sounded like Zashian to the ignorant—rang out from the same direction.

The men by the fountain drew closer together, a subtle but telling movement.

"We're surrounded!" Gelon yelped.

Phaia leapt to her feet. "They're Sasians! Daughters of Night curse you, Helenos! You've brought the Sasians down upon us!"

"Where did they come from?" one of the fishermen quavered.

"From Boukos!" a student answered, doing Nione and Aradne's work for them. "The city is lousy with Sasians."

"That's right, and the ship this morning came over from Boukos!"

"I didn't see any Sasians on the beach."

"They must have been sneaking up here already."

"They know we stole from them."

That last sentence rang out into an unexpected silence.

"Stole from them?" a fisherman repeated, voice high and unsteady. "Stole what? Do you know what they do to thieves in Sasia?"

"We didn't steal anything," Helenos said silkily, at the same time that one of the other students, more loudly, said, "We don't have it any more!"

"What do you mean, you don't have it any more?"

"We sold it on to a buyer. It's out of our hands."

At this point several of the porters, who had been whispering among themselves, seemed to have come to a decision. One of them stepped forward and dropped heavily to his knees before Nione.

"If you'll take us back, ma'am, we'll accept whatever

punishment we have coming to us. We've no quarrel with any Sasians. We're sorry for our disloyalty. We were following Sesna, our overseer, and he's dead."

"I will take that into account," said Nione sternly.

"You won't let them do anything to me, will you, Nione?" Phaia tried to dredge up some of her old, insouciant charm, and failed.

Nione said nothing, but Damiskos saw her lips compress into a tight line as if there might have been many things she would like to say.

Before the fishermen could get organized to join in the requests for mercy, Helenos spoke again, his voice cutting across the confused babble.

"I should mention. We have hostages."

There was another tense silence. Helenos's expression was wolfish.

"No," said a voice from the colonnade behind Helenos. "You don't."

Varazda strolled out of the deep shadow of the colonnade, one sword propped lightly on his shoulder. Except for the bandages on his right arm, he looked as fresh and relaxed as if he hadn't just fought ten men on the shore with two blunt swords and run all the way up to the villa afterward. He was followed by the rest of Nione's slaves, a dozen men and boys, bruised and haggard and blinking in the sunlight after spending two days in the cellars. Kleitos was with them, looking as bedraggled as the rest.

Helenos sagged visibly at the sight, and for once had nothing to say. Beside Damiskos, Aradne gave a little gasp and grabbed his arm.

"He got them out! How did he do that?"

"I don't know," Damiskos admitted, a smile spreading across his face. "I don't know how he does half of what he does. He's amazing."

Varazda came on, flicking his sword down off his

shoulder and twirling it gracefully around one hand. The men nearest him shuffled back.

Ah-yah, Damiskos thought.

"Tie their hands," Varazda instructed the male slaves.

They came forward prepared with ropes and even a few pairs of shackles. The students were all quickly restrained, including Phaia, and Gelon had his good hand tied to his waist.

"I'm arresting you and taking you back to Boukos to stand trial for murder," Varazda explained when one of the students demanded what he was doing. "I work for the Basileon, you know."

Turning to Nione, he said, "I've no interest in the rest of them, but would you like to have them tied up too?"

"Do what you want with us," one of the fishermen blurted. "Just don't let the Sasians in the woods have us!"

There was a little pause while a glance flickered between Nione and Damiskos.

"I wonder," she said, "if the Sasians in the woods should come out now?"

Damiskos looked over the prisoners, who were securely restrained and now quite outnumbered. He nodded.

"Why don't you call them, Aradne?" Nione suggested.

"Girls! Time to show yourselves!"

The women of Nione's household came out from the trees, grinning and giggling, some of them wearing Varazda's clothes, one leading Damiskos's horse. Damiskos felt his heart swell with pride in them, as if they really were a troop he had led into battle. They had played their part magnificently; it hadn't been done better at Abadoka's stronghold in the year '93. He doubted it had been done better at Sumuz in the year '75.

"I knew it!" Gelon wailed. "I knew there weren't really any Sasians!"

"No, you didn't," Helenos snarled back.

They were still arguing about it as the slaves, under Varazda's direction, led them off to deliver them to the guards on board the Boukossian ship.

The garden had cleared out. The repentant porters and fishermen had been herded inside, and Nione and Aradne had followed, arguing over what should be done with them. "They wouldn't have turned against me if they hadn't had something to complain of," Nione had said, and Aradne just snorted. The women were dispersing, some going into the house, some gathering up their props from the woods, others going down to the beach to bring back the children from the fortified huts. Niko, his grandfather, and the other men who had been hiding in the slave quarters came in from the yard, laughing over the success of their ploy with the horses. Kleitos and his wife had gone in, embracing tearfully. Someone had been dispatched to take the urn with Aristokles's ashes on board the Boukossian ship.

Damiskos and Varazda were in the summer dining room, where they had met. Varazda had sat down on one of the couches, perched on the edge as if afraid to let himself become too comfortable for fear he wouldn't be able to move again. Damiskos knew that feeling well.

"If I'd known you planned to go in and free the men from the cellar … " Damiskos began.

Varazda looked up at him with a tired smile. "I know. You'd have told me not to."

"No. I'd have worried about you more, that's all."

"Ah."

"How did you manage it, anyway? Were they not guarded?"

Varazda shrugged, one-shouldered. He was favouring his

injured arm much more now that he wasn't trying to keep up appearances. "They weren't guarded *very well.*"

Damiskos laughed, but he felt rather weak and as if he would like to sit down himself.

"You, um, may need stitches for that arm."

"What? Oh, the … Yes. It hurts quite a lot."

"Have someone look at it on the ship, if you can—don't wait until you get back to Boukos. And take it easy. You lost a good deal of blood, and then did a lot of running around—it would be abnormal if you *didn't* feel a bit unsteady on your feet. It's nothing to be ashamed of."

"Yes, First Spear."

Damiskos sat on the couch next to Varazda, not very close. He wanted to make this easier for Varazda, however he might do that. He didn't want to burden Varazda or leave him with regrets. But what could he say?

You can go. Don't worry about me. You can withdraw your invitation, and I won't feel hurt.

"You must be tired yourself," Varazda said.

"Pff. I just got to stand around being decorative. I didn't even have to shout at anyone. But I would like a bath."

Varazda laughed. "You've earned it. You were … down on the jetty … I was in awe."

"What? No, you weren't."

"Well, it felt like awe. Maybe that's not the right word."

There was a little silence between them. Damiskos realized, of his own accord, that Varazda was not going to withdraw his invitation. He felt choked with emotion. After all, it had really happened. This was not the end.

"I have to go, Dami," Varazda said finally. "I don't want to. Write to me as soon as you know when you can come?"

"Of course."

"You can send it care of the Zashian embassy."

"Yes. I'd have thought of that myself eventually."

"God. Dami, the look on your face. How is it that we make each other so happy?"

"I don't know how I make you happy—if I really do—unless it's that you enjoy having brought a wretched man back to life."

And finally he allowed himself to reach for Varazda and fold Varazda in his arms, silky and strong, delicate and steel-cored, all the gorgeous complexities of him. Varazda leaned against Damiskos, just resting in his embrace, and Damiskos held him gently until it was time to let go.

Saffron Alley
Sword Dance Book 2

A month ago, eunuch sword-dancer and spy Varazda collided with ex-soldier Damiskos at a seaside villa during a dizzying week of intrigue, assassinations, and a fake love affair that—maybe—turned real. Now Varazda is back home in Boukos, at the centre of a family and community he dearly loves, and Damiskos is coming to visit.

Things aren't going according to plan.

Varazda's family members suspect Damiskos's motives. Varazda grapples with his own desires. Add in a horrible goose, a potentially lethal sculpture, and yet another assassination plot, and any man other than Dami would be boarding a ship straight back to Pheme.

It's going to take all of Damiskos's patience, and all of Varazda's strength, to make this new relationship work. After all that, solving one more murder shouldn't be too hard.

JOIN THE CLUB

Join my *Fragments Club* list to get exclusive short stories and snippets!

Sign up at **ajdemas.com**

LIST OF PLACES

Sword Dance is set in a fictional world loosely based on the cultures of the ancient Mediterranean. Here are some details about the places mentioned in the story.

Pseuchaia: A group of city-states, mostly on islands, with a common language and religion, usually in alliance with one another but not always.

Pheme: An island and a very large city on that island. Pheme is a republic and the most powerful city-state in the region. The city is located on the west coast of the island; the interior of the island is mountainous, and there are villages and seaside estates around the coast.

Boukos: A city on an island of the same name, a short sea-voyage to the northwest of the island of Pheme. For the last eight years, Boukos has had a trade agreement with the kingdom of Zash. A permanent Zashian embassy was established seven years ago. None of the other Pseuchaian states has an official alliance with Zash.

Zash/Sasia: A sprawling kingdom on the mainland to the east of the islands of Pseuchaia. Their language, religion, and culture are very different from those of Pseuchaia. Zash is what they call their kingdom; Pseuchaians find this difficult to pronounce and so call it Sasia.

Suna: The main seat of the king of Zash.

Deshan Coast: A politically volatile region in the west of Zash. Pheme has colonies and a military presence in the region, where they cooperate unofficially with the king of Zash to keep the peace.

Rataxa: A famous cultural centre in Zash. Called "Ratases" in Pseuchaian.

Gudul: An obscure provincial palace and city in Zash.

Seleos: One of the Phemian colonies on the Deshan Coast of Zash.

Laothalia: Nione Kukara's villa on the north coast of the island of Pheme.

Laokia: A village near Nione's villa.

Kos: Another island city of Pseuchaia, famous for its arts and learning.

Ariata: A mainland state, culturally Pseuchaian but often at war with the island cities, famous for austerity and military discipline.

Tentines: A chain of small islands between the larger islands of Boukos and Pheme. There is a shrine to Opos on one of them. They provide the best route to and from Boukos and Pheme, because they allow ships to stay within sight of land for the entire journey.

Gylphos: An ancient kingdom in the south, once powerful but today subordinate to Zash.

SOMETHING HUMAN

They met on a battlefield and saved each other's lives. It's not the way enemies-to-lovers usually works.

Adares comes from a civilization of democracy and indoor plumbing. Rus belongs to a tribe of tattooed, semi-nomadic horse-breeders. They meet in the aftermath of battle, when Rus saves Adares's life, and Adares returns the favour. As they shelter in an abandoned temple, a friendship neither of them could have imagined grows into a mutual attraction.

But Rus, whose people abhor love between men, is bound by an oath of celibacy, and Adares has a secret of his own that he cannot share. With their people poised for a long and bitter conflict, it seems too much to hope that these two men could turn their fleeting happiness into something lasting. Unless, of course, the relationship between them changes the course of their people's history altogether.

Something Human is a standalone m/m romance set in an imaginary ancient world, about two people bridging a cultural divide with the help of great sex, pedantic discussions about the gods, and bad jokes about standing stones.

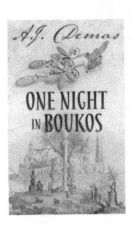

One Night in Boukos

On a night when the whole city is looking for love, two foreigners find it in the last place they expected.

The riotous Psobion festival is about to begin in the city of Boukos, and the ambassador from the straitlaced kingdom of Zash has gone missing. Ex-soldier Marzana, captain of the embassy guard, and the ambassador's secretary, the shrewd and urbane eunuch Bedar, are the only two who know.

Marzana still nurses the pain of an old heartbreak, and Bedar has too much on his plate to think of romance. Neither of them could imagine finding love in this strange, foreign city. But as they search desperately for their employer through the streets and taverns and brothels of Boukos, they find unexpected help from two of the locals: a beautiful widowed shopkeeper and a teenage prostitute.

Before the Zashians learn what became of their ambassador, they will have to deal with foreign bureaucracy, strange food, stranger local customs, and murderers. And they may lose their hearts in the process.

One Night in Boukos is a standalone romance featuring two couples, one m/f and one m/m.

ACKNOWLEDGMENTS

I'm grateful to have had the help of a number of wonderful, talented people in the writing and publication of this book.

Alexandra Bolintineanu talked me into returning to this story when I was bogged down in a different project, and pointed me toward the source for Eurydemos's "philosophy" —thanks, I guess? Lee Welch, beta-reader extraordinaire, gave me feedback that led to a major overhaul of the plot. Victoria Goddard spent a weekend talking over the second draft with me while driving me around Prince Edward Island. May Peterson helped me with that crucial last step of the recipe, "season to taste."

Aud Koch drew the absolutely perfect cover art, and Lennan Adams of Lexiconic Design completed the beautiful design of the cover.

Thanks to all!

ABOUT THE AUTHOR

A.J. Demas is an ex-academic who formerly studied and taught medieval literature, and now writes romance set in a fictional world based on an entirely different era. She lives in Ontario, Canada, with her husband and cute daughter.

Find out about upcoming books and more here:
www.ajdemas.com

A.J. also publishes fantasy and historical fiction with a metaphysical twist under a different name (her real one). You can find those here: www.alicedegan.com